Swan Lake

Jane Leaves the Wells

by
LORNA HILL

Illustrated by
EVE GUTHRIE

LONDON
EVANS BROTHERS LIMITED

First published 1953

To Edward, my Son-in-law,
with love and gratitude.

Printed in Great Britain by
Latimer, Trend & Co. Ltd., Plymouth

Contents

Illustrations

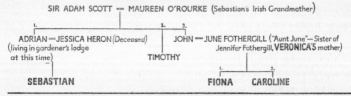

SCOTT FAMILY TREE

SIR ADAM SCOTT — MAUREEN O'ROURKE (Sebastian's Irish Grandmother)

1.
ADRIAN — JESSICA HERON (Deceased)
(living in gardener's lodge
at this time)

2.   3.
JOHN — JUNE FOTHERGILL ("Aunt June"—Sister of
Jennifer Fothergill, **VERONICA'S** mother)

TIMOTHY

SEBASTIAN

1.
FIONA

2.
CAROLINE

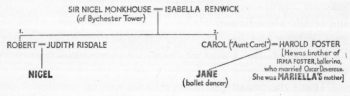

MONKHOUSE FAMILY TREE

SIR NIGEL MONKHOUSE — ISABELLA RENWICK
(of Bychester Tower)

1.
ROBERT — JUDITH RISDALE

NIGEL

2.
CAROL ("Aunt Carol") — HAROLD FOSTER
[He was brother of
IRMA FOSTER, ballerina,
who married Oscar Devereux.
She was **MARIELLA'S** mother]

JANE
(ballet dancer)

1

Backstage

"A-т-sнoo! A-t-shoo! Has anyone seen my hankie?"

"Dar-leeng, you push 'im down your front. I see eet." Carmencita's large dark eyes opened wide, her plump white hands gesticulated. Everything Carmen did was spectacular; she made even the loss of a hankie dramatic. "I theenk 'e 'as gone right down by now. The last *pas de deux* weel 'ave finished 'im off. You 'ad bettaire shake like a jelly!"

Jane laughed.

"Carmen, you *are* funny! But I can tell you it's no joke dancing the Princess Aurora with a streaming cold, and not even a hankie! All the same, shaking's a good idea. Here goes!" She shook herself until the frills of her ballet dress flew up round her slender figure like the corolla of a flower, but nothing happened.

"'E 'as stuck, yes!" Carmen said solemnly. "That ees the worst of a *tutu* made all in one with the panties. Ah, but what we dancers suffeur! All frills, and not one leetle, small pocket! Darleeng, I offer you a piece of cotton-wool. Eet ees much more of the hygiene. You can burn 'im when you 'ave finish wiz 'im."

"Oh, *thank* you," Jane said gratefully. "And now I must put on some powder—lashings of it. . . . Oh, thank you, Gladys!" she added to the dresser, who stood ready with a tray containing all the make-up a dancer needs—grease-paint, powder, mascara, cotton-wool, besides hair-pins, hair-grips, and, most important, a needle and thread. "I've got a red nose and watery eyes. What a blessing I'm not an opera singer. At least I don't have to *speak*! But I do feel awful. I'd give anything to be at home where I could just *flop*."

"That's the penalty of being a ballet-dancer, my dear," said

Canadian Sadie McPherson, leaning perilously against a "flat" of Coppélia's cottage. "One can't even have a cold in peace. Never mind, to-morrow is Sunday. A whole day off for you."

"Oh, but I wanted to go to church to-morrow."

"Can't be done," said Sadie. "You'd far better stay in your nice, cosy bed out of people's way. The congregation wouldn't thank you for giving them all 'flu."

"No, I suppose they wouldn't."

"Besides, don't forget you're one of the principal dancers at the Wells now. Golly! The luck some people have!"

"Yes, I *was* lucky, and it was a terrific thrill," admitted Jane. "All the same, I was frightened, too. You can't imagine how frightened I was—having to step into Veronica's part like that at a second's notice. One moment Veronica was dancing, and the next she was lying on the stage, her finger pricked by the spindle—only her faint was a real one. After that—well, it's all like a dream. I just remember being hustled round and pushed on——" Her voice tailed away, and Sadie knew she was re-living the dramatic moment. "Of course, I was Veronica's understudy, but no one ever expected——"

"No, of course not," put in Scottish Janet. "Not many understudies have the luck you had."

"One thing helped enormously," went on Jane. "No one actually knew I wasn't Veronica until the end of the performance, although you'd have thought they'd have guessed. Veronica is so much more brilliant and finished than I am. But they didn't guess—no one did except my cousin, Mariella, and Nigel Monkhouse."

"Nigel Monkhouse?" exclaimed Sylvia Green, appearing out of the wings in her White Cat costume. "Is he your boy-friend?"

Jane grimaced.

"Nigel my boy-friend? How he would laugh if he heard you! He's my enemy. At least, we used to be enemies when we were children. Incidentally, he's my cousin on Daddy's side. Well, Nigel said he knew it was me dancing and not Veronica because of my soapy expression!"

A low ripple of laughter ran round the company. Then a burst of subdued chatter came from the wings.

"How priceless! . . . Have you got enough powder on, miss? You look a lot better now, if you'll excuse my mentioning it. Not so *damp*. . . . Sylvia, you look nice in that get-up. Your face is the right shape—round! A lot better than Vera. She had a face like a horse. She always looked as if she was one kind of animal masquerading as another, if you know what I mean. Philip makes a grand Puss in Boots, too, don't you think? . . . I always said you talk too much, Delia. . . . Do you think I can possibly get over to the 'Mouse-Trap' by eleven-thirty? What? You've never heard of it? Darling, where have you been all this time? *Everyone's* heard of the 'Mouse-Trap'. The food's wonderful! Well, do you think I could possibly get over there by then—it's in one of those back streets round Soho—if I took a taxi? Really, it's *frightfully* important. You see, I promised to meet Peter for supper. Yes, Peter Wainwright. He's in that show, *Hey Diddle Diddle!* It's been running for ages. Peter says if it runs much longer he'll be turning into a cow! You see, he's the hind legs. . . .

"Does anyone know how you make the buttonholes down the front of a cardigan? It says in the pattern: . . . Gosh, I'm hungry! No time to get my lunch. Anyway, have no money, not till pay-day, and that's not till Friday. Yes, I know to-day's only Saturday, but you see I had a lot to pay off: instalments on my red coat. Well, a girl must dress decently. Oh, don't worry, I'll manage somehow. . . . Poor old Kathleen! It was like that with me last week-end—had to send most of my pay home. Dad's been out of work. Got some all right now, though. Had a letter this morning from Mum. By the way, if you like to crash up to our dressing-room and rummage in my bag—it's the tartan one with a zip pocket in the front—you'll find a couple of sandwiches, left over from the day before yesterday, somewhere. Oh, and there's a piece of sausage, too, wrapped up in a bit of greaseproof paper to keep it off my tights. I couldn't eat it all at lunch-time—they do you well at Lyons Corner House—but it seemed a pity to waste it. See how my Scottish nationality will keep cropping up! . . . Thanks, awfully,

Janet—that will just save my life! . . . Listen, everybody! Where have they got to, now? . . . Second Act, near end of Scene One, Lilac Fairy's entrance. . . . You on next, Jane. . . ."

But Jane was no longer there. She had quietly withdrawn from the laughing, chattering group, and had turned before their eyes into a dreamy, fairy-tale princess. She was standing in the wings, ready for her entrance as the Vision of the Princess Aurora. Her cold had vanished, her eyes, red-rimmed and watery only a few minutes ago, had miraculously become large and sparkling. She was as a fairy-tale princess should be—a creature far above all human ills. Not for her, aching muscles and sore toes; not for her, coughs and sneezes. She was the Princess Aurora, preparing to appear to her fairy-tale prince as a dazzling vision.

"Och! Doesn't Josef look bored!" commented Janet. "I wonder if it's good acting on his part—he's *supposed* to be looking bored just here, of course—or if he really *is*?"

"He really is, I expect!" laughed Sylvia. "Josef is only happy in the company of the Great Ones. Look! He's seen Jane! Behold, dear Josef has come to life! What did I tell you?"

"Yes, but he's *meant* to do that," argued Anna, a pale girl with a far-away expression. "You can't blame him for miming well, can you?"

"No, but knowing dear Josef as well as I do—one just wonders," pursued Sylvia. "Of course, you've only just come into the company, so you're not to know that Josef is really a nasty bit of goods. . . ."

"You'd better not let Jane hear you say that!" warned Janet. "She's awfu' fond of him."

"I know," answered Sadie, "and it worries me. She's a nice kid is Jane. She leapt to fame in the night, as you might say, but she's just the same to us small fry. Some people wouldn't be. Moreover, she's so decent, she judges other people by her own standards. It just doesn't occur to her that our dear Josef may be a climber, and that if anyone appeared likely to eclipse her, he'd transfer his affections in a trice. It would never do to tell her, either."

"I should just think not!" declared Anna in nineteen-year-old

*Jane was standing in the wings, ready for her entrance as
the Vision of the Princess Aurora*

wisdom. "That would be the worst possible thing to do. She must learn to judge people by experience. We all have to go through it. It's the penalty of youth!"

"You'd better be putting some powder on your nose, my dear, or another penalty will be yours!" laughed Janet. "The curtain's rising on the last scene, and it's the White Cat in a minute. Then your Blue Bird *pas de deux*, and after that it's me —Little Red Riding-hood. I think mine is a wonderful rôle— not important enough to weigh one down, but very rewarding. The end, where Toni carries me off, is so dramatic, the audience is carried away, too, and they quite forget how awfully I danced the first part. . . . Look out, Daphne! You know you're not supposed to sit in Carabosse's carriage, even if it *is* only an old soap-box! I saw the tail of a fox sticking out from behind that flat over there. It *might* be Madame!"

"Oh, Janet! You *are* awful! Poor Anna! She's gone quite white. Don't worry, Anna darling; I saw that 'fox fur' ages ago, and it was only Puss in Boots's tail sticking out—not Madame at all. As a matter of fact, Madame is still in Turkey or some- where, getting completely covered with roses. It was all in the paper. But Janet was quite right—it's nearly your entrance. Listen! That's the end of the White Cat's music. It's you now!"

The ballet drew to its end. Then came the "curtains".

"More than ever to-night," whispered Dorothy Mayfield from where she stood as a Court Lady behind the throne. "Oh, *no*! Not another one! I shall miss my bus. Oh, well, that's the last, thank goodness! It's all very well for Jane Foster—she gets all the bouquets, and a taxi to go home in—but for us, poor *corps de ballet*, who have our last buses to catch . . ."

"Who knows—you may be principal dancer some day," whispered her companion. "I said *may*!"

"I heard you, darling!" retorted Dorothy. "Candidly I quite agree with you. The accent *is* on the 'may'!"

While on the other side of the curtain crowds of people in evening dress were filing in orderly fashion out of the amphi- theatre and stalls, descending the great staircase from the Grand Tier, and crowding down from the gallery and the "gods", here, behind the stage, all was hurry and bustle. Scene-shifters, dressers, and other workaday people, crowds of Court Ladies in voluminous dresses, girls in peasant costumes, dancers in *tutus*, huntsmen, fairies, animals, not to mention the King and Queen of Fairyland itself, surged towards the dressing-rooms with but one thought in their heads—namely, to get home as quickly as possible. For them, another day of hard work had ended, and they were ready for a late supper and bed.

Jane, in her Princess Aurora costume, went with them. No longer had she to climb those endless flights of stone stairs to a chorus dressing-room. She was now in possession of a dressing-room of her own—softly carpeted, with shaded lights, and banks of flowers—her own flowers, the flowers that had been showered upon her to-night, and, in fact, every night since she had taken over Veronica's role in this ballet, the *Sleeping Beauty*. Yes, Veronica's dressing-room! Jane had certainly never thought she would be powdering her nose in Veronica's own mirror at Veronica's own make-up table! Her face turned quite pale under her make-up as the unbelievable fact was borne in upon her, as it was every time she opened the door. She felt she ought to bow to somebody—perhaps Veronica's ghost, standing over there beside the long-curtained window! Someone *was* standing there. It was Josef Linsk, looking unbelievably handsome in his Prince Floristan costume. He was a consummate artist at make-up, was Josef, and he had taken good care to accentuate his best features—his glittering dark eyes, and his thinly-bridged nose with the sensitively curving nostrils.

"Oh, Jane," he began, "I wished so much to congratulate you upon a very fine performance to-night. It was"—he hesitated slightly as if seeking for words with which to express himself—"it was of an extreme beauty. As you say in English— it lifted me up." He held out a spray of pale green orchids. "I wish to give you these."

Jane smiled as she took the flowers. Dear Josef! His English was very funny sometimes, but he was so serious that one had to be careful not to hurt his feelings by laughing at him.

"I'm so glad if I had an uplifting influence!" she said. "It was sweet of you to come and tell me, Josef. And thank you for partnering me so well, and for the flowers. I shall wear them on my coat."

"It was to me a pleasure," murmured the young man, bowing slightly. "Both to be the partner, and to give the flower." He murmured something in a foreign language.

"What did you say? I don't understand."

"We have a saying in my country which means 'flowers to the flower'. You are so very like a flower! And now good night, *chérie*. You must be very weary, *n'est-ce pas?*"

"Oh—a little," admitted Jane. "But very happy, too. Good night, Josef!"

As the dressing-room door closed softly behind the young man, Veronica's dresser came bustling in.

"Oh, Miss Jane—you were that lovely to-night, miss, I could have wept! Of course, you weren't the least bit like Miss Veronica, but all the same I could have cried aloud. You looked that *young*!"

"Well, I don't see why being young should make you cry," laughed Jane, stepping out of her *tutu* and handing it over to the dresser.

"No more I don't myself, miss," said Gladys. "But it do. Now here's your house-coat—you mustn't go catching more cold! Oh, and I hate to tell you, miss—knowing how tired you must be, and a cold on you as well—but there's two gentlemen of the Press here. I tried my best to get rid of them, but it was no use. Said they were from a couple of weeklies, and the copy had to be in by to-morrow at latest, so they had to see you to-night. I wouldn't have listened to them if it hadn't been that one of them were the spit and image of Our Albert. . . ."

Jane turned away to hide a smile. "Our Albert" was a back-stage joke. Everyone, from *ballerinas* to call-boys, knew all about "Our Albert". He was the black sheep of Mrs. Coggan's family and, as is the case with most ne'er-do-wells, he was the apple of old Gladys's eye. When, at rare intervals, Our Albert was working, he was referred to proudly as "my youngest son, Albert". Whenever, as was usually the case, Our Albert fell from grace, he was "Our poor Albert what's been took up for no fault of his own. Our Albert always was the unlucky one."

Yes, thought Jane, if either of the gentlemen of the Press resembled Our Albert, it was no wonder he was granted an interview by the all-powerful Gladys. No mere principal dancer would dare to deny him one!

As the two pressmen were ushered in, she studied them curiously, wondering which was Our Albert. One of them was a large, aggressive young man, with bright blue eyes and a ready smile. He introduced himself as Bertie Wingrove from the *Woman's Window*. The other was pale and dark, with a weak chin and sad, dark, frightened eyes. He looked rather like a spaniel who had been ill treated, thought Jane.

"He must be Our Albert," she said to herself. "I don't wonder Gladys couldn't bear to turn him away. He's the sort of young man any woman wants to take care of and 'mother'!"

2

News of Veronica

AFTER the pressmen had gone, Jane proceeded to take off her make-up, with the help of wads of cotton-wool and remover cream, finishing off with cleansing cream. Not for her a luxurious hot bath with scented soap and bath salts.

"I should come out in a rash if I washed at night after I'd been made up," she explained to Gladys.

"Miss Veronica was just the same, miss," said Gladys. "Some dancers with tough skins can wash all right, but most can't. Did you give the pressmen what they wanted, miss?"

"Well, I hope so," laughed Jane. "But they wanted to know such funny things—like was I engaged to be married? Or had I a boy-friend? You'd think people would realise that a dancer is wedded to her art."

"That's as may be," declared Gladys. "Take Miss Veronica, now. Proper wedded to her art was Miss Veronica, till Mr. Scott appeared. And then what happens? First an engagement, then a wedding——"

"Oh, that reminds me," Jane exclaimed, pulling a piece of cotton-wool off the large bundle at her elbow and trying vainly to get the last traces of make-up off her eyelashes. "Gosh! I look as if I'd had a night out, don't I? Talk about heavy-eyed! That reminds me—I mean, what you said about Veronica—my Aunt Carol sent me a copy of the local paper with a wonderful account of Veronica's wedding. It came just as I was leaving Fortnum Mansions this morning, and, as I knew I wouldn't be back there again till nearly midnight, I brought it along with me, but I haven't had a minute to read it, so far." She rummaged in her case, found the paper, and spread it out on Veronica's make-up table.

"The *Northumbrian Times*," read out Gladys. "Oh, here it is, right in the middle of the very front page, and a photograph, too! Isn't she lovely? Oh, Miss Veronica!"

"Why, Gladys—you're crying!" exclaimed Jane. "Whatever for?"

"I'm one of them as always cries at weddings, miss," said Gladys. "Many a one I've seen at St. Margaret's and West-minster Abbey, and Brompton Oratory, too, and I always cry. Why, at Princess Elizabeth's wedding—I should say the Queen's now, of course, only I can't never think of her as the Queen—I couldn't hardly see her I cried that much! I'd waited there all night, too. It was with her being that *young*!"

But Jane wasn't listening to Gladys's reminiscences. She was poring over the newspaper with its picture of a radiant bride, standing hand-in-hand with her bridegroom at the door of the little village church.

"A wedding of great local (as well as national) interest took place on Thursday, 18th September," read out Jane. "Two young people, known to all of us since their childhood, were united in the bonds of Holy Matrimony, in the ancient village church of Bracken. The service, which was fully choral, was conducted by the Vicar of Bracken, the Rev. Samuel Dickson, M.A., and Mr. Antony Pardell, L.R.A.M., was at the organ, the choir sang 'Love Divine all Loves Excelling'. The crowds of fashionable London friends who came to see such well-known—we may almost say world-famous—personalities as Veronica Weston and Sebastian Scott united in wedlock still did not prevent it from being in all senses a real village wed-ding. The church was beautifully decorated by friends of the bride and groom with flowers from the Bracken Hall gardens, the bridegroom's home. It will be remembered that the bride spent several years of her childhood at the Hall with her aunt, Mrs. John Scott, and her cousins.

"The bride was a radiant figure in ivory satin and tulle. She carried a bouquet of deep red roses. Her lace veil, which had been in the Scott family for generations, was held in place by a crown of orange blossom. The four bridesmaids were Miss Patience Eliot of Dewburn Hall, Miss Mariella Foster of Monks

B

Hollow, Miss Caroline Scott, cousin of the bride, and Miss Elizabeth Lister. Mrs. Ian Frazer, known to most of us as Miss Fiona Scott, was matron of honour. They were clad in high-waisted dresses of pale blue satin, with cream lace redingotes. They carried posies of pink anemones and maidenhair fern. The best man was Mr. Angelo Ibañez. He and Miss Caroline Scott are the well-known Spanish dancers, and it is rumoured that they are secretly engaged to be married. They flew from Madrid for the wedding, and left immediately after the cere-mony. The groomsmen were Messrs. Nigel Monkhouse, Guy Carlton, Toni Rossini and David Eliot.

"The wedding reception was held in the gardens of Bracken House, the new home of Mrs. June Scott, the bride's aunt. At night a dance was held in the church hall for the whole village. The bride's going-away ensemble was a brown corded silk suit with cream accessories. With it she wore a cream straw bonnet, trimmed with cream and pink roses. Mr. and Mrs. Scott left for an unknown destination on the Continent. The honeymoon will last several months.

"It may be a matter of interest (and also satisfaction) to many local people to know that the bride's home will be at Bracken Hall, the Scotts' ancient family seat. For many years the bride-groom resided with his father at Bracken Cottage, the original gardener's lodge. Mr. Scott junior is to be congratulated on having raised the family fortunes in a manner worthy of Dick Whittington!"

"Oh, dear! Doesn't it sound lovely!" said Jane, pausing for breath. "What a shame I couldn't have been there! But, of course, it wasn't possible—not when I was dancing in Veron-ica's place. It's strange to think that if Mariella and I hadn't changed places all those years ago, I'd have been at Veronica's wedding, dressed in a bridesmaid's frock, and perhaps Mariella would have been dancing here."

"Oh, no, miss—I don't think so, begging your pardon," said Gladys, who, like most other theatre people, had heard all about the dramatic change-over made by the two cousins in their school days. "I don't think Miss Mariella would ever have made a dancer. Her heart wasn't in it. It seems funny, though, with her mother that famous Irma Foster, but there you are! You can't always step into your mother's shoes, can you? All the same, miss, it's a real shame you couldn't have been there."

"I've had such a job trying to explain to the pressmen," sighed Jane. "Naturally, they wanted to know all about Veronica's wedding, so they came along to me because they knew we were such old friends and that I lived so near Bracken Hall, Sebastian's home. They kept on saying: 'Of course, you'll be taking a couple of days off to see her married?' I just couldn't get them to understand that one can't take days off when one's in the middle of the season—not unless one's so ill one can't move."

"No, miss. Them as aren't in the profession don't know the privations a dancer endures," said Gladys, who liked long words. "Well, it's nice to read about it, miss; makes it seem quite real. Can I have the paper, miss, to show to Our Albert, or will you be wanting it?"

"Oh, no—you can have it," said Jane generously. "I'll get another one somehow. Oh, and there's a box of wedding cake for you. It was sent with mine. Good night, Gladys, and thank you!"

"Thank *you*, miss. It's been a pleasure, I'm sure, to dress a young lady like yourself. Good night, miss."

"Oh, by the way," added Jane from the dressing-room door, "that Press reporter—the thin dark one like your Albert—he said I had to thank you for getting him the interview."

There was an explosion from the dresser.

"That dark one like Our Albert, miss—that long, thin, streak of misery! Never in your life! Not in a month of Sundays! Why, Our Albert——"

Jane escaped while the going was good. "It's funny," she thought, as she ran down the stairs to the stage door, "how one can get a preconceived idea of a person. I was quite sure Our Albert was pale and thin, with sad dark eyes, and now it seems I'm quite wrong. Our Albert is big and bouncy, with blue eyes and a "way" with him!"

"Good night, miss!" shouted George, the janitor, as she passed him. "Taxi waiting for you, miss! Still some people hanging about outside for autographs. You'd have thought they'd have gone away home to their beds long ago, wouldn't you? But no—must have their autos!"

"Oh, dear!" thought Jane with a twinge of conscience. "While I was reading about Veronica's wedding, all those poor people were waiting for me."

Patiently, and with a sweet smile, though her back ached, and her head felt as if it was made of a lump of lead, Jane signed the books presented to her by the balletomanes still waiting at the stage door to see their idol emerge. Only when she had signed the last book and had answered the last shy: "Oh, Miss Foster—would you mind telling me what it feels like to step into a principal part at a moment's notice?" and: "Please, Miss Foster, when are you dancing again?" or: "I wonder, Miss Foster, if you could tell me whether our little Elsie is too tall for a ballerina. She's twelve, and she's five feet four——" Only when Jane had answered all their questions, and the crowd had melted away, was she free to step into the waiting taxi and sink back upon the cushions with a sigh of utter weariness.

"It's no fun being a dancer when you've got a streaming cold!" thought poor Jane as the taxi bowled away.

3

Lunch at the "Dragon"

"THINGS are awfully flat after a wedding," thought Mariella as she turned out of the gates of Monks Hollow, the beautiful country house where she had lived with her aunt and uncle since she was fifteen, and rode down towards the village. "At least, not *straight* after because there are still guests floating about—staying at the village inn, and parked at various people's houses, and some of them are quite entertaining. That funny Mrs. Crapper, for instance, that Veronica and Sebastian insisted upon asking to the wedding, and boarded out with the blacksmith's wife. I believe she really had the time of her life, sitting on the village green, complete with umbrella, a hat with a veil, and an enormous handbag, telling all the villagers about the 'goings on' in London, and the time she saw the dancer, Stcherbakof, slip on the ice at Covent Garden. . . . 'And it's no use telling me there isn't no ice at Covent Garden, for I saw it with me own eyes, I did. That poor young man, skating to the manner born one minute, and the next carried out on a stretcher as like a corpse as makes no difference!' But now they're all gone," mused Mariella, "and everything's straight again, it's awful. I've nearly forgotten what my bridesmaid's dress looked like!"

She dismounted at the village shop, which was Post Office as well as general stores, and tethered her horse to the hitching-post outside the door: "Let me see—there were dozens of things Aunt Carol wanted. Packet of soap flakes, chocolate biscuits, reel of brown silko—what a blessing village shops sell everything!—tube of tooth-paste, and what was the other thing? . . . Oh, yes—I have to pay for the daily papers."

There were several people in the shop, as usual. Two children, who had been sent over from the village school during mid-morning playtime on errands for the school mistress, greeted Mariella effusively. A rosy-cheeked, hill-shepherd's wife from out-bye, who had come down on the daily bus and was packing a large string-bag with yeast for breadmaking, oatmeal, a monthly supply of tea, cocoa, and other daily necessities, together with a large packet of "sweeties for the bairns", gave Mariella a cheerful "Nice morning, Miss Foster. Looks as if we're going to have a fine back-end."

Mariella smiled at the colloquial term for autumn and helped Mrs. Fairbody to pack away the tins and packages in her bag. It was like an ever-open door, she thought. No matter how many things you put in it, there always seemed room for just one more! She had just helped Mrs. Fairbody to stagger through the door with her load when a tall, thin girl, with straight, dark hair cut in a fringe across her forehead, came into the shop. She wore a rather lumpy, tweed costume that bulged in the wrong places and sagged considerably at the back.

"Oh, hullo, Mariella! I was just off home when I turned round and spotted you coming in here, so I came back. Look what I've got here! You'll never guess." She waved a magazine in front of Mariella's nose.

"Oh, yes, I will, then, Ann Musgrave—if it's in the *Women's Window*," declared Mariella. "It'll be Veronica's wedding. It specialises in ballet."

"Oh, what a shame! I was sure you'd never guess!" exclaimed Ann. "There's a long paragraph, and a gorgeous picture of her. There's a lot about Jane Foster too. A whole article written by a journalist who interviewed her. It's called 'Spotlight on a Star's Dressing-room'. Oh, isn't it *romantic*? Imagine having reporters coming to your dressing-room to interview you. I think it's just wonderful!"

"U-um," Mariella said unenthusiastically. "You get fed up with it after a bit. At least, Mummy did, though of course she never said so—not outside the family. What does it say, about Jane?"

"It says——" Ann flicked over the pages of the magazine. "Here it is—no, it isn't, that's an article on ice-skating. Yes, here we are! . . . Bertie Wingrove, of the *Women's Window*, gets the low-down on Jane Foster's private life. Mr. Wingrove said that he had no need to ask lovely Jane Foster whether she was attached to her clever partner, Josef Linsk. The answer looked out of her beautiful eyes. 'There isn't anything definite between us,' she told him with an arch smile. . . .'"

"I don't believe it," Mariella said indignantly. "Jane couldn't look 'arch', as he calls it. I know these reporters! They say *anything* to make a good story. Besides, Jane wouldn't be idiot enough to fall for Josef Linsk—not now she's grown up. She'd have more sense!"

"All the same, it sounds terribly romantic," sighed Ann. "Imagine your dancing partner becoming your partner for life."

"Well, it wouldn't be romantic to marry Josef," declared Mariella realistically. "You'd end up by being his wardrobe-mistress cum laundry-maid cum slave-in-general! Josef only loves one person, and that's——"

"Yes?" said Ann eagerly.

"Josef Linsk," pronounced Mariella.

"Oh——" A sigh of disappointment ran round the little company. As is generally the case in village shops, everyone had been listening, open-mouthed. Mariella couldn't help wondering what sort of stories would be circulating round the countryside as a result of Ann's rash conversation!

"Never mind—there's a lovely picture of Veronica and Sebastian. Quite a good account, too—all about her life, and the ballets she's been in, and how she rode on horseback to her audition in a mist. By the way, did she, really?"

"Oh, yes," said Ann, glad to be able to tell Mariella something she didn't know. "Sebastian rode with her, and saw her on to the train. She would be about fifteen, and he sixteen. I do think it was *so* romantic, don't you?"

"U-um," said Mariella. "Yes, I suppose it was—especially to ride on horseback. I don't suppose anyone has ever *ridden* to their audition before. It beats me, though, how she could bear to leave her pony and go on by train. I'd have turned round and ridden back again jolly quickly . . . Well, I think I'd better be collecting up my stuff—it's after eleven o'clock. Have you any toothpaste, Bella?"

"Toothpaste, Miss Foster?" Bella came down to earth with a bump. It certainly was a bit of a come-down from High Lights of Stage and Screen, as you might say, to common or garden toothpaste! Bit of a shame, too. Just when she was hearing a few interesting tit-bits to buzz round at the Girls' Handwork Club that night. Miss Jane Foster engaged to her dancing partner, Joseph Somebody. . . . "Toothpaste? Oh, aye—there's twa sorts. The peppermint flavour, and t'other sort that makes your gums pink. That sort's real lov-ely. They say all the film stars use it, and it comes out in Technicolor beautiful!"

"No, I think Aunt Carol would rather have the peppermint, thank you, Bella," said Mariella firmly. "And then I want——"

When she had done her shopping and stowed away the parcels in her saddlebags, she mounted, and, nodding good-bye to Ann, rode off across the village green in the direction of a distant signpost.

"I'll just have a short ride up towards the North Wood," she said to herself, "and see if the blackberries are ripe." But all the time she knew that this wasn't the real reason she had turned down this particular road. The real reason was that Nigel lived at Bychester Tower, and this was the road to Bychester. "Everyone knows," thought Mariella, "that one wedding makes three more. I wonder if Nigel noticed I looked rather nice in pale blue, with my hair?" Then she sighed. "I don't expect he noticed me at all. He's too *used* to me. That's the worst of growing up with a person! The trouble is it doesn't seem to apply to *me*. I noticed Nigel when I was twelve, and I've gone on noticing him ever since." She sighed again. "I can't help thinking I'll notice Nigel till I die!"

At the far side of the green, rather like a policeman directing the traffic, as somebody once said, stood the school mistress's cottage. The school mistress, whose name was Goodall (no one ever dared to call her by her Christian name—in fact, it was doubtful whether anyone knew what it was), was an excessively tidy person with rather hard, dark eyes. Her house and garden echoed her personality. They were excessively tidy, too—the walls of the cottage were honest-to-goodness stone, with no crack or cranny anywhere where a creeper could find a friendly niche in which to hide. The garden was a square of grass, divided down the exact middle by a brick-edged path, each brick having been carefully measured for size and shape. No weeds were allowed to raise their ugly heads in Miss Goodall's garden. It was no use pointing out to her that not *all* weeds had ugly heads, that some were distinctly decorative. She would have none of it! A weed was a weed, according to Miss Goodall, and that was that. There were very few flowers in the garden, either, for the matter of that. The only touch of colour, apart from the grass, was a couple of straight lines of lobelia flanking the brick path.

"Lobelia is such a nice tidy plant," said Miss Goodall complacently when someone offered her a packet of lupin seeds to brighten up the corners. "No, thank you, Mr. Smith. I think I shall stick to my lobelia. Lupins are rather messy plants, don't you think? They need sticking, for one thing, and then you have to let them die down. I do so like a garden *tidy*."

"Well, she's certainly achieved her object," thought Mariella. "I believe even her grass is measured with a foot rule, and woe betide a blade if it dares to grow a fraction of an inch higher than its neighbour!" She sighed when she thought of the last occupants of the cottage—Mr. Glyn Jones, the late schoolmaster, his large-bosomed wife, and their six rampaging children. The school house certainly hadn't been tidy then. In fact, it had been nearly hidden under masses of rambler roses, virginia creeper and ivy. A clematis, with purple flowers the size of plates, sprawled over the porch, and flowers of all colours, shapes, and sizes jostled each other in the untidy flower-beds, and nodded in at all the windows as if saying how-d'you-do to the flowers inside the house. For there were flowers everywhere: roses in the front room, spilling out of a hideous china vase with "A Present From Blackpool" on it, lupins in a cracked water-jug in the tiny hall, and jam jars filled with buttercups all over the kitchen. One of the rampaging children had nearly drowned itself gathering marsh marigolds in the brook, and these filled a soup tureen on the middle of the front-room table and shed a mantle of yellow pollen on the polished surface. In the spring, a laburnum tree had stood sentinel over the gate like a huge golden umbrella.

"It makes the cottage so dark," said Miss Goodall as she gave orders to her jobbing gardener to cut it down.

"Oh, well—I suppose it *was* all rather untidy," thought Mariella with another sigh. "Still——"

She rode slowly up the road. It was very quiet. The long rides of the fir-wood to her left were filled with deep blue, misty shadows, the cobwebs hung their jewelled nets on every bush, tall fronds of bracken on the north side of the road, where the sun never shone, sparkled with hoar frost. It was a lovely autumn day, perfect as only autumn days in Northumberland can be. There was a wide grass verge to the road, and Mariella's horse's hoofs made no noise on the springy turf. Apart from a slight creaking of leather as she swayed easily in the saddle, there wasn't another sound. Even the cushats in the wood had stopped cooing, now that autumn had come.

"I wonder where Nigel is?" thought Mariella.

And then, as if in answer to her question, she saw him riding towards her. For a second she almost wanted to turn her horse and gallop back towards the village. She wanted to meet him, and yet she didn't. Then she pulled herself together firmly. It was silly, she thought, to be suddenly shy of Nigel. Why, she'd known him ever since they were children. Why should she be suddenly shy of him now? He certainly wasn't shy of *her*! He gave her a view-hallo that went echoing through the wood, and made a couple of cock pheasants rise in alarm, and came cantering towards her.

"Oh, hullo, Mariella! I wondered whether I'd run into you this morning. Got over the festivities yet?"

"Oh, yes," said Mariella, feeling with annoyance the colour flooding into her cheeks. "Oh, yes, I think so."

"Well, I'm glad it's over," declared Nigel. "A more silly affair I never saw. Weddings are the dickens of a waste of time. First there's the stupid bride tittupping up the aisle——"

"Oh, Nigel—she didn't tittup!" giggled Mariella. Then she

stopped herself firmly. "I mustn't—I *mustn't* giggle," she thought. "Men hate girls who giggle."

"Veronica couldn't tittup, as you call it," she went on. "Why, she's a dancer!"

"Yes, I believe you're right," Nigel laughed. "I believe she walked up it like a blooming ballet-dancer doing the—I forget what you call it."

"You mean the mime-walk?"

"Yes, that's it. Anyway, she looked like Odile—or is it Odette? I never can remember which is which—dressed up in wedding togs."

"Oh, Nigel—she *didn't*!"

"Yes, she did. But enough of Veronica. She gives me the willies! Ha! Ha! That's a good one, isn't it? Look here, Mariella, I've a mind to ride over to Bridgend to look at a horse. Like to come? We could have lunch at the 'Dragon'."

Mariella's eyes shone like stars. Would she like to come? Would she, indeed! She wheeled her horse and rode back with Nigel to the village. They crossed the green side by side, and set off down the narrow winding road which led to Bridgend.

Lunch at the Dragon Inn—that famous inn, beloved by artists and fishermen—was lovely. Nigel certainly knew how to choose the nicest things to eat. He didn't consult Mariella, but ordered jellied soup in a lordly manner, to be followed by grilled trout and fresh fruit salad with cream. "And cider," he added to the hovering waiter. "Oh, and we'll want coffee afterwards of course. Black with cream."

Mariella sighed happily. It was wonderful to be with someone who knew his own mind. Of course, it would have been even more wonderful if he'd remembered that she couldn't eat raspberries because she came out in spots, but after all, spots were a mere nothing compared with the thrill of having lunch with Nigel. He sat opposite her—tall and fair (like a Greek god, thought Mariella rapturously), narrow-hipped, with wide, powerful shoulders.

"Oh, there's George!" he exclaimed when, half-way through the meal, a young man looked into the dining-room and, seeing the couple, disappeared discreetly. "Chap I came to see. About the horse, you know. Hi, George! . . . Look, Mariella—I simply must speak to George. Shan't be long!" He rose without apology, pulling the cloth a little askew, and disappeared after the young man, leaving his fruit salad untouched.

Mariella straightened the cloth, finished her own sweet, and set herself to wait in patience. The waiter appeared at her elbow and inquired if she would have her coffee now or wait for the gentleman's return.

"Oh, I'll wait until Nigel—I mean Mr. Monkhouse—comes back," she stammered.

"Very good, madam," answered the waiter, deftly whisking away her dirty plate and flicking the cloth with his napkin.

The grandfather clock on the inn's shallow oak staircase struck two. There was no other sound except the buzzing of a bee on the window-pane, and the faint clatter of dishes being washed beyond the swing-door that led, Mariella guessed, into the kitchen. There was a bookcase over by the fireplace. Mariella approached it and examined its contents: *The Pickwick Papers, The Complete Angler, Sketches by Boz, Tally Ho, and Away!* by an author she had never heard of. The collection was rounded off by a complete set of *Encyclopaedia Britannica.*

"Oh, well," thought Mariella, "there ought to be something interesting in *that*, at all events." She tried to unlatch the glass doors of the bookcase, but they were evidently locked.

She shrugged her shoulders and wandered round the room. On the massive mahogany sideboard, flanked by two enormous cruets and a perfect forest of bottles of sauce, stood a curious object in a jar. Mariella examined it idly, then turned away with a shudder of disgust. It was obviously a locust, brought home from the East by some soldiering son, maybe, bottled in spirit.

"Ugh!" exclaimed Mariella. "How horrid!"

She sat down at the table again and picked up a pile of magazines and newspapers: *Farmers' Weekly, The Farmer and Stockbreeder, Financial Times.* . . .

"Oh, dear!" she sighed. "I wonder where Nigel is, and how long he'll be."

The autumn afternoon wore away. The sleeping world began to wake up, as it grew cooler. The hens cackled, and Mariella

saw a girl in a lilac cotton dress, with bare, red arms, go out to
feed them, calling: "Chuck! Chuck!" and clattering the dish.
The cows began to moo, as milking time approached. A cascade
of children, released from the little village school near the
church, pelted down the road, shouting and singing. The sun
sank in a blaze of glory behind the grove of fir trees across the
river. Still no sign of Nigel. When at last he did appear, he
didn't apologize. Mariella was to discover, as time went on,
that Nigel was one of those people who never do. He stared at
her as if she herself had done something rather stupid.

"Oh, hullo, Mariella! Don't say you waited for me? Why, I
imagined you'd have gone home ages ago! . . . What? No
money for the bill? Well, good lord! You had only to explain.
They know me. I'd have been back before, but it took longer
than I thought to put the mare through her paces. Grand chap
that George! Forgotten more about horses than most people
ever knew. Say, Mariella, now you *are* here, would you like to
help a chap out of a difficulty? George wants me to go into
Hexham with him in his car. The trouble is, what to do with
Bess. I suppose you could take her along with you? Yes, that's
a good idea. You'd better ride Bess, though—she's a bit tricky.
Easier to ride than lead, especially when you meet anything. It
would be all right to lead that nag of yours, I suppose? She's
as staid as they make 'em."

"You mean—you mean, you're not coming back with me?"
faltered Mariella, trying valiantly to keep the sick disappointment from sounding in her voice. "You mean, I'm to go home
alone?"

She needn't have worried for fear that Nigel would notice
the tears in her voice. There was nothing at all sensitive about
Nigel.

"Yes, that's the general idea," he agreed. Then he added as
an afterthought: "It would be doing me no end of a good turn.
You see, if you don't take Bess, I shall have to leave her here,
and I shan't be able to hunt to-morrow. Or at any rate, I'd have
to come all the way over for her. Now, do get a move on,
there's a good girl!"

"Yes," thought Mariella, gingerly mounting Nigel's high-stepping Bess, "that's what I am to Nigel—'a good girl'. I have about as much glamour in Nigel's eyes as—as the kitchen stove! And yet," she added when she got home and was taking off her riding-jacket in the hall, "and yet I'm supposed to be quite good-looking. Other people seem to think so, anyway. Why, Ronnie Wainwright told me I was beautiful at the Golf Club dance!"

The girl in the looking-glass above the hall table stared back at her seriously. "Yes, I *am* beautiful," thought Mariella. "My hair isn't really ginger now—it's toned down a lot. It's more gold than red, and I have a lovely complexion. My eyes are quite a nice deep blue, not insipid like a lot of red-headed people's are, and I have a wonderful figure, due, I expect, to all Mummy's ballet training! Now, why—*why* doesn't Nigel like me? He *used* to like me."

But the girl in the glass had no answer to this question, and Mariella went upstairs to her room to finish changing with a heavy heart.

4

Fiona's Party

IT had been a lazy summer—not hot, because no summer is really that in rural Northumberland, but warmer than usual. In Newcastle it might sizzle, but up here, on the Border, even in the middle of a heat-wave, there was always a welcome breeze, full of the scent of wild thyme and meadowsweet.

Of course, it hadn't suited everybody. The farmers grumbled that the hay crop had been thin, that the wheat and oats weren't filling out, that the streams and springs had dried up; the land was parched and cracked, and water had to be pumped and carried to the stock. The reservoir at Catclough, on the Roman Wall, which supplied Newcastle with water, had fallen to an alarmingly low level, and warnings about wasting water were blazed in all the local papers. People were forbidden to water their gardens. No, it hadn't suited everybody, but it had certainly suited Mariella. Her red-gold hair blazed with life, and her blue eyes shone. She'd gone about sniffing the scented air, and thanking her lucky stars she wasn't in London. All through the long, warm summer she'd thought of Jane treading the blistering London pavements, and breathing the fumes of petrol and oil, and pitied her from the bottom of her heart.

"I must make the most of it," she thought, as she walked in the shady fir woods on the hillside above Monks Hollow, gathering fir-cones to put on the fire that evening. "It's nearly the end of September, and I shall be going up to the University soon to begin my veterinary training. This is the very last holiday in my life that I shall be completely free. Of course," she added, "living in Edinburgh will be fun—not like London —but all the same I shall miss all this."

She stopped at the edge of the wood, perched herself on the

fence, and looked down at the beautiful countryside spread out
before her eyes like a giant patchwork quilt. Half-hidden in the
hazy blue distance rose the Border hills. Nearer, and over to the
right, were more hills. Mariella could pick them out as Simon-
side, and the Rothbury heights. Between them, through a gap,
was a blue streak. The sea, thought Mariella. She could just
imagine it on this September morning—deep blue, with a hint
of green, and the waves creaming in and spilling over the firm,
golden sand. She could see in her mind's eye Bamburgh with
its hoary castle, and the Inner Farne, lying to the south like an
enchanted fairy island. To the north lay a dark, misty streak
that was Lindisfarne, with its ancient priory and wonderful
beaches.

"Oh, Northumberland!" thought Mariella. "Beautiful, re-
mote Northumberland! I would die if I had to leave you for
ever and go to live in a town!" But, of course, she wouldn't
have admitted this to anybody—even Jane. She hardly admitted it to herself. Outwardly, Mariella was a very matter-
of-fact young lady, intensely practical, who rode to hounds
and wanted to be a veterinary surgeon. But deep down, under
the practical crust, the real Mariella was intensely romantic
and beauty-loving. In this way she was like the Scot who
earns his daily bread in some drab, industrial English city but
who for ever dreams of his native Highlands with their wild
and beautiful mountains and foaming cataracts.

The wonderful weather had lasted all through July and
August, providing the people who held fêtes in their gardens
for charity, and wayside stalls on their village greens, with a
series of perfect days for their functions. They had made more
money for the church, the waifs and strays, or the Sunday
school outing, or whatever it was, than ever before, and now
that it was all over, they were going about with satisfied smiles
on their faces, rather like a cat that has been given a large
saucer of cream.

But now it was nearing the end of September, and the
twenty-eighth was Fiona's birthday—her twenty-first birthday.
It was hard to realize, thought Mariella, that Fiona, Veronica's
cousin, had been married for three whole years, and was only

now twenty-one. Fiona seemed to think it was queer, too.

"I do think it's awful," she grumbled, "to have one's twenty-first when one's *married*! Especially when one has a baby. A baby is an awful nuisance at any time, but at one's twenty-first——"

Mariella didn't retort, as she might well have done, that no one had *asked* Fiona to get married at eighteen. Nor did she point out that Fiona's mother had offered to look after the baby, Flora, at her home at Bracken House so that Fiona could have her party in her own flat with no responsibility at all.

"But I *should* have responsibilities," argued Fiona. "I'd still have all the food to look after, and no one to do *anything* to help me except that stupid 'daily'. I really don't see how I could possibly manage."

"Well, have it at a hotel, then," suggested Mariella helpfully.

"Oh, no! A hotel is so awfully soulless, don't you think?" said Fiona. "I mean, it hasn't the atmosphere of 'home' about it."

Personally, Mariella didn't think that Fiona's flat had much of a homely atmosphere about it, either. The furniture was very elegant and expensive, and also extremely modern. The chairs had scarlet leather seats and backs, and their legs were twisted steel tubes that always surprised Mariella when she sat down. She expected them to collapse any minute, only they never did. Fiona's bedroom was like a Henry Moore exhibition —the furniture all made of chunks of queer-shaped wood that vaguely reminded you of something, but you never could quite say what. One whole side of the lounge was taken up by a cocktail bar, and over the fireplace (which wasn't an open one, because that made too much work) was a larger-than-life-size oil-painting of Fiona. The artist had been rather too clever, and had managed to catch a glimpse of Fiona's soul, and had put it on his canvas. So Fiona's personality met you—hit you between the eyes, as Sebastian put it!—the moment you entered the room, and indeed it dominated the flat. Nowhere—except in his dressing-room—was there any evidence of Ian, Fiona's husband. Fiona managed to keep Ian strictly in the background of her life. He provided the money to keep up the flat, and to

c

buy Fiona the expensive clothes to which she was accustomed, and which included a new fur coat each winter. Otherwise he was just a necessary evil. This was the sort of idea one got of Fiona's marriage.

Fiona's baby was certainly a surprise to everyone. She was nine months old, and the most contented, good-tempered baby that ever blessed the most loving couple.

"I expect she knows she jolly well has to be, poor little blighter!" Sebastian had said when he'd first seen her.

As Fiona's "nannies" never stayed more than a week or two, and the "daily" refused to baby-sit, nine-months-old Flora was trundled around in cars, buses, and trains, left for hours on people's beds in strange bedrooms whilst Fiona played bridge with their owners, dumped in ladies' rest rooms in shops whilst Fiona tried on frocks and hats, and even left in cloak-rooms while Fiona danced eightsome reels and Strip the Willow till two o'clock in the morning! She slept peacefully in her Moses basket while girls dashed in and out to renew their make-up and sew up ladders in their stockings, and most of them never even knew she was there. Occasionally one of them took a glance into the basket and made cooing noises at the baby within, but usually no one even bothered to glance in her direction.

"I always think a baby is so much better if you don't take too much notice of it," declared Fiona to her mother. "I never have the slightest bother with Flora—except, of course, dressing and feeding her, and so on, and I must say *that's* an awful bore. But, as I was saying, Mummy, I think a party in one's own home is much more cosy, so if you'd have Flora at Bracken for a day or two I might manage to get things ready here. A baby at my twenty-first *would* rather cramp my style. If she isn't there, I shall be able to forget I'm married. Of course," she added, "if you'd like to lend me Mabel to help with the washing up, that would mean that my 'daily' could fetch and carry, and I shouldn't have to slave *quite* so much."

"Of course you can have Mabel—as long as you don't arrange the party on a Thursday," said Mrs. Scott. "Thursday is Mabel's day off, you know, and she doesn't like to change it."

"Oh, all right," said Fiona ungraciously. "I suppose I shall have to choose another day for my party—though Thursday *is* the most convenient."

"But your birthday is on the Friday," said her mother. "Surely it would be nice to have your party on the right day? And in any case I thought Thursday was the one day you couldn't manage, owing to Ian being late at the office. I know when I asked you to help with the church jumble sale, you said——"

"That was ages ago," said Fiona smoothly. "Things are quite different now, and Thursday is my best day, but it's all right, I'll have it on the Friday if I must—I'll manage somehow. After all, why should anyone consider *me*?"

It was fun dressing for Fiona's party! Although Fiona wasn't exactly a favourite with Mariella, still, a twenty-first was a twenty-first, and you could always wear your prettiest frock for it. After all, there would be lots of people at the party. Nigel, for instance. Mariella wondered if Nigel would like her dress, the shot green-and-gold taffeta with the real lace yoke, and the jade necklace that her collector father had brought home for her from China. Would he notice that it looked nice with her hair?

"I don't care what the party's like," thought Mariella, vigorously brushing her red-gold locks till they shone like beaten copper, "as long as Nigel notices me. Anyway, he's taking me there, though I suppose he could hardly do anything else, seeing that he passes Monks Hollow on his way from Bychester, and Aunt Carol asked him to call for me." Gathering up her short white fur cape, her gold-brocaded vanity bag, and dabbing a little scent behind her ears, Mariella flew down the stairs. The unmistakable sound of a car in the drive had reached her ears.

"I don't know what time I'll be home, Aunt Carol," she said, putting her head in the lounge door. "You see, after the cocktail party, or whatever it is, we're going to the Theatre Royal to see the European Ballet. And after that, we're having supper somewhere, so I expect it'll be awfully late."

"That's all right," said Aunt Carol indulgently. "I know

you'll be all right with Nigel. I'll leave a flask of coffee and some sandwiches in the smoking-room. Have a good time, darling."

"Oh, please, God!" prayed Mariella, clasping her hands under her fur wrap. "*Please* make Nigel notice me! . . . Thank you, Aunt Carol! I mean, for the coffee and everything. . . . Hullo, Nigel! I heard your car coming up the drive."

"Oh, hullo, Mariella!" Nigel, looking very handsome in his big tweed overcoat, with a white silk scarf wound round his throat, appeared just inside the hall door. "Don't say you're ready for once? Wonders will never cease! Now just see you've got your bag, and your slippers, and so forth, there's a good kid. I warn you, I'm not coming back for them!"

"I'm quite ready, Nigel," answered Mariella meekly. Not at all a meek person really, Nigel seemed to cast a spell of self-negation upon her. "And I haven't forgotten anything—not even my hankie." He didn't notice my frock, she thought, even though I didn't fasten my cape till the very last thing so that he could see it. I expect God thought it was awful of me to ask for such a silly thing as for Nigel to notice me.

Mariella's large blue eyes opened even wider when she beheld Fiona's bedroom. The triple mirrors on the Henry Moore dressing-table reflected back a glorious conglomeration of expensive gifts. Silver ornaments jostled an amazing variety of crêpe-de-chine undies, boxes of talcum- and face-powder, flasks of jade green and pink bath salts, bottles of exotic perfume, jewellery of all sorts, and nylon stockings, fine as cobwebs, handbags, and lace hankies completely covered the bed. Drifts of tissue paper, lurking in corners, disclosed embroidered bedroom slippers, hand-printed head-squares, boxes of chocolates, and more than one spray of orchids.

"Many Happy Returns of the Day!" said Mariella, laying her offering—a morocco and silver manicure set—on top of a scent spray and a couple of china horses on the chest of drawers. "Goodness! What a lot of presents you've got!"

"Yes, haven't I!" exclaimed Fiona. "Not bad, are they? Oh, thank you, Mariella—for the manicure set, I mean. That's the

fourth I've got so far. Whatever I shall do with them, I really
don't know! By the way, listen, everybody! I've got such a surprise for you. Guess who's coming to my party?"

"Princess Margaret," said one of the guests promptly, a
large, untidy girl with a big, good-humoured mouth.

"If you think you're being funny, Sylvia, you're not!"
snapped Fiona. "It isn't a bit amusing to make silly jokes like
that."

Poor Sylvia subsided, crushed, and Mariella racked her
brains wildly.

"Well, it can't be Veronica, or Sebastian, because they're on
their honeymoon," she said at length.

"No, of course not," Fiona said crossly. "Really, you are
stupid, all of you! Veronica and Sebastian wouldn't be the
least bit exciting. I wouldn't give *that*"—she snapped her slim
white fingers contemptuously—"for either of them!"

"They *are* rather famous," put in a tall dark girl who was
dabbing powder rather wildly on her nose in front of the
mirror. "I'd adore to meet Sebastian Scott. Of course, I *saw*
him at the wedding, but only from afar—worse luck!"

"Well, it's someone much more thrilling that either of them,"
said Fiona. "It's——" She paused dramatically, "It's Vivien
Chator."

There was a short silence.

"Sorry! Never heard of her," said Sylvia, applying lipstick to
her mouth with more zeal than artistry.

"What? You've never heard of the principal dancer in the
European Ballet?" exclaimed Fiona. "But, of course, you
hardly ever go to the ballet, do you, Sylvia? Having a farm the
way you do, and thinking of nothing but pigs and cows——"

"And tennis," put in Mariella firmly. Sylvia was one of her
particular friends. "You forget what a splendid tennis player
Sylvia is."

But Fiona wasn't listening. More guests had arrived, and she
was busy examining the presents they had brought her.

Fiona had been determined to have a very sophisticated
party. The guests were all announced by Ruby, Fiona's "daily",

in a high, nervous, Tyneside squeak. After which they were plied with glasses of various drinks by Mabel, Mrs. Scott's cook-general. It was plain by the sniff on Mabel's honest, Northumbrian face that she didn't approve of what she called "these goings on". She was thinking: "Why, Miss Fiona"—Fiona was always "Miss" to Mabel—"couldn't have had a right and proper dance for her twenty-first, with a sit-down supper, and a birthday cake with candles, and 'Happy Birthday To You' sung by everyone, and a silver key hung above the door, and everything, I can't imagine! All this standing about drinking things! Folks nowadays have no idea how to enjoy theirsel's!"

Yes, even to Mariella's eyes, the party seemed a bit slow. Everyone stood about, talking brightly, cigarettes and glasses in their hands. Some of them looked as if they'd never done it before, thought Mariella critically—me, for one! I'm dead scared of dropping my cigarette, or my glass, and spilling cigarette ash or tomato juice all over Fiona's expensive carpet! Really, one needs three or four hands for this job! I wonder if I dare risk one of those funny little green things like snails on toast. Oh, dear! How I wish I could sit down! Even one of Fiona's uncomfortable chairs would be better than nothing! But no one seems to sit down at this sort of a party. Anyway, there aren't enough chairs, and I expect they'd be shattered if I sat on the floor!

The party began at a quarter to six and was to finish at a quarter to seven, in order to allow people to collect their wraps, pile into taxis or cars, and get to the theatre in time for the ballet. At half-past six a stir announced the arrival of the guest of honour. "The Guest Artist," said Mariella, who still thought balletically.

"Miss Vivien Chator, Miss Fiona," announced Tynside Ruby, adding maliciously and audibly: "Aye, and that's the lot! I'll gan back to me washing up, noo, if it's arl reet with you, Mrs. Frazer, hinny."

"Oh, do come in, Miss Chator," gushed Fiona, ignoring Ruby. "I was beginning to think you'd got stopped or something."

There was a queer little silence as the newcomer swam towards Fiona—"swam" is the only word to describe the effortless grace of her walk. Barely eighteen, she was as poised and as
unself-conscious as a society beauty twice her age. Slipping her
fur cape slightly back from her shoulders, she disclosed to the
fascinated gaze of Fiona's friends a frock of white and gold
brocade, cut so simply and yet so perfectly that it was obvious
it had been created by a master hand. It was held up round her
slender white throat by a halter of glittering amethysts. Her
low contralto voice, with a slight American accent, held the
room spellbound, as she explained to her hostess why she
hadn't been able to get there sooner.

"I came along as soon as ever I could," she explained. "We
only finished rehearsing at six o'clock, and I have to be back at
the theatre at seven. I'm dancing to-night, you know—after the
first interval. So I only have a bare half-hour. Oh, thank you *so*
much! Just a sandwich. No sherry for me, if you don't mind.
You see, I'm a dancer. I don't smoke, either. A glass of lemon
squash, if it isn't too much trouble." She accepted the glass
held out to her, and stood sipping the pale yellow liquid,
seemingly quite unaware of the spell her husky voice had cast on
the company. With sheer amazement Mariella watched Nigel
dancing attendance upon the newcomer. . . . Was she warm
enough? Would she have one of these sandwiches? No? Then
one of these? Or perhaps a *paté*? Oh, no trouble at all . . . de-
lighted . . . what ballet was she dancing in to-night? . . . most
fascinating. . . .

Since when, thought Mariella, had Nigel been fascinated by
the ballet? Not until this last five minutes! Why, he didn't know
the very first thing about it. He'd only once been to the ballet,
and that was to see Veronica dance, and then he was as bored
as bored! He'd said so! She listened as he talked vivaciously to
Miss Chator. Miss Chator was dancing in *Sultan's Story*? Oh,
yes—a very modern ballet. She was the Artist's Model.

"It takes me quite a long time to make up," she explained.
"You see, I wear a blue wig, and a lot of pale green on my
face."

"Oh, what a shame!" declared Nigel, so softly that no one

but Mariella heard. "I mean the wig. You've got such beautiful hair, if you'll forgive my mentioning it. It seems a pity to cover it up with a wig."

Miss Chator smiled at him, and Mariella thought how silly Nigel was. As if it matters what one's hair is like in a ballet! Why, the audience can't see it, anyway. One's hair is about the only thing that *doesn't* matter. But, of course, Nigel doesn't know the first thing about ballet, and never will!

The European Ballet Company wasn't by any means a first-class company. The principal dancers were either too fat or too thin, or had enormous thighs, or short necks. The *corps de ballet* were under-rehearsed.

"Oh, dear!" said Mariella to herself, as she listened to the very earthly thumps made by a heavy group of *sylphides* in the ballet of that name. "Oh, dear, whatever would Daddy say? They ought to be prevented by law from dancing in that ballet! It's sacrilege! They're as unlike sylphs as anyone *could* be. They haven't got the atmosphere in the very least. It's an awful disadvantage," said Mariella, "having a ballet critic for a father. One simply *has* to pick holes in everything. Blood will out! . . . That girl in the front row is the best of them. In fact, if she wasn't so awfully 'mannered' she'd be quite good. She's obviously been well trained. I wonder who she is?"

When the lights went up, Mariella studied her programme.

"Now let me see—I don't seem to have heard of any of them, except, perhaps, Gloria Higgins. That name seems to ring a bell! Perhaps I've heard Jane mention her, which means, of course, that she was at the Wells. Yes, that'll be it. She'll be the one I noticed. One can always tell a Wells-trained dancer. It sticks out a mile! . . . Ah, now for *Sultan's Story*. Let's see what Vivien Chator is like. . . ."

Vivien Chator was undoubtedly a very good dancer. Far too good for the European, thought Mariella, forcing herself to be strictly fair. She was a brilliant technician, and far above the silly modern version of the *Arabian Nights* in which she danced the principal rôle. In her blue wig and green make-up she dominated the stage—"just as she had dominated Fiona's party," thought Mariella jealously. "Just as she'll dominate everything she does, and stand out a mile everywhere she goes. . . . Oh, dear! One wonders why she stays with this terrible company? I'm getting so *bored* with these hefty young women bounding about in slacks and berets, and—yes, mackintoshes! But I suppose it's modern ballet!" Her thoughts ran on until, with a shock, she realized that the ballet had really come to an end, and the curtain had fallen on a mass of writhing and twisting arms and legs, leaving a slightly bewildered audience not knowing whether to clap or not, and wondering what it was all about.

"I refuse to!" said Mariella aloud. "I think it was awful! Well, the programme's nearly over now, thank goodness!" Another short interval, and then the classical *pas de deux* from *Swan Lake* —Vivien Chator and someone called Serge Yougmann. "She'll have to be quick to change out of that modern costume, and get all that ghastly make-up off. She certainly couldn't dance *Swan Lake* with blue hair and green make-up! At least, not unless she toned it down a lot—the make-up, I mean."

Again Vivien Chator charmed the audience, and completely filled the stage with her personality. She had that air of authority and showmanship that marks out the classical *ballerina* even from her earliest days in the *corps de ballet*.

"Oh, lovely! Lovely!" sighed Mariella, as the *pas de deux* ended. She joined in enthusiastically with the burst of applause, quite forgetting the sore feeling she had had when Nigel had completely forgotten her and given his whole attention to the dancer. Mariella was nothing if not generous in nature.

As Fiona's party slowly filed out of the front rows of the dress circle and followed the ranks of theatre-goers into the foyer, Mariella found Nigel at her elbow.

"I'm going round behind to see Vivien in her dressing-room," he announced, just as if, thought Mariella, it was the most natural thing in the world. Also, it's "Vivien" now, is it? "So if you would go on to Tilley's with the others, we'll follow as soon as Vivien can manage. I expect there will be a lot of autograph-hunters, and so on, to deal with, but we'll be as quick as we can."

"Very well, Nigel," said Mariella meekly. How was it, she wondered, that although she wasn't at all a meek girl, she was a positive doormat where Nigel was concerned? "All right, I'll go in the taxi with David and Elizabeth. Or perhaps Fiona and Ian could squash me in their sports car. Anyway, I'll manage."

"Good!" Nigel said cheerfully. "You're a decent kid, Mariella. I'll see you home somehow—that is, if you don't mind coming round by Jesmond. I shall be taking Vivien up there, of course. She's staying with friends while the company's here."

"There's nothing so funny as men," thought Mariella. "Now, here's Nigel—he met Vivien Chator for the first time to-night, and already he's talking about taking her home, 'of course', as if it were the most natural thing in the world! He's always telling me how much he hates sophisticated girls who use bright scarlet lipstick and nail varnish to match, and pluck their eyebrows, and yet look at him now—positively falling at the feet of the first really sophisticated girl who crosses his path! Yes, men are very queer!" sighed Mariella.

Mariella was a very popular girl. Her bright good looks, coupled with her extreme good nature, made her a favourite with both sexes. She had no difficulty in getting a lift to the restaurant where Fiona had booked a whole floor for her supper party.

"Plenty of room for you in here, Mariella! . . ." This from David Eliot. . . . "My car, such as it is, is at your service, your ladyship!" Richard Lister yelled from underneath his ancient sports car, where he was lying full length on an old rug. "If I can only get her to start!" . . . "Come with us, Mariella!" shouted Sylvia, remembering with gratitude the way Mariella had stuck up for her in Fiona's bedroom. "There's loads of room!"

"I think I'll wait for Richard," said Mariella. "Perhaps I can help him to start up. Shall I press down the clutch pedal, or waggle the accelerator, Richard, while you crank?"

"Oh, thanks, that'll be fine! You're such a decent girl, Mariella. You don't mind if a chap has a spot of bother with his car. You *understand*!"

"Some people," thought Mariella with a surge of gratitude towards the recumbent Richard, "some people don't seem to think that. Some people don't seem to remember I'm there at all! Yet, that's not fair. Nigel *did* say almost those exact words to me in the foyer, only it was the way he said them—as if his mind was somewhere else, and he was speaking to a small child —that made it different."

"Squash in, Mariella!" ordered Nigel in a brotherly manner, as he carefully arranged rugs over Miss Chator's lap. Incidentally, he had appropriated for the purpose the back passenger's rug as well as the front. "Now are you quite sure you won't be cold, Vivien? Shut that window, Mariella! Miss Chator might feel a draught down her neck."

Looking at Miss Chator's neck, swathed to the chin in silver fox furs, Mariella didn't think it likely! Looking at Miss Chator herself, wrapped in every rug in the car, Mariella didn't think it likely that Miss Chator would feel anything at all! In amazement she watched Nigel carefully shutting the car door on Miss Chator, then walking round to his own side. Never had he done this for her, Mariella, in all the times he had given her lifts. It had always been: "Jump in, Mariella! Be careful of that door, you clumsy oaf! It's not shut properly. . . . What a nuisance the field-gates are, though of course it's not so bad when there are two in the car. It's a good thing you've got your gumboots on! It won't matter if they get a bit muddy." If it had been Vivien Chator, thought Mariella, he would have jumped out at all the gates and opened them himself—Miss Chator would just have sat there and let him. That's the way to treat Nigel, evidently, only I just don't seem able to do it. When one's fond of a person, one is so afraid he'll be offended and never offer to take one in his car again.

"Hounds are meeting to-morrow over at our place," Nigel was saying as they drove up Northumberland Street, "and it's my free day. I suppose you don't hunt?"

Miss Chator laughed and shook her head.

"Oh, no—I'm not allowed! That's one of the penalties of being a dancer. There are so many things one mayn't do—like smoking, swimming, horseback riding——"

"Oh, really," said Nigel with interest—just as if I'd never

told him all that before, thought Mariella savagely. "I expect that only applies to a really famous dancer—like yourself?"

"Oh, no," said Miss Chator generously. Even Mariella had to admit that. "No, it applies to all dancers who have dedicated themselves to the art. One must give up most of one's private life if one wishes to succeed. I shall be practising to-morrow— oh, yes, we dancers go on practising all our lives—and I have a rehearsal in the afternoon. But after that—well, it's my free day, too. I'm not dancing to-morrow evening, so——"

"So you mean you'll be free to have a meal with me?" said Nigel eagerly. "Good! I'll ring up Tilley's and book a table. Or perhaps you'd rather go up north? I know a good place at Sea-houses—the Dunes Hotel. We could run up there in no time. The coast's rather fine in that part. We could have a look at Bamburgh Castle by moonlight."

"I wonder," thought Mariella, "if Nigel remembers he promised to play tennis with Sylvia, David, and me, to-morrow after tea?" She broached the subject going home, after depositing Vivien Chator in the arms of her friends, and it was evident that he hadn't remembered.

"Oh, I *am* sorry, Mariella, old girl—about that tennis, I mean. It completely slipped my memory. But even if it hadn't, you couldn't expect me to stick at home playing tennis, which I can do any night in the summer, when I could take Vivien out on her one free evening, could you?"

"No, of course not," said Mariella with a sigh. "It's all right, Nigel—we'll manage somehow. We might get someone else to make a four. Guy Charlton, perhaps, if he's not too busy. He's a wonderful tennis player."

"Oh, not too bad," said Nigel, jamming on his brakes as they turned into the drive of Monks Hollow. "He's a bit on the stolid side, but all things considered——"

"He's not stolid a bit," burst out Mariella. "He's steady, if that's what you mean."

But Nigel wasn't listening. He had stopped the car, and was examining a handkerchief that had been dropped on the floor.

"This yours, Mariella? No, of course not." He held it to his nose for a second. "It's Vivien's scent. There's something very attractive about that girl! Even the scent she uses is unusual. . . . What's that you were saying, Mariella? Yes, of course I shall be at the meet to-morrow—as long as I get home in time to change. Rather a special party," he laughed lightly. "Not like just anybody."

"Like just me!" thought Mariella sadly as she sat herself in the smoking-room and drank the coffee her aunt had left on the writing-table. "Oh, what a party! How is it that the things one looks forward to never seem to turn out right?"

That night her dreams were vivid and unhappy. They were all about Nigel, only he'd turned into a ballet-dancer like Serge Yougmann. He wore flesh-coloured tights and a riding-jacket in hunting pink, and he kept blowing a large hunting-horn which shouted in a human voice: "Tally ho! Tally ho! The fox is away!" But Mariella, who, in her dream, was sitting in the stage box, saw that the fox was a beautiful girl dressed in a classical *tutu*, and though she couldn't see her face, she knew that it was Vivien Chator.

5

The Meet

MARIELLA loved hunting. It wasn't the fact of chasing the fox that thrilled her: she had no interest in that. In fact, she'd have been just as pleased if there hadn't been a fox at all—"like the drag-hounds in the Lake District", as she had explained once to Jane, who had taxed her with being cruel.

"And I'm not cruel, Jane—really I'm not. I wouldn't be cruel to an animal for the world. Why, I'm going to be a veterinary surgeon, and a vet. has got to love animals or he'd be no good at his job, would he? I mean she. But I adore hunting, and I feel sure the fox loves it too. He's so cunning and cruel, and after all, he has a quick death. Of course I wouldn't dig a fox out when once he'd gone to earth. That's not sport. I think when he's given you a good run for your money, and out-witted you, he deserves to go free. But you've no idea how lovely it all is—the bright scarlet coats of members and hunts-men, the white flickering sterns of hounds, the beautiful clean smell of perfectly groomed horses and leather, and autumn leaves, and trampled earth. Oh, there's nothing half so lovely as a meet of the hounds on a fine autumn morning! Of course, I know you're not convinced, Jane, but that's how I feel. I think people do far more cruel things to animals—like keeping them in zoos and menageries, and overfeeding them."

Well, this was certainly a fine autumn morning! As Mariella ran lightly down the stairs of her aunt's house and picked up her crop and gloves from the table in the gun-room, she thought how exactly right it was for the first big meet of the year. There had been a touch of frost during the night, but now the sun was shining and bringing out the glorious autumn colours of the trees. Each beech tree in the belt of park-land surrounding

Monks Hollow shone and glinted, and the Canadian maple in the middle of the lawn had a ring of burnished copper round it where the leaves had fallen during the night. A blue haze hung in the hollows of the fir woods, and the moors above and beyond the house blazed in the glory of dying bracken and heather. Against the dappled, morning sky the shattered crag of Ravens' Eyrie stood out black and clear-cut as an etching.

"What a day for a hunt!" said Mariella aloud as she saddled up. "And joy of joys! Miss Vivien Chator isn't going to be there! Even if she was, I don't expect she'd be able to ride like I do. Between you and me," she added to her reflection in the harness-room window, "I ride rather well. And I look quite nice, too. This riding get-up becomes me!" She was quite right about that. She made a lovely picture—a slim and graceful girl, mounted on a perfectly groomed, chestnut filly, her red-gold hair neatly tucked under her black bowler, and her blue eyes shining. "Yes, I look my best on horseback."

As she nibbled sandwiches and drank coffee in the Bychester morning-room, along with a score of other followers before moving off, Mariella reflected that it was good to be alive on a morning like this—especially when people like Vivien Chator were busy practising their *pliés* and *battements* far away in the town. . . . "Oh, yes, Nigel—I'm just coming! Hounds have arrived? . . . What's that you say, Lady Repton? Another cup of coffee? Of course I'll get it for you. Shan't be a second. Do you take sugar? . . . I *must* get away from her. Nigel wants me. . . . Oh, yes, Lady Repton, I'm starting at Edinburgh at Michaelmas; that's in October . . . yes, next month. . . . I must dash . . . yes, I'll tell Aunt Carol. . . . Good-bye, Lady Repton. . . . Coming, Nigel!"

Mariella fled, leaving old Lady Repton looking after her in some annoyance. "Really those modern girls! They have no idea of manners. I wanted to explain to her about the jumble-sale. Now I shall have to ring up her aunt. . . ."

"What a time you've been!" exclaimed Nigel crossly, swinging himself into the saddle. "Look—will you do something for me, Mariella? You see that kid over there—the one on the piebald pony? Her name's Mainwaring. Well, will you keep an eye on her—see she doesn't break her blessed neck or anything. I promised her mother—Imogen Mainwaring, you know—I'd see she—Imogen, I mean—had a good day with the hounds, and one can't have a good day with a kid tagging alongside, can one, and she's got no one she can leave the brat with. So I told Imogen you adored kids, and that you'd be tickled to death to act as nursemaid. Ginny was so grateful."

"Oh, but——" began Mariella, but Nigel had ridden off, leaving Mariella face to face with a hard-faced child mounted on a small pony.

"Are you Miss Foster? I'm Meg. Mummy said you'd look after me. Well, you don't need to, 'cos I can look after myself all right. Get *up*, Tinker! He loves antirrhinums, Miss Foster—especially the yellow ones! Oh, no—I shan't break my neck, but if I did I don't expect anybody would mind much—I'm a bit of a curse! Mummy would just say: 'Get up, Meg. You're far too big a girl to cry.' That's what she said when I broke my collar-bone last year. I adore huntin', though, don't you, Miss Foster? I think it's worth it, even if you do break your neck or your collar-bone."

"I think it might worth a collar-bone, but not a neck," said Mariella firmly. "Which is your mother, Meg?"

"Oh, she's the one on the black," said the child. "She always rides a black, 'cos it looks well. Mummy's got fair hair, you see. Mummy adores huntin', too—even after Daddy was brought home on a hurdle. She says it's all in the game, and you can't help havin' accidents sometimes. Mummy says you can have accidents crossing the road, so why not have a thrillin' time with the hounds even if you *do* end up by being brought home on a hurdle!"

"Yes, I see her point," said Mariella, looking at the lovely face of Meg's mother as she talked animatedly to Nigel. Then she added, half to herself: "She's very beautiful, but I really don't see why she couldn't look after her own kid. I didn't come here to be a nursemaid! Oh, well—I suppose it can't be helped. I believe it's quite a nice kid—even if it *has* a hard face, and it's not its fault."

But Mariella found that keeping an eye on Meg Mainwaring

wasn't so easy. The child obviously didn't intend to have an eye kept upon her. She was here, there, and everywhere, darting about on her little piebald pony like a piece of quicksilver. More than once Mariella got a telling-off for pressing hounds or crowding the gate, which hurt her pride, for she had beautiful manners as a general rule. But what was one to do when one had been told to keep an eye on the child, and the child kept vanishing and then popping up again in the most unexpected places?

"She's gone again now, for instance," said Mariella with a sigh, as hounds checked and she looked round vainly for the tiny jockey-cap bobbing about above the little stocky pony. "Oh, dear! I wonder where on earth she can be? Oh, *good*! They've found! Now I expect she'll turn up somewhere in the front of the Field! . . . Yes, there she is! Oh, my goodness! I hope she doesn't try jumping that wall. It's miles too high for her, and there's a ditch on the far side."

The Field fanned out to the right towards Corbie Fell, and well in front of Mariella on her chestnut filly raced the little Mainwaring girl on her stocky pony, determined to be as near the front as possible. Over the wall she went, the pony grazing the top with his hind feet and bringing down a shower of small stones.

"Oh, she's fallen!" cried Mariella with a catch in her breath. "She's fallen! I knew she would! Oh, Meg! Why did you have to do it when you were in my charge? Nigel! . . . Imogen. . . . Somebody come quickly!"

But both Nigel and Mrs. Mainwaring were far away by this time, over by the spinney on the edge of Three Tree Common. Hounds had cornered a fox, and both Nigel and Imogen were determined to be in at the kill.

"Darling!" said Mariella, kneeling beside the dreadfully still figure lying on the edge of the ditch. "Please, Meg—speak to me. Oh, please, somebody! Isn't anybody a doctor?"

A tall boy flung himself off his horse and pressed forward.

"I'm a veterinary surgeon. I'll see what I can do. I'm afraid there isn't a doctor here. . . ."

"Oh, Guy!" said Mariella. "Do you think she's dead?"

D

"Dead? Not a bit of it!" said Guy, kneeling down on the other side of the child. "Now don't get in a flap, Mariella. She's concussed, that's all, and I think one of her arms is broken—if not both. I can strap them up and get her on a hurdle or something before she comes round. Save her a lot of pain. Will some of you chaps range round and get something for splints?— anything will do. A bit of fencing, or some straight sticks. Thanks—a riding-crop. The very thing! Anybody got a rug?"

Nobody had a rug, but willing followers stripped off coats and pullovers and Guy tucked them round the unconscious child.

"Now for a hurdle—or a gate will do."

Several men took a gate off its hinges, and Meg was laid gently on it.

It was at this moment that Mrs. Mainwaring burst into the little group.

"Oh, my darling! My little, little girl! What happened? I left my little Meg in charge of Miss Foster. Where *is* Miss Foster? How *could* you be so careless, Miss Foster! If anything happens to my little girl you'll be a murderess!" she shrieked hysterically.

"Be quiet!" said a voice behind her—the voice of the tall boy who had rendered first aid, and there was something in it that effectively silenced Mrs. Mainwaring. "If there's anyone to blame, it's the child's own mother, who ought to have been looking after her. Mariella did all she could, but naturally the child didn't recognize her authority. I saw what happened, and Mariella was in no way to blame."

"Oh, Guy—you *are* decent!" said Mariella with a sob.

"No, I'm not. I'm fair, that's all! If a mother can't look after her own child—then she oughtn't to have one," said Guy in a voice that made Mrs. Mainwaring's shell-like ears turn decidedly pink at the tips. For the first time in her life she felt that public opinion was against her. Even Nigel was looking disapproving.

"It's not fair!" she thought. "It was he who asked me to ride with him." She learned, at that moment, a new side to Nigel's character. He never took the part of the loser.

"I'll take the child over to Bridgend Cottage Hospital myself," Guy was saying. "There's a shooting-brake over on the road there. We'll commandeer it. I don't expect the owner will mind when he knows the circumstances." He had turned his back contemptuously upon Mrs. Mainwaring, and was busy with the child on the improvized stretcher. "If the kid recovers consciousness I'd like to be there."

"Oh, I must go, too!" sobbed Mrs. Mainwaring. "I must be with my little girl!"

"As you like, Mrs. Mainwaring," said Guy off-handedly, and his voice implied that he wouldn't have been at all surprised if Meg's mother had preferred to finish her day's hunting rather than sit in a hospital waiting-room waiting for the verdict on her sick child. As for Mariella, she rode soberly homewards. The sound of thudding hoofs reached her ears before she left the open country.

"Oh, Nigel—what an awful day! That poor little girl!"

"Don't worry—she'll be O.K.," Nigel said easily. "A couple of broken arms won't kill her! As Charlton says, she'll be as lively as a cricket in a day or two. A fall in the hunting-field is all in the day's work to a kid like that. She's tough. Good thing Charlton was on hand—useful fellow in a case like that, and I must say he told Imogen where she got off! She's had it coming to her for a bit, has that woman—palming off her responsibilities on to someone else! As Charlton said—she ought to look after her own kid."

"But I thought——" began Mariella, then stopped. After all, perhaps Mrs. Mainwaring *had* asked Nigel to look after Meg, and, in that case, he'd had to ask her—Mariella—to step into the breach. Mariella's heart lifted. She had got Nigel with her again. He was looking down at her indulgently from astride his big hunter, and there was no doubt about it, he was trying his best to be nice to her.

"I'll be over for a spot of tennis to-morrow evening," he was saying. "You and I could be partners, and we could get the Listers to make up the set. How would that do, Mariella?"

"Oh, that would be lovely, Nigel," said Mariella with a sigh of happiness. "I'd adore that." She stole a glance at him under her eyelashes and thought how wonderful he looked on horseback, and her heart melted within her.

"He's really an awfully nice person," she thought. "After all, he can't help being popular, can he? He's got such a lot of natural charm."

She was right there! Nigel *had* got more than his fair share of natural charm, inherited from a long line of illustrious and charming ancestors. Moreover, it was charm which he could turn on and off, at will, like a tap. Jane could have told Mariella all about Nigel's famous charm, just as Mariella could have (and in fact already had) warned Jane against another excessively charming young man—Josef Linsk!

6

Jane and Josef

"Oh, Josef—I thought you were never coming!" A wave of relief passed over Jane's meadowsweet pale face. "I was beginning to think something had happened to you—that you'd had an accident."

"An accident?" The young man spread out his hands and shrugged his shoulders expressively. "You are right, *chérie*, it was an accident that prevented me from being here on the—how do you say it?—full stop."

"I expect you mean 'on the dot'!" laughed Jane. "But you don't mean that something really happened to you, Josef?"

"Oh, I do not mean that I was knocked beneath a bus—but I had a collision! I collided on the dressing-room stairs just as I was leaving the theatre with someone most important that we both know, and the upshot is that I am to dance the leading male rôle in the new production of *Daphnis and Chlöe*. Now is not that great news? You see now why I am late."

"You mean you've to dance the title rôle? How splendid," exclaimed Jane. "And I?"

"You, of course, are to be my Chlöe," said Josef tenderly. "That was understood. You are *right* for Chlöe. You have the personality—so tender, and sweet, and young. As for me——" he shrugged again. "Well, who was there who could dance that rôle as well as I?"

Jane smiled at him indulgently. Some people called Josef conceited—Mariella, for instance. But Jane knew he was just a child—a Peter Pan, who had never grown up. When he was pleased he crowed!

"What will you have to eat, Jane?" asked the young man solicitously. "I know that you do not drink anything, except perhaps a little orange-squash, yes?"

"Please, Josef," said Jane, running her eyes down the menu of the tiny restaurant where she and Josef and other members of the company went for meals. "And if you don't mind I want something very *simple* to eat to-night. Not hors-d'oeuvres, thank you. Grapefruit, I think, and after that roast lamb and green peas. Oh, yes, and potatoes just the way they are."

"You mean, not mashed, or *sauté*, or——"

"I mean *the way they are*!" repeated Jane, laughing at the young man's astonished face. "Just potatoes."

"But, *ma chérie*, how peculiar!" exclaimed Josef. "I never heard of anyone eating potatoes the way they are. *Alors*, we shall do our best to procure them for you." He beckoned to the waiter and explained Jane's wishes. "The lady desires potatoes *ordinaires*."

"Yes—just the way they are," added Jane with a sigh. "Surely that ought not to be difficult?" Then, when the waiter had vanished with a puzzled look on his face, she laughed again. "Gosh! I seem to have shattered this restaurant by demanding ordinary potatoes! By the way, who are to dance the other rôles in the new ballet—Lykanian, for instance?"

"Oh, the new girl is to dance Lykanian—Vivien Chator. As you know, she has just joined the company. But of course she is a star already. She comes to us with a reputation. She was, until a short time ago, with the European Ballet. She is the latest 'find'. She is good—there is no doubt about that. I have seen her dance, many, many times. She will make a wonderful Lykanian. But of course," he added hurriedly, "she is not a dancer like you, my dear Jane. She is as far below you as the least big light in Piccadilly Circus is below the Evening Star."

"You do say pretty things to me, Josef," said Jane.

"If I say pretty things, it is because you, yourself, are so pretty," said Josef gallantly. "But no—that is all wrong! Pretty is not the right word for you. You are beautiful, Jane, from the tantalizing winged eyebrows to the arch of the little ballerina foot. It is so! And, by the way—I hear other things of interest while I remove my make-up this afternoon. It is that the second company—the Theatre Ballet—is to visit Edinburgh for two weeks at the New Year, and that you accompany them as guest-artiste."

"Oh, Josef, what fun!" exclaimed Jane. "I've never been to Edinburgh, and I've always wanted to see it. Besides, Mariella is at college there." Then her face fell. "Oh, but of course, it will be in vacation time. Never mind! Edinburgh isn't so very far from Northumberland, is it? I might be able to dash down and see them all at Monks Hollow, and perhaps Veronica and Sebastian will be there too. I wonder when Veronica is coming back to the company?"

"Not for some time," said Josef. "The doctors say she must have a long holiday. That is the worst of being a ballet-dancer —one works and works until one drops. Then it takes one a very long time to recover."

"It's funny," mused Jane, "to think of Veronica coming back from her honeymoon to live at Bracken Hall, instead of her cousins, Fiona and Caroline."

"Caroline?" repeated the young man. "Where have I heard that name before? Ah—I have it! She is that girl who was at the Wells school and turned into a very wonderful character dancer, is she not? Her name, it is now Rosita?"

"Yes, that's Caroline," said Jane.

"She will be a good dancer," declared Josef. "I know personality when I see it, and I am never wrong!"

"You knew I would dance leading rôles, then?" said Jane.

"Certainly I knew it," answered Josef, pausing with a piece of roast lamb half-way to his mouth. "Have I not watched you in the *corps de ballet*? Is it not plain to see that there was something 'different' about you, *ma petite*? That is why——"

"Why what?" prompted Jane.

"Oh, nothing. It was just something that occurred to me, and that is of not much interest," said the young man. "What would you wish for a sweet, *chérie*? Something just 'ordinary'—like the potatoes?"

"Yes," laughed Jane. "I want a peach just ordinary. Not Peach Melba, or Peach Delight, or Peach Surprise, but just a peach. And I must eat it quickly, Josef, if you don't mind. It is six o'clock, and I must be back at the theatre at half-past."

"Oh, yes—it is the *Princess Aurora* to-night," said Josef. "Let us hope it is better than last Wednesday when Taylor and Beaucaire did it. Dear Basil got nerves and let Her Ladyship down too quickly in one of the lifts. She was not too pleased, that Belinda, I can tell you! She is not all of the sweet temper. She smile to the audience oh so sweet, but behind her hand she glares like a tigress!"

"And they say women are catty!" teased Jane. "I don't believe Belinda glares."

"It is true, nevertheless," persisted Josef. "I dance with that Belinda at first in my career—many times."

"Why did you stop dancing with her?" asked Jane curiously. "I thought when one had a partner——"

"You thought they dance with each other for ever?" said Josef. "Ah, no! Sometimes it is so, sometimes not. If one finds it is no longer one's inspiration to dance with a person, then that is the time to stop dancing with her." He rose from the table and began shrugging on his coat. "*Allons*, let me help you, Jane. What was I saying?"

"About Belinda."

"Ah, yes—at first we dance together. Then *you* come along, my little Jane, and I see that my inspiration is to dance with you. *Que faire?* It seems to me that I must dance with Belinda no more!"

"I see——" Jane said soberly. "And—and what about Veronica? Don't you wish to dance with her?"

"Ah, Veronica Weston? Naturally one would wish to dance with the great Veronica! But there is Toni Rossini—always Toni is there. He choreographs—makes up the ballets for her. It follows, of course, that he dances in them, and is for her the partner."

"But if he didn't?"

"If he did not? Ah, then, who knows!" Josef shrugged his shoulders. "Perhaps then I should dance with Veronica some-times. Who would not wish to dance with the *prima ballerina assoluta*? But do not be so jealous, little Jane! There is only one Veronica, and only one Jane. When they were made, the Potter"—he crossed himself reverently—"broke the mould.

Come, Jane—as you say, it is time we left for the theatre."

Outside the snug little restaurant, Jane pulled up her coat collar and shivered. Already the nights were getting cold. In her home in far-off Northumberland the last leaves would be falling from the trees, the blackbirds and thrushes would be sitting with their feathers ruffled as if waiting for the first snow-flake to fall. Here in London, fog had closed down over the city, making its inhabitants cough and sneeze. The lighted shop windows glimmered eerily out of the gloom. Winter was coming.

Down the street walked the two young figures, side by side. Anyone passing them—the graceful, handsome young man, with his slightly aquiline features and slanting black eyes, and the girl with her pale, childlike face—would merely have thought: "What a nice-looking couple!" No one except an expert would have guessed that here were two of the world's most famous dancers. The tip of Jane's nose grew pink with the cold, and Josef thrust his thin, sensitive hands into the pockets of his greatcoat. No one would have thought of a *ballerina* with a red nose, or a *premier danseur* with blue hands! Or, for that matter, a *ballerina* with chattering teeth, let alone watery eyes!

The long façade of Covent Garden Opera House loomed up before them—that historic façade, before which so many famous people have passed. Foreign royalty, English royalty, world-famous singers, dancers, impresarios, diplomats. All of them have paused for a brief moment before that long and—let us admit it—somewhat dingy façade, before being engulfed by the light and warmth within. Josef and Jane walked quickly round the building to the stage-door. A few dauntless autograph-hunters, who had braved the fog, were waiting patiently for their idols to appear. They caught sight of the young couple, and pressed forward eagerly.

"Oh, Mr. Linsk—if you would be so good! Miss Foster— *would* you be so kind——"

Quickly, with fingers trembling with cold, the two young dancers signed the books held out to them.

"One day," whispered Josef, as they slipped in at the stage

door, "when we have been famous for a long, long time, we shall, perhaps, be able to afford to arrive in a taxi, like prosperous business men! Well, Jane—*chérie*—*au revoir!* I am all impatience for my fairy princess to appear!"

"*Au revoir*, dear Josef!" said Jane dreamily. Already her thoughts had flown ahead to her dressing-room and to the stage where her work awaited her. Already she was shedding her own personality and becoming a fairy-tale princess. Josef watched her change before his eyes, and as she disappeared up the stairs, he murmured to himself: "Ah, yes—she is the one! It must be so! As a dancer she is perfection. Perhaps one day she will step into Weston's shoes, and become *prima ballerina assoluta*, and then I, Josef Linsk, will come into his own as her partner—perhaps even her husband. We shall see! I do not often make a mistake, though I grant that I was deceived in Belinda——" Still musing, he went his way, and no one saw the almost crafty smile on his face except old George, the stage doorkeeper, who saw many things but seldom spoke of them.

7

Rehearsal

COVENT Garden Opera House during a rehearsal is a very different place from Covent Garden Opera House just before the curtain rises on an evening performance.

Instead of warmth and bright lights, and crowds of expectant balletomanes, the exciting sound of the orchestra tuning up, the soft burst of clapping upon the entrance of the conductor, the glitter of jewels from the boxes and the stalls, the gleam of white shirt-fronts and the glowing colours of silks and satins—instead of all this, imagine a darkened auditorium, a lighted stage crowded with people dressed in the queerest costumes—black tights, laddered pink tights; in fact, tights of all colours, knitted cross-overs, black hip-length jumpers, crushed *tutus* that had taken part in many a ballet now forgotten, faded pink satin ballet shoes whose blocked toes had grown soft but were still beloved because they were "so comfortable, my dear—you'd think they were bedroom slippers!" Imagine the famous Josef Linsk in a cricket shirt and white flannel trousers, with a red cummerbund to keep them up instead of a belt! Imagine his partner, Jane Foster, in a skating skirt of royal blue flannel, with tiny skating figures *appliquéd* in scarlet felt all round the bottom. "Wherever did you get it, Jane? I never saw anything so breathtakingly smart! Was it that shop in Regent Street? You know—the one with the Swiss blouses and things? . . . Oh"—with a sigh of disappointment—"your Aunt Irma brought it back from America? Then it's no use my trying to get one like it in another colour. I do think that's too bad! . . ."

Yes, ballet dancers are simple, naïve people. Let one person turn up in a new style of dress, and everyone else blossoms out in exactly the same thing in a few days' time! Remember the rage for tartan? Scottish Janet Sanderson had started that craze down at the Wells by wearing a kilt of her mother's clan, the MacLeod's. Within a week nearly everyone in the company was kilted, until, as the ballet mistress sarcastically remarked, one felt as if one were conducting a rehearsal of *Brigadoon* instead of *Le Casse Noisette*. The tartan rage had spread to other things besides kilts. The girls had turned up with tartan handbags, and tartan linings in their coats, Scottish purses with silver thistles ornamenting them, Cairngorm brooches, pocket-mirrors and combs in tartan cases, with "A Present From The Highlands" written upon them in sprawling silver letters. Even Scottish brogues, with a famous Scottish shoemaker's name inside, became *de rigueur* down at the Wells. Even the men wore tartan shirts!

The first company, at Covent Garden, wasn't above these sudden fads and fashions, either. It might be large-brimmed trilby hats for the men, or high-necked, small-waisted Edwardian blouses for the girls, or it might be scarlet Russian boots with high heels and astrakhan round the tops for the girls, and for the men overcoats with fur collars, or embroidered waistcoats. But you might be sure of one thing—when the fashion started, it went right through the whole company, from the soloists down to the programme-sellers and the people who swept the floor!

"So it's clear," said Canadian Sadie McPherson, "that we're going to look like the 'Ballet on Ice' for quite a long time—judging by the interest people are taking in Jane's new skirt! I must say, Jane, you don't look very much like Chlöe, a Greek shepherdess. More like Belita, the skating star!"

But Jane wasn't listening to Sadie's chatter. She was sitting, together with several other members of the cast, in one of the boxes on the Grand Tier, watching the dance contest between Daphnis, the shepherd boy, and Dorkon, his rival, and thinking how wonderful Daphnis—Josef—looked as he danced holding his crook, his finely cut profile lifted to the morning sun rising over the cave in front of which the scene was taking place. Her own dance with her lover, Daphnis, had taken place earlier.

"You'd better go, Jane," whispered Sadie, as the tinkling

notes of the one lonely piano announced the end of the contest. "You come on again soon after this, you know."

But Jane had already disappeared.

Jane had, of course, seen quite a lot of Vivien Chator, the newest member of the company. She had trained at the Wells School. After this, not being technically good enough for the Wells companies, she had joined the European Ballet. Perhaps it was because she had been slow in developing, or perhaps it was the extra training she had received under Probrajenska in Paris—be that as it may, she had certainly made a startling come-back, decided Jane, watching her critically as she danced the role of Lykanion.

"She does it an awful lot better than *I* ever could," thought Jane, watching the girl's movements. "But then perhaps it's more her type, and that, I suppose, is good casting. Josef is a wonderful actor, too. He makes it look as if he is almost in love with her." She gave a little sigh. "Gosh! I'm so tired!" The rehearsal had begun at ten o'clock, and now it was after one. "And oh, so very, very hungry! Breakfast seems years away. I can't even remember what I had for it," she added aloud. "Surely we must stop soon for lunch. If we don't, it'll be tea-time!"

"You ought to know by now that time stops when rehearsal begins," said Sadie, leaning, chin on hand, on the velvet ledge of the box. "Especially first rehearsals. By the way, Janet, I saw a review of the *Sleeping Beauty* last night, and it said you and Pater Martyn were excellent as the Blue Birds. It called you 'Sanderson' and 'Martyn'. Surnames, mark you! Janet, you've 'arrived'!"

There was a moment's awed silence in the box. To be called by one's surname is every dancer's dream.

"What was it in? The review, I mean?" said a chorus of voices.

"Oh, the *Ballet Weekly*, I think," answered Sadie. "What's the matter, Janet? Why the disappointed 'oh!'?"

"Because," said Janet with a wry smile, "I know now the reason for the honour. That review was written by Antony

Solway, and he's a friend of mine. I expect he imagined he was giving me a leg up on the ladder of fame! I thought at first you meant a *real* review by someone like, say, Oscar Devereux."

"Oh, well, cheer up!" said Sadie. "After all, only your friends know the horrid truth! Anyway, it wasn't as awful as what happened last night during the performance of *Lac*."

"What did happen?" came a chorus of voices. "Tell us what happened."

"My dears——" Sadie paused dramatically. Then she went on: "It was the most devastating thing you ever saw! Belinda Beaucaire was dancing Odette-Odile, and at the end of the performance she got a huge bouquet."

"Well, what about it? Why shouldn't she? Doesn't everyone get a bouquet when they dance the principal rôle? Even Belinda!"

"Do be quiet and let me finish my story," begged Sadie. "At exactly the same moment another bouquet—exactly the same, my dears, flowers, wrapping, ribbon, and everything!—was handed up to Mavis Shipley."

There was a horrified silence. Then Delia McFarlane burst out: "But why on earth should anyone give Mavis Shipley a bouquet? And on the stage, too! It's just not done! Not to give a bouquet to a mere member of the *corps de ballet*, cheek by jowl with the *prima ballerina*."

"That's what *you* think!" drawled Sadie. "But perhaps if you think just a little harder, you'll remember that young Mavis is about to marry the Marquis of Somebody-or-Other in the near future. Well, I expect the bouquet was from his Reverence, or his Excellency, or his Grace, or whatever you call a marquis, and no one dared to tell his Holiness he ought to have it sent to dear Mavis's dressing-room." She yawned loudly. "Hey ho! We seem to have finished Act One at last! Cheers! It's only a quarter to two. There's still time for lunch. Come on, folks! We must be back at three. Oh, by the way, Jane, I've just heard on the most reliable authority that your dear Josef is going to be the male part of the guest-artist fit-up for Edinburgh. Of course, it was only to be expected, but aren't you lucky!"

Poor Jane blushed. For one thing, she had an idea that Sadie was laughing at her, and for another, the very idea of dancing for two whole weeks with Josef as her partner away from the rest of the company sent her heart singing.

"How lovely! How lovely!" she thought. "I shall be able to dance as never before with Josef to partner me. I must tell him straight away, although I expect he knows."

But when she got to the stage-door lobby, where she and Josef always waited for each other, she found it deserted.

"Bit late, aren't you, missie?" said George with a grin. "The young gentleman has gone off for lunch with that new Miss Cheetah, or whatever her name is." It was quite evident that George hadn't taken kindly to the newcomer.

"Miss Vivien Chator," Jane corrected soberly, all the happiness dying out of her eyes. "Oh, well—I expect he was tired of waiting for me, George. I *have* been rather a long time."

"There's some folks that's worth waiting for, be it never so long," pronounced George, "and there's some as isn't, you being of the first group, miss, if you'll forgive my saying so. Now that Miss Cheetah——"

"Chator, George."

"That Miss Whatever-her-name-is—now *she's* definitely the other group. And if you were to ask me," added George, "the two of 'em won't spoil two houses! Don't you go frettin' your little heart about the likes of that young man, miss. Take it from old George, who's seen quite a bit of young men and young women, too—take it from old George, he's not worth your little finger."

"I'm not fretting," expostulated Jane. "I only wanted to give him a message. I wanted to tell him——" She stopped suddenly. If she didn't go quickly she would cry. "Oh, never mind —I'll tell him about it later. I'm dancing with him to-night." She dashed past the old man, and out into the street. George looked after her and nodded his head.

"Dance with him, miss, by all means," he muttered to the empty air. "But don't you go a-marrying him, that's all! Don't you go a-doing it! He's not the right young man for a sweet missie like you!"

Mariella Visits Bracken Hall

WINTER had come to Northumberland. As Mariella led her horse out of the Monks Hollow stables, and swung herself into the saddle, her breath hung upon the still, cold air like a cloud, and the frost caught the tip of her small nose, tingeing it with pink. Above the old country house the high moors wore their white mantle, and Raven's Eyrie had a cap of snow on his frowning brow.

"Oh, Mariella," said her aunt, suddenly appearing round the end of the stable-yard, "are you going anywhere particular for your ride this morning?"

"No, Aunt Carol," Mariella answered. "Is there anything you want me to get in the village? I took the W.I. magazines out yesterday."

"I know you did," Aunt Carol said with a smile. "You're very helpful, Mariella. You've no idea how much I miss you, now you're away at college. I feel dreadfully guilty, asking you to run errands for me on your half-term holiday."

"Oh, I don't mind a bit," Mariella assured her cheerfully. "I like having something to do. After all, I couldn't spend a whole week-end—Friday morning till Tuesday night—doing nothing, could I? I *like* riding round and seeing people, Aunt Carol; so if you want anything——"

"It's old Sally Carruthers in Up And Down Cottage," explained Mrs. Foster. "You know the one I mean? It's about a mile from the road, across the moor. Yes, of course, you know it—everyone does! Well, poor old Sally's legs are worse than usual, and she can't call at the shop for her groceries. I promised I'd take them as far as the stile and leave them there for her, but with this snow I don't think we could get the car up there. So——"

"So I'm to ride, you mean?" said Mariella good-naturedly. "Of *course* I'll do that. Poor old Sally! She's a particular friend of mine. I'll take them right up to her very door, dear old soul." She held out her arms for the large carrier-bag her aunt produced. "And while I'm in that direction I'll look in at Bracken and see how Veronica and Sebastian Scott are getting on. They're old married people now! It's quite a month since they came back from their honeymoon. I might hear some news of Caroline as well. She and Angelo are due back from Madrid at the beginning of next month, I think—just in time for Christmas."

"Oh, and if you *do* happen to pass the village shop, you might get my *Country Life* and your uncle's *Field*," said Aunt Carol apologetically, opening the gate for Mariella. "But just if you happen to be passing. You mustn't go on purpose, dear."

"All right," Mariella laughed. "Just if I happen to be passing! 'Bye, Aunt Carol!"

She cantered across the field, sniffing the cold air joyfully. The fine, powdery snow flew up round Jasmine Flower's hoofs, and glittered in the morning sunlight. It was a blue and silver day—a Swiss day, thought Mariella. Just the sort of day she loved best. A day to make one's heart sing and one's pulses leap.

"I meant to ride down the Bychester road"! she thought, "to see if Nigel was anywhere about. And here I am doing Aunt Carol's odd jobs for her! But after all—I owe a lot to Aunt Carol. If it wasn't for her, I shouldn't be here at all. I should be in London doing *barre* work at a ballet studio! Anyway, tomorrow's Sunday, and I shall see Nigel at church. Thank goodness for church! Not that I don't like church for its own sake, of course, but when Nigel's there it's extra specially nice. I love to see Nigel in church, sitting in his family pew, with all his illustrious ancestors around him—their tombs, I mean. And the stained-glass window of St. George and the Dragon above his head—the one his great-grandfather put up in memory of Douglas Monkshouse who died in the Black Hole of Calcutta.

E

I always think that Nigel, with his fair hair shining in the dark church, is rather like a knight of old—like St. George himself!" Mariella sighed happily at the thought, and sent Jasmine Flower into a headlong gallop across the corner of the field to the gate.

She delivered Sally Carruthers's groceries and had a chat with the redoubtable old lady, who, ninety if she was a day, lived in the moorland cottage with its earth floor and tiny windows. The cottage was condemned, of course, and when old Sally had gone, it would be pulled down, and the sheep would wander in and out of the ruins of old Sally's kitchen and nibble the raspberry bushes in her tiny strip of garden. The authorities had tried their best to get old Sally out of her cottage. They'd tried to persuade her that a modern hospital or a Home for Old People would be better for her than a condemned hovel. That was how they described Up And Down Cottage! But old Sally would have none of it.

"An auld body is best in the place she knows," she argued with the doctor, the vicar, and all the authorities who approached her. "An auld body gets used to her ain hearth-stane, and her ain bits of sticks." She meant her furniture. "What would an auld body like me do in a hospital ward, or a Home, be it never so clean? They wouldna let me keep me cats. 'Sides, I couldna see Cheviot, and the Nob. How could I tell when a storm's brewin' if I couldna see yon cloud o'er Cheviot? Nay— I was born and bred here, and here I'll die, mister."

The doctor shook his head, thinking of himself being called out on cold winter's nights to visit a dying Sally, but the vicar smiled and understood. Rugged old Sally was part and parcel of that wild and rugged landscape. Take her away from it and she would die, just as surely as a moorland plant, pulled up and planted in a civilized garden. So he made his visits to her especially long, and sat talking to her in front of the peat fire about her family, now all married, and scattered over the earth. There was George in Canada. He had four children, had George —Sally's grandchildren. One of them was grown up, had married, and had a son himself—Sally's great-grandson. Not that she'd seen any of them, mind you, but she had their photos.

Just bide a wee while, and she'd get them. She opened a drawer in the old bog-oak cupboard, and the vicar looked down, for the hundredth time, at the much-thumbed, faded picture of George and his family outside the door of their summer cabin on Lake Michigan, at George's son's son riding round his ranch in Ontario. Yes, George had done well. One day he would come home and see his old mother, and bring his wife and the kids. Sally lived for that day.

Then there was Adam in Australia, with his own sheep-farm, and Bessie, a nurse, in London. Jack was the son who had died in South Africa, but he had a son—Sally had his photograph, too, and he was so like Jack that it hardly seemed as if Jack had died. Then, of course, there was Thomas. He was in the Merchant Navy. He never forgot his old mother. Why, only last week he'd sent her a pair of bedroom slippers all the way from Singapore: "Look you, Vicar—them's nice, ain't they? No, a course I couldna wear 'em mysel—they're far too fine— but they's nice to look at, so I keeps 'em here on the mantel-shelf. They look real pretty!"

Yes, old Sally was a local character, and many a one, feeling "down in the dumps", looked in at her cottage to be cheered up by the old lady. Having nothing to live for, as you might think, Sally lived on, supremely happy in her memories, and in the thought that outside her door stretched her beloved moorland. The summer was coming, she would say, as soon as December was past, and very soon she would hear once again the chuckle of the peaty burn, frozen now and silent. Not long now, said old Sally, before she would see the butterflies taking the nectar from the cuckoo flowers growing in the moorland grass, and smell the tang of the bracken outside her garden wall.

Mariella left Up And Down Cottage on her right, and rode off across country towards a clump of trees, above which a plume of smoke hovered, betraying the presence of a house, Bracken Hall, where the Scotts had lived for centuries. Times had proved hard for Sir Adrian, and at last he had been forced to let the house and estate to a younger brother who had made money in trade. So, for all their childhood Fiona and Caroline Scott, the children of that younger son, had lived in the ances-

tral home, while their cousin, Sebastian, who ought by rights
to have been living there, had lived with his father, Sir Adrian, in
the little gardener's lodge. But at last the tables had turned, and
Sebastian, now one of England's most famous composers and
conductors, had taken back his family home, and he and his
young bride, Veronica, equally famous *ballerina*, were living
there. They were still on a prolonged honeymoon, Veronica
having been ill with influenza, and unable to dance for the
present. But she intended to return to the stage before very
long, so it was unlikely that Bracken Hall would see much of
the young couple except during their short holidays. Still, as
everyone agreed, it was fine to have the heir back where he
belonged. Sebastian's father refused to leave the lodge, saying
that the big Hall was meant for a family, and not for a lonely old
widower like himself.

Mariella, being a friend of the family, unlatched a gate at the
back of the house and led her pony into the stable-yard, where
she left her in an empty loose-box. After that, she made her way
round to the front door. Just as she was about to ring the bell,
she heard a well-known sound from within—the tap-tap of
point-shoes on polished floor.

"Oh, Veronica's practising again!" she said to herself, and
pushed open the door. Inside was a lobby, and through the
glass doors Mariella watched, entranced, the dancing figure in
the hall within.

"There never was, and never will be, anyone to equal her!"
she said aloud. "Lots of dancers are beautiful to look at and
dance wonderfully, but there's only one Veronica. She lives
every rôle she dances. She possesses such extraordinary musi-
cality that she can tell by the way a note or a chord is played
exactly what it means. She's—she's just the *essence* of music!"
The critic in Mariella (inherited from her father, Oscar Devereux) made her recognize and understand these things, made her
realize just what she was watching as she stood there. "I'm
watching one of the most famous dancers of all time. Perhaps
greater even than Pavlova, or Ulanova, or Fonteyn. Who
knows?"

The Odette solo from *Swan Lake*, with its preceding mime

scene, ended, the radiogram stopped, and Mariella opened the glass doors. She stood in the well-known Bracken entrance-hall, but everything was changed. Gone were the thick carpets, the settees heaped with cushions. Now all was austerity. Gleaming parquet floor replaced the carpets, a polished wood *barre* took the place of the settees, a rosin-box stood where Aunt June's famous hydrangeas had reigned supreme.

"Oh, hullo, Veronica!" said Mariella. "Getting down to it already?"

Veronica's eyes flew wide. It was obvious she was still Odette in *Swan Lake*. Then she smiled—an enchanting smile, half-gay, half-wistful.

"Oh, hullo, Mariella! I wasn't expecting you. You took me by surprise."

"Yes, if I'd walked in, covered with feathers, and quacked —only do swans quack? I'm not sure. Anyway," added Mariella wickedly, "if I'd waddled in like a swan, you wouldn't have been half so surprised. Now would you? Confess it, Veronica!"

"I expect you're right," said Veronica shame-facedly. "I'm afraid I'm an awful person when I'm dancing. And so is Sebastian. I mean, he's awful when he plays, and even more awful when he composes. He just forgets I'm there at all, so I have to do *something* to get my own back. You don't know how badly Sebastian treats me, Mariella!"

Mariella laughed.

"You seem to thrive on it, anyhow. And by the way, where *is* Sebastian now you come to mention him?"

"Oh, he's back in London," said Veronica. "You know he's conducting at the Albert Hall on the tenth, so he had to be back at least a week before. I'm off, myself, on Saturday. I want to be there to hear his Woodland Symphony. It's the first time it's been played at the Albert. Besides——"

"Besides what?"

"Well, I'm dancing again at Covent Garden, you know," answered Veronica. "The season starts in January, and I'm appearing in Toni's new ballet *The Emperor's Nightingale*, and afterwards at the Gala performance of *Lac des Cygnes*. It's my come-back—after my illness and my marriage. I must go back to dear Madame and get into training. What with 'flu and my honeymoon, I'm dreadfully out of practice."

"You certainly didn't look it when I was watching you a moment ago," declared Mariella. "But, of course, if you say so —by the way, have you got friends staying, Veronica? I thought I saw someone out there in the sun-room."

"Oh, that would be Stella!" laughed Veronica. "You remember Stella Mason? She was at the Wells School with me. She married my dear friend Jonathan Rosenbaum. He's Sir Jonathan Craymore, really, but one's apt to forget it. Jonathan Rosenbaum sounds so much more like Jonathan! Well, he and Stella live in Cornwall—when they live anywhere settled—but they come north occasionally, because Jonathan owns a huge estate on the Border, and Stella's granny lives in a little cottage at the foot of Cheviot. She's eighty-five, but she's still hale and hearty. When Stella knew that I was left a 'grass widow' so early in my married life, she and Jonathan came over to keep me company. We're all going back to London on Saturday. . . . Stella!" she called. "Do come and meet Mariella, one of my dearest friends . . . Lady Craymore, Mariella Foster."

"Oh, no—'Stella', please!" laughed the shy girl, who came forward to meet Mariella. "I hate to be called Lady Craymore."

"Of course I've heard of you," exclaimed Mariella. "And you're just like your picture—I mean the famous one that's been exhibited in all the art galleries—the one of you sitting backstage on some 'props', and your sardonic-looking partner in the background."

"Oh, that was poor Josef!" laughed Stella. "Josef Linsk, you know. He was at Sadler's Wells with me, and that was the first real rôle he danced. He was Harlequin in the ballet *Carnaval*. I'm afraid I wasn't really Columbine." She sighed, and a shadow came over her face. "I never got as far as that at the Wells, but Jonathan used a bit of poetic licence, and painted me so. Have you seen Jonathan's picture of Veronica? It's in here——" She led the way back into the shadowy hall, and stood in front of the great fireplace. A picture had been let into the oak panelling — a picture of a small girl, painstakingly darning an old satin bal. t-shoe. "It was Jonathan's wedding present to Sebastian and Veronica."

"You see how plain I was when I was a small child," put in Veronica. "There's no denying it!"

Mariella, looking down from her graceful height of five feet four inches at the slim dancer, in her tights and practice tunic, thought with amusement: "Why, she's only a small child now! It's quite true what Daddy says—a famous *ballerina* always has a childlike, unworldly look about her—even when she's married. Yes, even when she's a mother, and a grandmother!" It was certainly true with Veronica. Whether it was that her life was dedicated to her art—even her marriage coming second—or that she naturally couldn't lead a gay, sophisticated life, but must practise every morning, and go to bed early each night when she wasn't on the stage, the fact remained—the pale oval face, with the big dark eyes and sweet sensitive mouth, was still that of a child.

"Very plain!" sighed Veronica, her eyes on the portrait.

"Very interesting, though," said a warm, deep voice from a little behind the group.

"Oh, Jonathan! How you startled me! . . . Mariella, this is Jonathan Rosenbaum. His real name is Craymore—but, of course, you know that."

Mariella turned round and beheld the most splendid figure she had ever seen. He even eclipsed her own Uncle Elmer! Jonathan Rosenbaum was an enormously tall young man with flashing dark eyes and a little black beard. He laid two large, gentle hands on Stella's shoulders, and she leaned her fair, shining head against his chest. Mariella felt a strange little pang shoot through her heart. For a second—just one brief second— she wished that Nigel was a large, gentle person like Jonathan —someone you could lean on, someone who would comfort you if you were in trouble. But the wish only lasted an instant. Nigel was Nigel, and Mariella didn't want him changed. If he was gentle and considerate, he just wouldn't be Nigel, and that was all there was to it.

"You know it's a queer thing," Veronica was saying, "when Stella had to dance for a living, why, she just couldn't! She was much too gentle and polite to force her way to the top, the way you have to do in ballet. Now she's married, and has Jonathan to back her up, she's improved no end. Her dancing's really very good. I believe she could get back into the company now, if she liked, and she'd get on like a house on fire. We were both practising yesterday, and really you wouldn't have thought she was the same person. I mean as regards dancing, of course."

"You may be right," said Jonathan, "but don't think you're going to tempt my little Stella back on to your cruel stage, Veronica! I know you'd do it, if I gave you half a chance. I see I must remove my wife out of the temptress's path! No, Veronica, we are not going home to Cornwall. Even the south of England is too cold for my north-country primrose. She needs warmth and sunshine. We are to spend Christmas in Italy." He drew himself up to his full height and flung his arms wide in a magnificent gesture—totally unselfconscious. "Then I shall paint. How I shall paint! I shall paint Stella in St. Mark's, feeding the pigeons; Stella seated on the steps of some ruined temple; Stella dreaming by the Tiber; Stella in a gondola, her fair hair falling over her face. Always Stella—Stella——"

"It sounds wonderful," said Mariella. "But I don't envy you. I love Northumberland in the winter. So cold, and clean, and sparkling! I wouldn't miss it for anything. Goodness! Is that the time? Nearly twelve o'clock! I must dash! Aunt Carol asked me to call at Monks Hollow for some magazines, and they close at half-past twelve for lunch. 'Bye, Veronica! Good-bye, Stella and Jonathan!"

"I'll come round to the stables with you," cried Veronica, dashing into the cloakroom, and pulling a coat over her tights, and fur-lined bootees over her ballet slippers. "I have some more news, but I don't want to make you too late for the shop, so I'll tell you as we go. Caroline and Angelo are due back from Madrid at the week-end. Oh, won't it be lovely to see them again! They're booked at the Four Stars Theatre for two weeks before Christmas, and at the New Globe, Hammersmith, for four weeks, beginning on the sixth of January. I'm longing to see how Caroline dances now. Angelo says she's wonderful! He says he's rapidly becoming merely the famous Rosita's partner, and not a dancer in his own right! But, of course, that's just Angelo! He'll always be a dancer in his own right. . . . Oh, look at the lake! Isn't it beautiful in the winter sunshine, and the frost sparkling on the fir trees? You're right, Mariella, nowhere could be quite as beautiful as this. Perhaps it's because I'm Northumbrian born, but even Switzerland and Austria can't beat it. I wouldn't exchange even the Matterhorn or the Jungfrau for Raven's Eyrie on a December day, as it towers frowning over the Border moorland."

9

In the Village Post Office

ALTHOUGH Monks Hollow was several miles south of Bracken round by the road, it was only a short distance across country, and Mariella arrived at the little post office with ten minutes to spare. She tethered her horse and went inside.

"Oh, hullo, Ann!" she exclaimed. "I always seem to meet you in here! But I suppose it's natural, really—the Post Office *is* the place to meet people in a country village. I was afraid I'd never get here in time—I mean in time to catch the shop before it closed for lunch. I must have come over from Bracken Hall in record time!"

"Bracken Hall? You mean—you've been to see Veronica and Sebastian?" said Ann in an awestruck voice. "Oh, Mariella, you *are* lucky! I mean lucky to know them well enough to call, when they're still, so to speak, on their honeymoon. How are they?"

"Flourishing," pronounced Mariella, taking her purse out of the pocket of her riding-breeches. "At least, Veronica is. Sebastian has gone back to London to get ready for his big concert at the Albert. . . . I'll take Mrs. Foster's *Country Life*, please, Bella. . . . Oh, and the *Field*, too, if it's in."

"Aye—it's in, Miss Mariella," said Bella, appearing from behind a festoon of paper streamers, newly put up in readiness for Christmas, now not so far away. "And there's your dancing book, too. You can take that an' all."

"Oh, thank you, Bella." Mariella took the ballet magazine from the pile of other papers on the counter—Bella called them all "books"—and opened it. Ann Musgrave craned eagerly over her shoulder.

"Oh, look!" exclaimed Mariella, flicking over the leaves. "Belinda Beaucaire as Myrtha, Queen of the Wilis in *Giselle*. She looks wonderful, doesn't she, with those slanting green eyes and cruel fingers! Now that's exactly the right rôle for Beaucaire. She can't do anything with soul in, because she hasn't got any—any soul, I mean! I should say the Queen of the Wilis will perhaps be her best rôle. . . . Another ballet by Toni Rossini. Good old Toni! It's been on television. I wonder how I came to miss it? It says here: 'Mr. Rossini's ballet, taken from Hans Andersen's *Little Matchgirl*, showed what can be achieved in the medium of television with a ballet plus a little imagination. The first scene, which shows the little Match-seller offering her wares at a street corner, was exceptionally well done. The snow, blown up in gusts and eddies round her feet, and falling off a nearby lamp-post, was most effective. The Match-seller, herself, danced by Jane Foster of the Sadler's Wells Ballet, was an entrancing creation. The Dance of the Poor Children was one of the most touching things ever seen in ballet. Especial mention must be made of the beautiful dancing and miming of Sara Linklater, who danced in the ballet and was also assistant producer. Let us hope to see more of Mr. Rossini's work on television. We foresee a great future for this young and sensitive choreographer. . . .' "

"Oh, Mariella!" exclaimed Ann, pushing strands of unruly hair back underneath her unbecoming felt hat. "Mariella, you *are* lucky to have television! I do wish we had it! But it's much too expensive, of course. Mummy and Daddy would have a fit if I suggested it. And I suppose they're right—we ought to get a new car first. The one we're running now is fifteen years old, and it's in danger of conking out at any moment. Still, wouldn't it be lovely to see Jane on television!"

"You can come and look-in at ours," offered Mariella. "But as for me, I'd rather see her ordinarily. But, of course, television *does* make it possible for lots of people to see first-class dancers who wouldn't otherwise, because it's a fact—we don't see much of the first-class companies up here—except Edinburgh, of course. And talking of Edinburgh, here's something rather interesting. It says that the guest-artists for the short Edin-

burgh season at New Year of the Sadler's Wells Theatre Ballet
are to be Jane Foster and Josef Linsk. It says something about
that new dancer, too—Vivien Chator. You remember—she was
at Fiona's party. She's evidently joined the Wells. I thought she
was far too good for the European Ballet. Fancy Jane dancing
as guest-artist in Edinburgh! I may see something of her. Oh,
but, of course, I'll be on vacation. Isn't that like life? Here am
I up at Edinburgh University most of the year, and Jane has to
come one of the few weeks I'm on vacation!"

"Oh, well, Edinburgh isn't as far away as all that," said Ann
consolingly. "Perhaps Jane will be able to dash down here to
see you all at Monks Hollow. By the way, I think Bella wants to
close the shop. It's after half-past twelve."

"Oh, is it?" Mariella came to earth with a bump. "Golly! So
it is! I must dash—lunch is at one!"

Outside the shop the two friends said good-bye, and Mariella
had already swung herself into the saddle when Ann exclaimed:
"Oh, Mariella—how dreadful of me! I've only just remembered. You know Nigel Monkhouse of Bychester Tower, that
tall, fair, good-looking boy?"

"He's my cousin," said Mariella. "At least he's Jane's
cousin, and Aunt Carol is his aunt, so I *count* him as my cousin,
though he isn't really."

"Oh!" Ann said. "You *are* lucky, Mariella! You seem to be
connected to all the most interesting people—Sebastian Scott,
and Veronica, and of course your mother, Irma Foster, and now
Nigel Monkhouse. Well, I met Nigel yesterday, and he said he'd
been trying to ring you up, but their phone's off. A tree in the
drive had fallen on the wires, or something. Anyway, he gave
me a message for you. He said I had to tell you there was going
to be a Charity Ball at a place in Scotland called Dalmally, in
Argyll, and would you like to go? He, Nigel, has promised
Lady Blantosh—she's the person who's organizing it—to get
up a party for it. He asked me if I'd like to go, too." Ann's eyes
shone. It was plain that Nigel was her hero, as well as Mariella's and half the other girls in the county. "I said I'd adore to,"
she added.

"When is it?" demanded Mariella. Not that it made any

Belinda Beaucaire as Myrtha, Queen of the Wilis

difference. If Nigel was going, of course she'd go, too—no matter how inconvenient it was.

"New Year's Eve," pronounced Ann, pulling on a pair of woolly gloves, and wriggling the middle finger to hide the hole in it. "Hogmanay, they call it in Scotland. Of course, as Nigel says, we'd go up a day or so beforehand. He says it's an awfully nice hotel—where the dance is to be held, I mean. Oh, isn't it romantic! Think of dancing at a Charity Ball on New Year's Eve with—with all one's friends."

"U-um, yes," said Mariella. "I don't know what Aunt Carol will say about my being away for New Year, though. She and Uncle don't see very much of me as it is. Still, if Ni—if everyone else is going, I expect it'll be all right. I wonder exactly when the ballet season opens in Edinburgh? It would be lovely if Jane could come to the ball, as well. After all, Edinburgh is half-way there." Mariella dismounted, and flicked open the *Ballet Weekly* again. "Let me see, there's a Balletomanes' Diary somewhere. Oh, yes—here it is! 'Edinburgh, Sadler's Wells Theatre Ballet, 30th December to 11th January. 'Well, that rules out Jane! Oh, no, it doesn't! It says here: 'The first appearance of Jane Foster will be on Thursday, 2nd January, as Columbine in *Carnaval*. Before going up to Edinburgh, this young dancer is having a short, well-earned holiday after her strenuous season at Covent Garden, when, as balletomanes will remember, she took over the rôle of the Princess Aurora from Veronica Weston at a minute's notice.' . . . It's almost too good to be true!" exclaimed Mariella. "I must write to Jane straight away! Thank you, Ann, for giving me Nigel's message. I'll get in touch with him somehow—I expect by now they'll have removed the tree and mended the wires. Good-bye, Ann! I really must dash—it's ten to one! . . . I always seem to be dashing," she added as she cantered along the grass verge towards Monks Hollow. "Golly! I do seem to lead a hectic life! Ballerinas are nothing compared to ladies of leisure in the country!"

10

Jane Writes a Letter

In her dressing-room at Covent Garden Opera House, Jane sat writing letters.

"That's the one to Mummy," she said aloud, folding it and slipping it into an envelope. "It was sweet of her to send me some country butter to 'make me a little less skinny,' as she puts it! I must write a note to Gloria Higgins as well. Mariella told me she was at the Prince's Theatre, Newcastle, with the European, and she was quite good. I've been meaning to write to her ever since, but I've never had time. It *does* make all the difference when people notice that your dancing has improved. Oh, well—I'll write to her after I've written to Mariella." She took up another sheet of paper and began:

"*Covent Garden,*
"*In my dressing-room,* 9.20 *p.m.*

"Dear Mariella,

"Thank you for your lovely long letter. What a wonderful idea about the Charity Ball! Of course, we must all support dear Lady Blantosh! As a matter of fact, it works in wonderfully with my plans. I'm to get nearly a whole week's holiday before I join them in Edinburgh. Oh, but of course you know all about that—you said so in your letter. You'd seen it in the *Ballet Weekly* or somewhere. Sometimes I think that these journalists know more about one's movements than one does oneself! Anyway, I could come home to Monks Hollow on the Friday night and have two whole days at home, and we could all travel up to Scotland together. I'd have to leave Dalmally on the Wednesday (New Year's Day) so as to be in Edinburgh for the Thursday, which is the first time I dance there. You say in your letter to bring a partner. Well, I don't know anyone I could ask, except Josef. He's dancing with me in Edinburgh, so perhaps he would oblige, if I asked him very nicely. I think I'd better not ask him to stay at Monks Hollow, though. Somehow I don't think he'd fit in there! He might enjoy the riding, but I have an idea he'd hate the rest—walking over wet fields and gardens, feeding the hens, perhaps having snow drop down his neck! I simply *can't* imagine Josef feeding the hens, can you? And even riding—he's used to such perfectly trained horses. I expect if he rode Mummy's Satan, he'd be in the ditch in a trice! And think of his lovely riding clothes! No, I think we'd better arrange for Josef to join us in Scotland.

"We are frantically rehearsing the new production of *Lac des Cygnes* in readiness for the coming season. The Gala performance is to be early in the New Year, and Veronica is dancing Odette-Odile, with Pamela May as the Queen Mother. There are to be twice the usual number of swans. Oh, it will be most wonderful—Veronica so beautiful, and May so regal! Her mime is splendid to watch—you can understand every 'word'. I'm not dancing any leading rôles in this production—at first, anyway, though when I come back from Edinburgh I may, perhaps, get a *matinée*. They always give you a *matinée* when you dance a leading rôle like Odette-Odile for the first time. But perhaps I shall have to wait a little longer. It's a most exacting rôle—more difficult than the Princess Aurora. Not technically, but emotionally, if you understand what I mean. And, after all, I *have* gate-crashed, so to speak, so it may well be that Madame may think I'm not ready yet. She doesn't believe in forcing her dancers.

"I was interested to hear all about Fiona Scott's twenty-first birthday party, but am terribly ashamed to realize that it was all that time ago and I haven't written to you since. It's strange that you should have met Vivien Chator. She has just joined the first company, you know. She trained at the Wells School, of course. In fact, she was there just before me. She wasn't good enough technically to get into the company, so she joined the European to get stage experience. She also did a lot of work with Vera Volkova in London, and Preobrajenska in Paris, and

I must say she's improved beyond recognition. She's better than I am, technically, and I shouldn't be surprised if we saw great things from Vivien. Josef thinks so, too, and he's usually right. He's got a 'nose' for dancers—if you can say that!

"I was also glad about Gloria Higgins. Although she wasn't one of my particular favourites, she was awfully keen on her art. Her people were very poor, and Gloria was their only hope. Yet she refused to go into musicals, where she'd have made oodles of money. I'll always remember that, on the dreadful day when I was unmasked at the Wells, she offered me her powder to powder my nose! Those are the sort of things one doesn't forget. Getting back to your letter and the Charity Ball, I see that John and Lilian Moffit are going. Also Guy Charlton, Richard and Elizabeth Lister, and 'several others'. I wonder who the 'several others' are? Nigel, I expect, and perhaps Fiona and her husband. Are you going as Nigel's partner? My goodness! I've just been brought back from Northumberland by the Call Boy, and the music at the end of Symphonic Variations! It's my Princess Aurora *pas de deux* next. I must dash!

"Love always,

"JANE"

11

Mariella Visits Bychester

"ONLY a week to Christmas!" said Mariella to herself, as she rode down the lane which was a short cut to Bychester Tower, Nigel's home. "I wonder if I dare send Nigel a Christmas card? He sent *me* one last year, only it was a joint affair—to the family as a whole—so perhaps I'd better not send him one all to himself. It's queer how only a year or so ago I'd have sent Nigel a picture of my pony, drawn by myself, and put 'Love and Christmas Greetings from Mariella' on the back. Now I can't even send him the most sedate photograph of Jasmin Flower signed 'Best Wishes from Mariella'. That's the worst of being a girl! Of course, I dare say lots of girls send Christmas cards to young men before the young men send cards to them, but I'm pretty sure Aunt Carol would say it was 'forward' and not what she did when *she* was a girl! Well, the problem doesn't arise this year, thank goodness, because I shall be in Scotland, and Nigel will be there with me. I wonder if we shall all go up together—Jane, Nigel and me—all in his car? How lovely that would be!"

With a shock, Mariella realized that her dreams about Nigel had lasted so long that here she was at the lodge gates of Bychester Tower. She rode up the long, shadowy drive, and after a while the grim, battlemented roof of Nigel's home came into view. The ancient peel-tower looked wicked indeed as it stood there, its stern, battlemented walls reflected in the dark, still waters of the moat below. One of Nigel's ancestors had added a curious lopsided pepper-box top to the peel, which somehow made it look more wicked than ever—"like a bandit with his hat on", as Jane had once remarked to Mariella when, years ago, they had ridden over to Bychester together. But to-day Mariella didn't even notice the hoary old building. She had taken longer riding over than she had expected—perhaps because she'd been thinking so hard about Nigel that she'd walked her horse solemnly all the way, and not even cantered along the grass verges. If she didn't hurry, she'd be late back for tea.

She left the drive when in sight of the front door, and made for a gateway in the wall.

"Lady Monkhouse will be round by the kennels or the stables," she said to herself. "So I may as well go there straight away to save time."

She was quite right. When she reached the stable-yard, her horse's hoofs clattering on the cobbles, someone came out of a door near by and hailed her loudly.

"Oh, hullo, Mariella! You've just come at the right moment. Like to feed the dogs for me? Dickson decided she was tired of Bychester, so she's gone to Bridgend to the McFarlanes'—you know, the vet's. I suppose they offered her a bigger wage! How curiously inconsiderate these people are nowadays—they think of nothing but money! I'm sure we were kindness itself to the girl—she got every Wednesday afternoon off, except when there was anything special on, and though it was very incon-venient for me, I willingly fed the dogs myself so that she could be away by tea-time. What more could the girl want? Well, now she's gone, and I've had everything to do. I've had to groom Castor and Pollux, and exercise them, and muck out the stables, and tidy the harness-room. You should have seen the mess it was in! Really, what that girl did all day long I can't think. I've had to feed the hens, and clean the car, and—oh, dozens of jobs. The work that stupid girl has given me! It's a good thing I'm hale and hearty."

Yes, thought Mariella, Nigel's mother was certainly hale and hearty. She was of a stocky build, and Mariella couldn't help smiling as she remembered Richard Lister's description of Lady Monkhouse: "A behind like a battleship, and a front like a breakwater on Brighton beach." "Yes, and a very clean, well-scrubbed face," supplemented Mariella, "as if she's washed it a great many times with carbolic soap!"

Nevertheless, although Mariella wasn't especially fond of

Nigel's formidable mother, she was a kind girl, and always willing to lend a hand.

"Of course I'll feed the dogs for you, Aunt Phyllis," she said. Although Lady Monkhouse was no real relation, Mariella called her "aunt" out of courtesy. "And the hens as well, if you like. What do they have? Corn or mash?"

"Mash at this time of the day, of course," said Lady Monkhouse. "Some people swear they get better results by giving them mash in the mornings, but they're quite wrong. I've proved it over and over again. My hens laid eight eggs yesterday. Eight eggs from twenty hens, a week before Christmas. That speaks for itself!"

Mariella smiled inwardly. As a matter of fact, Aunt Carol's twenty hens (fed by mash in the *mornings*) had laid eleven eggs only yesterday, and had been doing so for a bit, but Mariella was far too diplomatic to say so. She found the bin of meal, made the crowdie, and carried a large dish of it down to the hen-house in the South Field. After which she came back to the stable-yard.

"I've got a letter for you from Aunt Carol," she announced. "I think it's about the Christmas Fayre they're having in the village. Aunt Carol wondered if you would run the Comic Dog Show. Oh, and the committee want to know if you would open the Fayre, as usual?"

"Well," began Lady Monkhouse, slitting open the letter Mariella held out with a large, horn-handled pocket knife, "yes, I suppose I shall have to open it—everyone expects it, don't they? As for the Dog Show—tell her I'll do it on one condition only—that there are separate pens for the dogs. *Separate* pens, mind you, Mariella. They get excited if they can see each other. The last Comic Dog Show we had, I got nipped on the leg by that beastly dachshund of Jean Cartwright's. I have a mark still on my calf." Lady Monkhouse thrust forward one sturdy leg clad in a thick, hand-knitted woollen stocking of a violent shade of green for Mariella's inspection. "*Separate* pens, Mariella. Tell your aunt that!"

"Very well, Aunt Phyllis," said Mariella, trying not to laugh. "Oh, by the way—Nigel isn't anywhere about, is he?"

"Nigel?" Lady Monkhouse peered round Castor's flank as she spoke. "No, he's over at Crossways, looking at a horse."

"Oh, but I thought Wednesday was his free day?"

"It is," answered Lady Monkhouse. "I didn't mean looking at a horse in *that* way. I meant he was looking it over with a view to buying it."

"Oh!" Mariella couldn't help thinking how funny Nigel's people were—always complaining about how hard up they were, yet for ever adding yet another hunter to their already full stables. "Well, could you ask him to ring me up when he comes in. It's about that dance in Scotland. He knows all about it, but there are still some arrangements to be made."

"I'll tell him," promised Nigel's mother.

"Thank you," said Mariella. "Well, I think I'd better be going, Aunt Phyllis. Have you any letters you want posting? I can drop them in the letter-box on my way through the village."

"Letters? No, thank goodness!" said Lady Monkhouse, hissing between large, white teeth (rather like marble tombstones, thought Mariella!) as she plied the dandy-brush. "Never write letters unless I have to. 'Phone much more convenient! In any case, John always takes my letters along with the estate ones. Thanks, all the same. Good-bye, Mariella!"

Mariella stayed in all that night, hoping that Nigel would ring her up, but he didn't. It was the following evening that the 'phone rang and she heard his voice at the other end of the wire.

"Oh, hullo, Mariella! This is Nigel. Mother said you'd been over. I was at Ploverswood—you know, the Jessops' place— looking at a horse. Beautiful animal. Not too long in the back. Powerful action. Go well in the dog-cart. . . . What's that? Oh, yes, of course I bought her. Couldn't let a bargain like that slip. Only seventy guineas! Dirt cheap! Look, Mother said you want-ed to know about Scotland. Well, I can't go till the actual day, so you'd better get a lift from the Listers. And Jane as well, of course. Or you might try Guy Charlton. . . . Don't be ridicu-lous, Mariella! Of course Charlton won't think it queer of you to ask him. Why the dickens should he? After all, you're only kids. . . . What, eighteen? I can't believe it! It only seems the other day since I boxed your ears for losing Jimmy, my ferret, and nearly put Jane across my knee for going after that stupid sheep on the Roman Wall. . . . Well, even eighteen isn't really grown up, is it? I'm sure Charlton wouldn't mind giving you two a lift, if there's no one else he's taking. If there is, well, I expect he'll tell you quick enough! Anyway, it's the only thing I can think of—unless you like to go by train. . . . No, sorry, I can't, Mariella. You see, it's like this. You remember Miss Chator—Vivien Chator? Yes, I thought you would. She's not the sort of girl one could easily forget, is she? Well, she's coming to the dance. Are you there, Mariella? I said Vivien—Miss Chator—was coming to the dance, but she's appearing at Covent Garden on the Monday *matinée*, so she's coming up from London overnight, and I'm meeting her in Newcastle on the Tuesday at crack of dawn—almost! Then we shall travel up to Scotland together by car and arrive just in time for the festivities. Good idea, isn't it? Yes, I thought you'd think so. And by the way, you must have a partner for this affair, you know. Jane has fixed on some dancer or other, I believe, so you'd better ask Charlton. I don't suppose he's got anybody yet. Well, cheerio, Mariella! See you in Scotland! 'Bye!"

The 'phone clicked, and Mariella put down the receiver slowly. All her gay dreams about herself and Nigel dancing together were shattered. It would be Vivien Chator who would be dancing with him, and not her—Mariella—at all.

"Oh, how miserable I am!" she said aloud. "Here I am going to that glorious Charity Ball on a romantic night like New Year's Eve, and I'm as miserable as miserable! I wish I wasn't going! I wish I was staying here with Aunt Carol and Uncle Harold—I do indeed!'

But it was no use wishing. However much she didn't want to go, she had said she would, and pride forbade her to back out. She picked up the telephone receiver again, and dialled the Listers' number.

"Oh, hullo! Is that you, Elizabeth? Mariella speaking! I was wondering about the Ball on New Year's Eve. You see, Nigel —Nigel Monkhouse, you know—well, I thought he might have given Jane and me a lift, but he can't. No, you see he's waiting behind to drive Vivien Chator up. She only arrives early Tuesday morning from London. Well, to cut a long story short, I wondered if you and Richard . . . Oh, I *see*. No, of course not. I forgot about Lilian Moffit. At least, I knew she was going, of course, but I thought that John, her brother—oh, he can't go, after all? What a shame! But of course you must give Lilian a lift, and of course you haven't room for two more—not with all the suitcases. I'll try somebody else. . . . No, of course not. Well, I shall see you all at Dalmally. Good-bye!"

Poor Mariella laid down the receiver with something like despair. Should she sink her pride and ring up Guy Charlton? Was it very unladylike to ask a young man to give one a lift? Surely not if there were two of you. Still—— While she was debating the matter, the 'phone at her elbow rang, making her jump, and a young man's voice at the other end said:

"Is that Mariella? I thought I recognized the voice! This is Guy Charlton speaking. I was wondering about Scotland at New Year. Do you know if there's anyone who would be glad of a lift? It seems stupid to travel up there by car all by myself."

"Oh, Guy!" said Mariella, covering the mouth of the receiver with her hand so that he shouldn't hear. "You always seem to turn up in the nick of time—just when you're needed!" Then, taking her hand away, she said eagerly: "As a matter of fact, Jane and I—yes, Jane Foster, she's coming up for the dance—would be most awfully glad of a lift. I'd just been wondering how on earth we should get there. Nigel says it's a bit tricky if you go by train. You have to be sure to get on the right coach, or you have to change at Edinburgh, or something, instead of going right through to whatever the name of the station is."

"Tyndrum," supplied Guy promptly. "You change there for Dalmally, and then there's a long walk at the other end—to the hotel, I mean. Of course, you *can* go on to Loch Awe Station, beside the big Loch Awe Hotel, then go across the loch by boat to Inveross. That's the name of the little village where our hotel, the Allt nan Ros, is. On the other hand, I'm not sure whether trains stop now at Loch Awe Station. No, much better for you both to come with me by car!"

"Oh, *much* better," agreed Mariella, with a sigh of relief. "If you're sure you don't mind having two of us, and all the luggage——"

"No, of course not," said Guy. "I'll come over there for you."

"Oh, no!" exclaimed Mariella. "We'll come across to Hordon. At least, I expect Aunt Carol will bring us in the car. It's miles out of your way, Guy, to come all the way over here for us."

"Not a bit of it!" said the warm voice at the other end of the wire. "That's settled, then. I'll be over at your place on the Monday, bright and early, and woe betide either of you if you're still in bed! It'll be a wet sponge if you are!"

"In this weather? Ugh!" said Mariella with a shiver. "I shall certainly be up all right! I'll leave the cold sponge for Jane!"

"Oh, and there's one more thing," said Guy. "I believe we're each supposed to have a partner for this affair. If you're not already fixed up, why not come as mine?"

"Oh, yes, please, Guy," said Mariella. "I mean, no, I'm not fixed up, and I'd like you to be my partner."

"Right ho! So long, Mariella, and a Happy Christmas!"

"Good-bye" said Mariella, stopping herself just in time from adding: "dear Guy." It suddenly occurred to her that Guy had waited until she had rung off herself before putting down the receiver. When she talked to Nigel, it was always he who rang off first.

"It's true," said Mariella. "Nigel still thinks I'm about twelve, so he doesn't bother about being polite to me."

12

Meeting Jane

JANE was now one of Covent Garden's *prima ballerinas*, and she could afford to travel in comfort. She left her first-class sleeper at Newcastle station in a positive fever of excitement. It was nearly a year since she'd been home, and, although she was very happy living in London, and, as she had so often told Mariella, wouldn't live anywhere else, yet there *were* times when she longed for a glimpse of Monks Hollow, her north-country home, nestled amongst its woods, with the lonely moorland stretching away as far as the eye could see. Also she ached to see her father and mother. Yes, Jane was very often homesick.

"It's queer," she thought as she followed a porter down the long platform, "when I lived here, I didn't appreciate it one little bit! All I wanted to do was to get away from it. I didn't think I loved the country at all, but now I know I do. I suppose it's in my blood. . . . Oh, there's Mariella! How pretty she is! I love her with her hair like that—all short and curly. She's awfully like Mummy. Oh, and there *is* Mummy—and Daddy, too! How sweet of them all to come and meet me so early in the morning!"

She ran forward to greet them, and people turned round to stare at the slender girl with her sweet, pale face, and graceful carriage. Many of them wondered idly who she was, but not one of them guessed that here, under their very noses, was one of England's greatest dancers, a girl whom many of them had stood long hours in theatre queues to see.

"Oh, Jane—how lovely to see you again!" cried Mariella. "I don't believe you look any older than you did the day I first saw you in this very station! You're just like Veronica—you stay about fifteen!"

Jane didn't answer. She wasn't listening. She was far too busy hugging her father and mother, and then all three of them together.

"It seems such *ages* since I saw you! Oh, I know it isn't really. It's only a few months since you came to London to see me dance—the time poor Veronica collapsed and I took over her rôle in *The Sleeping Beauty*. Still, it's ages since I was actually *here*, in this darling, dirty old station! Are all stations dirty? I believe they are. What romantic places railway stations are, when you come to think of it! Imagine all the meetings and partings that have taken place on this very platform!" Jane gently brushed the dingy expanse of concrete with her little, flat-heeled shoe.

"Oh, Jane—you always did think the funniest things!" giggled Mariella, as they went through the barrier. "You make it sound as if the station was alive. I don't know what Nigel would say if he heard you!"

"*I* do!" laughed Jane. "He'd say: 'Wake up, Jane, you stupid girl! Oh, what did you do that for? You pulled his mouth, so of course he bucked!' 'He,' by the way, refers to that beastly little pony Firefly. Sorry, Mummy, I know he was your birthday present to me, but he *was* beastly, you must admit, and it's no use my pretending I wasn't scared to death of him."

"I thought he was beautiful," declared Mariella. "I loved him dearly, and when I grew too big for him and we gave him to the McFarlane kid, I cried like anything! Firefly and I were great friends. He'd do anything for me."

"Rather like Nigel," Jane said mischievously. "He'd do anything for you, Mariella, but nothing for me—except order me about!"

Mariella said nothing, but she sighed wistfully. Her thoughts had flown to Nigel. Would he do anything for her now? No—she seemed to have lost the spell that had made Nigel her willing slave.

"What's the matter?" asked Jane. "You looked quite sad for

a minute, Mariella. I've never seen you look sad before—not even on that awful day when Uncle Elmer spanked you!"

"Oh, I wasn't sad then," declared Mariella. "I quite enjoyed it, as a matter of fact! It's just that—oh, nothing, really. I'll tell you about it some day, Jane."

"Well, here's the car," said Mr. Foster, as the three of them emerged from the gloom of the station into the portico. "I was lucky to get a parking-place so near the main entrance. That's the reward of meeting a train so early in the morning! . . . Put my daughter's case here in the boot, please," he added to the porter. "Thank you. Now, get in, all of you. I shall drive straight round to the office, Carol. It's just a quarter-past eight, so I shall be really early for once in my life! . . . Have you got plenty of rugs in the back there? You'll feel the cold, I expect, Jane—after London?"

"Oh, it's pretty chilly in London, too," laughed Jane. "In fact, I often think the damp and the fog in London make it seem even colder there than it is here, where at least it's a dry cold."

"You haven't got very thick clothes on," said Jane's mother, glancing at her daughter's brown velvet coat and kid gloves. "Why not a fur coat? Surely you could afford one now? Anyway, I thought we gave you a grey squirrel last year for a Christmas present. Or am I wrong?"

"No, you're quite right, Mummy," Jane said. "You did give me one. But you see," she added apologetically, "I don't really like fur coats, although I know, of course, that they're beautifully warm——"

"Not like fur coats? But why on earth not?" demanded Mrs. Foster in amazement.

Jane's creamy cheeks turned a delicate pink.

"It's just that I can't bear to think of all the animals being killed to make me a fur coat," she said simply. "Pretty little squirrels, and little velvety moles, and all sorts of wild things. I think it's cruel!"

"Well, *I* think it's plain ridiculous," declared Mrs. Foster. "But then you always did have queer ideas, Jane! And I suppose that's why you're wearing those absurd kid gloves, instead of fur ones? I wonder you don't freeze to death!"

"Oh, they're lined with silk," explained Jane, spreading out one tiny hand and flexing the fingers. "They're beautifully warm. You wouldn't believe!"

"I certainly wouldn't!" laughed her mother.

"Pilgrim Street seems to have shrunk!" declared Jane, as the car threaded its way through the cold Northumberian dawn, in and out of the traffic, past the cathedral church with its ancient lantern tower, and up to the traffic lights at the cross-roads. "Even the castle doesn't seem quite so big, or the bridges so long. London dwarfs everything! Why, even the traffic seems to be in slow motion! And I'm sure the people don't scurry along to their work half as fast as they do in London! . . . Oh, here's Daddy's office. The same old brass plates on the door. . . . First Floor: Josiah Character and Sons, Advertising Agents—Second Floor: Airylite Mattress Co. Ltd. —Third Floor: Harold Foster and Sons Ltd., Egg Importers— that's Daddy!"

"It's the floors higher up that fascinate me," put in Mariella. "Fourth Floor—the headquarters of the Squeeze-eezy Corsets Co. Ltd. The lift doesn't go up there, so if you want to know how to squeeze your figure, you've got to walk! . . . Good-bye, Uncle Harold. Don't be late home. We're going to celebrate at dinner—in honour of Jane. . . . What was I saying? Oh, yes— I'd got to the Fifth Floor, hadn't I? Well, the Fifth Floor is taken over by some art students who rent it while they're in college, and then pass it on to the next lot when they 'go down'. You get a wonderful view of the river up there. In fact, you've got a bird's-eye view of the whole of Newcastle."

"How do you know?" demanded Jane, while her mother took over the steering-wheel, and edged the car out into the traffic stream once more.

"Oh, I went up there one day while I was waiting for Uncle Harold," confessed Mariella. "There was no one in the corset place, so I thought I might as well have a look higher up. It's awfully nice—I mean the artists' part—and frightfully interesting. They've had a skylight put in one of the rooms—they're attics, really—and they use it to paint in. The other one is their bedroom, and behind a partition there's a little kitchen, with a gas-ring, and one of those ovens you put on the top, and there's a bath——"

"*Mariella!*" exclaimed Mrs. Foster in horror, as they were held up at the traffic-lights at the bottom of Northumberland Street. "You don't mean to tell me——"

"Oh, *no*, Aunt Carol—I didn't dash up and snoop around while they were out," interrupted Mariella. "I just pretended I was wanting to order a Squeeze-eezy corset, and they—I mean the artists—asked me up and showed me everything."

"But who *are* these artists?" asked Mrs. Foster, letting in the clutch. "It's getting a little lighter now, I think. Or perhaps it's because we're almost out of the city."

"Derek and Bill," said Mariella promptly. "I'm afraid I don't know their other names. Come to think of it, I don't believe art students *have* other names. Have they, Jane?"

"I don't know," laughed Jane. "All I know is that in ballet you start off by being a Christian name and end by being a sur-name. I began by being Jane, and now I'm Foster! It always re-minds me of a boys' public school! . . . Oh, look! Here's the Ponteland Road. I think you can see the Rothbury hills from here. Oh, yes—and there's Cheviot, too! There's snow on him. Has there been any snow at home yet, Mummy?"

"Only a little," answered Mrs. Foster. "But according to the local weather sages—not to mention the B.B.C.—we're in for some before long. I don't know how far you can depend upon them. I hope it won't interfere with your plans. You're all going up to Scotland by car, Nigel tells me. I don't know how he's going to squeeze you both in that small car. You'll have to economize with luggage!"

"Nigel?" echoed Mariella. "You mean Guy, don't you, Aunt Carol? Guy Charlton. Nigel rang me up to say that he couldn't take us because of Vivien Chator. She's coming up from Lon-don by sleeper on the Monday night, and he's meeting her, and driving her up to Scotland on the Tuesday just in time for the dance. So Guy offered to give us a lift instead."

"Well, I met Nigel only yesterday," declared Mrs. Foster, "and he said he'd be over for the two of you bright and early on the Monday, and he hoped you'd remember his car wasn't a Rolls Royce six-seater, and travel light!"

"There must be some mistake," said Mariella, but her heart lifted. Perhaps she had misunderstood Nigel, and he wanted to drive her, Mariella, after all, and not Vivien Chator. Then it fell again. It was no use now—she'd arranged with Guy. Suddenly she became aware of a queer expression on Jane's face.

"Oh, need we? *Need* we, Mariella?"

"Need we what?"

"Need we drive up to Scotland in Nigel's car?" said Jane. "I know it sounds silly, but I still don't like Nigel very much. I'd an awful lot rather go up with Guy. I remember once——" She stopped suddenly, but Mariella knew from the expression on her small, expressive face that she was living again some incident that had happened in the past. "Guy is such a nice person."

"Well, I expect we shall have to go with him, anyway," said Mariella. Then her sense of fairness made her add: "And you're right, Jane—he *is* indeed a very nice person."

That night, before dinner, Mariella rang up Nigel. It was a long time before he came to the 'phone, and when he did he sounded more than a little disgruntled.

"That you, Mariella? I've been meaning to ring you up. I met your aunt yesterday, and she'd got hold of some stupid, cock-and-bull story about you and Jane not coming up to Scotland in my car. I told her that *of course* you're coming up in my car."

"Oh, but Nigel—you said the other day that Jane and I couldn't come with you because of Vivien Chator——"

"Did I? Well, perhaps I just said that I *might* give her a lift, but there was nothing actually settled. You *will* take up a chap all wrong—it's an awful fault you've got, Mariella. As a matter of fact, Vivien—Miss Chator—decided to go straight through to Tyndrum. Naturally that suits me down to the ground, because now I shall be able to take you and Jane——"

"Oh, *no*!" said Mariella faintly.

"What's that you say? Now I do hope you're not going to be

pig-headed, Mariella—just because you got me all wrong. I'll be over for you both, nine o'clockish on Monday, and don't be late!"

"But Nigel, it's impossible," said Mariella. "You see, Guy is taking us."

There was a short silence at the other end of the wire. Then Nigel exclaimed: "Guy Charlton? What on earth made you ask *him*?"

"Why, you told me to," burst out Mariella.

"Only after you'd tried the Listers."

"I did try the Listers, and they hadn't room. But, as a matter of fact, Guy asked *me*. I didn't ask him."

"The dickens he did!" exploded Nigel. "Well, anyway, you can tell him you've changed your plans, I suppose, and that you're coming with me, after all?"

"Oh, I couldn't do that," expostulated Mariella. "It was most awfully kind of him to offer. I was frightfully grateful at the time——"

"Oh, Charlton won't mind if you call it off," declared Nigel. "I expect he was just being polite. He'll be no end relieved at not having to tote a couple of girls all that way—not to mention all their luggage! You see, I know you and your suitcases, Mariella!" He laughed lightly.

"Well, I can't do anything about it, Nigel," said Mariella firmly. "It would be most awfully rude."

There was another short silence. Then Nigel said with what Jane would have called his well-known charm: "Look here, Mariella, don't you *want* to drive in my car? I know it's not a dashed great limousine like Charlton's, but you used to like it. I shall be most frightfully disappointed if you don't come with me, Mariella. Dash it all, couldn't Jane go with Charlton? You might ask her, and do a chap a favour."

"I can't," Mariella repeated firmly. "I can't really, Nigel—not even to please you. Not even to please myself."

"You mean you won't," said the voice at the other end, returning to its former petulant tone. "Oh, all right. Have it your own way, but don't expect me to dance with you, that's all. One good turn deserves another, remember, and the opposite applies, too!" The click of the telephone receiver going down on the stand told Mariella that this most difficult and aggravating conversation had come to an end.

"I gathered that was Nigel," said Jane from where she stood at the fireplace. "Of course you were perfectly right, Mariella. Oh, I'm so *glad* it's Guy we're going with, and not that horrible Nigel! So glad, and so happy!"

"*I'm* not!" said Mariella, half to herself. "I'm not happy at all. I'm terribly, terribly miserable! Oh, I wish—how I wish I'd never even heard of this beastly dance!"

13

Journey to Scotland

MARIELLA and Jane listened in anxiously to the weather fore-cast on the Monday morning. They had looked in the night before, and the television map hadn't been very reassuring. . . . "Snow showers all over the country," it had said, "especially on high ground." This morning's report was even worse. . . . "Considerable falls of snow in the north," said the announcer with relish. "The A.A. report icy conditions on many roads, and motorists travelling on these roads are warned that they may find themselves in difficulties." With a sigh of relief Mari-ella noted that the roads mentioned were mostly those across the Pennines, and over into the Lake District. Evidently the roads into Scotland were open as yet.

"All the same, I wish we were there!" she said as they fin-ished breakfast. "It would be awful to get stuck and have to see the New Year in, stuck deep in a snowdrift!"

Jane laughed.

"I don't think it's the least bit likely," she declared. "Guy Charlton is the sort of person who always gets you there. By the way, I think I can hear a car. Have you finished packing your suitcase, Mariella?"

"Yes, it's down in the hall beside yours," answered her cousin. "Of course, I expect I've forgotten loads of things—my tooth-brush, for instance, or my nightie. Gosh, I *have*! Tell Guy I shan't be a minute!" She dashed away upstairs again.

Guy didn't seem to be unduly worried, though he was obviously anxious to be off.

"Good morning, Mrs. Foster!" he said. "Hullo, Jane! It's grand to see you back again in Northumberland! So sorry to barge in right in the middle of breakfast, but I feel we ought to be on our way. I'll just put the cases in the car, shall I? Are these the ones, Jane? Right ho! Leave them to me! By the way, where's Mariella? I hope she isn't still in bed?"

"Oh, no!" laughed Jane, as they came back into the house after depositing the suitcases in the boot of Guy's car. "She's gone to fetch her tooth-brush."

"Trust Mariella to forget the most essential things," laughed Guy. "It's a wonder it wasn't her pyjamas!"

"As a matter of fact, it *was!*" exclaimed Mariella from half-way down the staircase. "At least, it was my nightie. And I'm afraid I've still forgotten these." She waved a pair of nylon stockings and an evening bag. "Do you think you could push them in somewhere, Guy? Oh, don't bother taking the cases out of the boot again. I can push them in the side—the stockings and things, I mean. I'm so sorry to make you open it again—I mean the boot—but I couldn't possibly go to a ball with thick stockings, could I? Goodness! Whatever have you got in there?"

"Climbing things," said Guy solemnly. "Couldn't possibly go to the Grampian country without a rucksack or a pair of climbing boots, now, could I?"

Mariella knew that he was laughing at her, and she laughed, too. In spite of the fact that Guy was a rather serious-looking boy, he had a strong sense of humour.

"But what on earth is this?" exclaimed Jane in her turn.

"Ice-axe," answered Guy. "And a climbing rope. Must have my nylons with me!"

"You don't mean to say that it's made of nylon—like my stockings?" Mariella said incredulously.

"Certainly it is. Much stronger than the other sort."

"How thrilling!" Jane said dreamily, as she settled herself in the back of Guy's car. "I adore mountains! At least, I adore pictures of them. I've never seen any real ones—except the Cheviots at a distance, and I expect you'd only call them hills."

"You've never been to Scotland, then?" asked Guy, as they sped down the drive.

"No, never. I've never been further than Galashiels, and you can't really call *that* going to Scotland, can you? Disgraceful, isn't it—especially for a Northumbrian, but you see, all my life I've been too busy dancing to do anything or go anywhere."

"Never mind," Guy said consolingly, "you're going to make up for it this time."

"I've been to Scotland several times," Mariella put in, arranging a rug over her knees. "I've even been to the Isle of Skye with Mummy years and years ago—when I was quite a little girl. I still can't imagine what on earth made Mummy go to Skye, of all places! *I* loved it, but I have an idea poor Mummy thought it was the last place on God's earth, and the most desolate!"

"Oh, I expect she'd heard that Sir Walter Scott went to see the famous Loch Coruisk, or something," put in Jane. "He wrote a poem about it, didn't he? She probably felt she ought to see it. Or perhaps she was doing some choreography—making up a ballet—about the Hebrides, and felt she ought to have some 'local colour'. Imagine what a thrilling ballet you could make about Skye, with a Scottish background, and a wonderful backcloth of mountains and mist. It would be better than *Les Sylphides*! You could bring in Flora McDonald, and Bonny Prince Charlie, and the spirits of the Cuillin Hills——"

"You've forgotten the waterhorses," said Mariella.

"The *what*?"

"Good gracious, Jane—it's well to be seen you've never been to Skye! You couldn't have a ballet about the Misty Isle, and not introduce one of their famous waterhorses! These fearsome beasts live in the depths of the lochs, and emerge every now and then to claim a victim. You'll be walking along a lonely moorland road—perhaps on the shores of Loch nan Dubrachan —that's the loch where a particularly savage waterhorse lives. . . . Well, you'll be walking along all unsuspecting, and suddenly you hear a clip-clop behind you. You turn round to say how-d'you-do to the horseman, but there's no one there! But you notice that the grasses by the side of the road are bending, and the tufts of heather are crushed. Then you know the horrid truth. It's a waterhorse come to carry you off to his lair in the depths of the loch at the foot of Blaven!"

"Ugh! You're making my flesh creep!" shuddered Jane. "What a horrible place!"

"It isn't horrible at all—it's wonderful," said Mariella indignantly. "The only trouble about Skye is that it baffles description. When you talk about the Black Cuillin with their shattered peaks, and the mist, and the lonely locans, and dark, stony corries, people say 'How dreary!' and yet Skye isn't dreary at all. It's got 'atmosphere'. Once you've been there, you die to go back. As the song says: 'The Black Cuillin are callin' me away' —by the way, Guy, we must be getting near the Border. We cross at Gretna Green, don't we?"

"Yes, as a matter of fact, this village is Gretna. Not a very inspiring place, is it?" commented Guy. "Anything less romantic one couldn't imagine! This is supposed to be the famous smithy where all the runaway couples got hitched up. For a small sum you can have the ceremony performed all over again, just as it used to be in the olden days, only of course it isn't legal now. I never can understand this place. There seem to be *two* 'original smithies'! Local competition, I suppose!"

"What is the next place we come to?" asked Jane.

"Well, there's a stretch of high ground up to Moffat," Guy answered. "We shall probably run into snow there."

His prophecy was proved to be correct. The road got whiter and the snow deeper until they reached the outskirts of Glasgow, when all traces of snow suddenly vanished.

"This is where we go over in the ferry. It's called the Erskine Ferry on this side, and the Old Kilpatrick on the other. It looks as if we shall have to wait. There's a long queue, as usual! Never mind—we can have a spot of lunch in the car while we wait. It will save time. There's a flask of coffee and some cups in the back there, Jane, if you can manage to pour out, and there's a packet of sandwiches in the cubby-hole, Mariella."

They ate the sandwiches ravenously. As Mariella said, breakfast seemed so far away that you could scarcely remember what you'd had for it!

"Oh, what glorious coffee!" exclaimed Jane. "Why don't we get coffee like this in London, or is it just that I'm so thirsty?"

"A bit of both, I expect!" laughed Guy. "Coffee always does

taste better when you're on a picnic, but naturally our coffee up here in Northumberland is miles better than your London stuff at any old time! Good! The queue is on the move at last!" He dug into his overcoat pocket. "I've got a Mars Bar or two on me somewhere if I can find them. Oh, here they are! Catch, Jane! Coming over, Mariella! You'll need something to help you to forget this next bit of road. It's a dreary stretch, but fortunately it's not for very long. We take the Dumbarton Road, and it's about forty-six miles to Balloch. After that Loch Lomond."

"Oh, is Loch Lomond as near Glasgow as that?" exclaimed Jane. "I always thought the famous Loch Lomond was in the heart of the Highlands."

"It's a longish loch, you see," explained Guy. "So, while the south end is nearly on Glasgow's doorstep, the north end is what you might call the gateway to the Highlands. Crianlarich is, anyway. That's where we're making for now. It looks as if we're in for more snow!"

The snow started to fall in earnest when they reached Balloch.

"Look!" Guy said, pointing out of the driving window. "See that?" A curtain of flying snowflakes had obscured the view of forested hills across the loch, and the water itself was cold and ruffled. "We're in for a storm!"

As they drove slowly round the loch, the road became more and more deserted, until at last they seemed to be the only travellers on it.

"This is Tarbet," Guy said, reading the name of the village as they passed. "We should be able to see Ben Lomond across the water, if it wasn't snowing so hard. Only another few miles, and we ought to be getting to the end of the loch."

"Ardlui," read out Mariella in her turn. "What a funny name!"

"It's the last village on Loch Lomond, I believe," said Guy. "Unless you count the tiny hamlet of Inverarnan. Yes, I thought so—this is the Inverarnan Hotel, at the entrance to Glen Falloch. I think we'll draw in here for a spot of tea. How queer it sounds!"

"How do you mean 'queer'?" asked Jane.

"Well, it's so silent," mused Guy. "Other times when I've been here, you could hear the waterfall over there," he nodded towards the precipitous wooded slopes of the mountain opposite. "But now I suppose it's frozen. The Glen seems strange, too—not nearly so noisy!"

"Oh, what a lovely place!" exclaimed Jane, as, having parked the car, they stretched their legs. "It looks awfully old."

"Yes, it *is* old," said Guy. "It used to be a coaching inn. I'll bet this was a wild place to live in in those days! This inn could tell you some stories, if only it could speak!"

They went into the inn, and it was obvious that Guy had been there before.

"Gosh! They've got electric light now!" he exclaimed as he led the way into a cosy dining-room, panelled from floor to ceiling in dark wood. "And running water, too! Last time I was here there was plenty of running water, to be sure, but only in the waterfall!"

While they were drinking their tea and eating a huge pile of hot buttered scones someone came in from outside, stamping the snow from his heavy boots, and shaking it off the brim of his deer-stalker.

"Have you any idea what the road is like farther up the Glen?" asked Guy. "Crianlarich way?"

"Ye're no going to Crianlarich?" exclaimed the newcomer. "I'll advise ye to bide here the nicht, for ye'll be main lucky to get as far as yon."

"It's bad up there, then?" said Guy.

"Bad? Why, mon, it's as thick as parridge! Ye canna see yer ain nose in front o' yer face!"

"Well, I'm hoping to get through to Inveross," Guy declared.

"Inveross?" The man shook his head. "Och, mon, ye'll no get to Inveross the nicht. Unless, mebbie, ye've got chains on yer car."

"Yes, we've got chains," said Guy.

"Ah, weel—then ye might manage it," said the stranger. "And then again ye might not. Onyways, I'll be wishin' ye the best o' luck, for ye'll be needin' it!"

"Thank you!" laughed Guy. "Well, if you others have finished, we'd better be off. It certainly looks as if our friend here is right, and it'll be touch and go whether we reach Inveross tonight. I'll just collect our thermos-flask—I left it in the kitchen to be filled. I thought we might need it! I'll be out to the car in a jiffy, if you'll just get in yourselves."

"Now for Glen Falloch!" Guy continued when he joined them. "This is one of the loveliest parts of the district."

Although it was only just after three o'clock, it was very dark under the arching trees, and Guy switched on the car's headlamps. Immediately the road ahead sprang into a glittering fairyland. All along the sides of the road the river poured itself down the glen in a series of waterfalls, but, as Guy had said, whereas in summer the water roared and tumbled over mossy boulders and fallen tree-trunks, now it flowed under great slabs of frozen snow, and slid down gleaming stairways of ice. The trees stretched motionless snowy branches across the road, and the road itself was now merely a hard white ribbon winding on and on into a deserted, frozen world.

Jane gave a sigh of pure joy at the unearthly beauty of it.

"Oh, Guy! Isn't it lovely! Could anything be more beautiful?"

"No, I don't think anything could," he agreed. "It's much more beautiful now than it is in summer chock-block full of tourists. The last time I was here we were meeting trailer-caravans at every turn of the road—goodness knows how they managed the bends! It's certainly narrow and twisting enough —especially up at this end! But you're right—it's worth seeing when it's like this. All the same, I wish——"

"What's the matter? You look worried."

"I was wondering what it would be like the other side of Crianlarich," he answered. "We've got a pretty wild stretch of moorland to negotiate before we get to Tyndrum and Inveross, and although it's quite still in here among the trees, I have an idea the wind is getting up, and there may be drifts." Jane followed his eyes, and saw that the tops of the fir trees overhead were bending and swaying, and sending down showers of snow which mingled with the flakes that fell in an ever-thickening curtain.

"I was also wondering where the others had got to," Guy went on. "I suggested to Ian in the first place that we should meet at Crianlarich and have a spot of tea at the hotel there, since he and Fiona were coming up by Stirling and Callander, but he said he didn't want to make any definite plans as he didn't know exactly when Fiona would be ready to start."

"They had to call at Bracken on their way you see," said Mariella. "Bracken Lodge, I mean. To park Flora. Mrs. Scott is looking after her while Fiona is away."

"That's a blessing, anyway," Guy declared. Then, seeing that Mariella looked mystified, he explained himself. "I mean it's a blessing for the kid—poor little beggar! She'll be a lot happier at Bracken than being racketed round Scotland with Fiona and Ian."

"Yes, I expect she will," Mariella agreed. "Look! Isn't this Crianlarich?"

"It is," answered Guy. "We'd better park the car outside the hotel, and I'll dash in and see if there's any sign of Fiona and Ian. There's no time to lose if we're to get to Inveross to-night— the road's rapidly filling up."

It wasn't long before Guy was back again.

"Ian and Fiona are on ahead," he told Jane and Mariella. "They had tea here, and left about half an hour ago."

🕸 14 🕸

Fiona in Distress

AFTER leaving Crianlarich, the road got more and more lonely. Great hills loomed up, looking even larger than they were in the gathering darkness.

"Ben More behind us," said Guy. "He's the one with the cloud on top. Ben Lui in front. You can tell him by his notched outline. The most lovely plants and ferns grow on Ben Lui."

"You've climbed him, then?" asked Jane.

"Oh, yes," answered Guy. "My father and I have climbed most of these mountains at one time or another—including the Cruachan group. They are the mountains on the north side of Loch Awe; they're really the tail end—the south-west arm—of the Grampian range. Ben Cruachan is the highest. You get a beautiful view of him out of the windows of the Allt nan Ros Hotel. . . . Golly! This snow is getting thick! It's almost blocking the windscreen wiper—even with the de-froster at work! The wind's getting up, too, as I feared, and the snow's drifting badly."

Jane glanced out of the rear window of the car. Infinitely lonely, the road stretched behind them as far as the eye could see. Infinitely lonely, it wound away ahead, a thin ribbon of white. On either side savage mountains raised their cloudy crests. Cataracts, hung with icicles, glittered eerily in the light of the car's headlamps, the soft hiss of the half-frozen water sounding like the swish of silken curtains blowing in the wind. Like a dream, silver-birch trees appeared by the side of the road. Dreamlike, they vanished into the darkness. The curdled sky drew down upon the car, and snowflakes drove in eddying waves against the windscreen. Once a couple of deer looked up in alarm as they ate their evening meal from the bark of a young tree, and then bounded away into the snowy wood.

"I think we'll certainly be the last car to pass along this road for a bit," said Guy. "We'll be lucky if we get through."

"Look out!" warned Mariella. "We're not the only people on the road. Here's a lorry!"

Fortunately it happened to be a sheltered part of the road. Guy edged gingerly into the side, whilst the lorry driver dashed past in a cloud of flying snow.

"He's in the dickens of a hurry!" Guy remarked, revving the engine, whilst the back wheels of the car spun round. "Gosh! We just managed to get out of there—even with our chains! I expect that lorry driver wanted to get back to Crianlarich while the going was good. It's New Year's Eve to-morrow!"

"We ought to have brought some sacks and a shovel," Mariella said. "But somehow away back at Monks Hollow it didn't seem necessary."

"I *have* brought some sacks, and a shovel, too. They're in the boot, along with my climbing things," laughed Guy.

"What did I tell you?" burst out Jane. "Didn't I say Guy was the sort of person who would get you there, no matter what!"

"I haven't got you there yet," teased Guy. "You may still have to spend New Year's Day in a snowdrift!"

"It's like the end of the world," put in Mariella. "Nothing but snow, and mountains, and great half-frozen waterfalls. Not a house for miles. Not a living being anywhere. . . . Oh, yes, there is! There's something in front. Look out, Guy! It's a car! It's——"

"It's *Fiona*!" shouted Guy. "What on earth is she doing there, standing in the road?"

"Something's wrong!" shrieked Mariella. "Something's happened to the car! It's in the ditch!"

A huge snowdrift was piled half across the road, and, slewed round, with one wheel in a deep hole by the side of the inevitable waterfall, and the other rakishly in the air, was the Frazers' smart little sports car. In front of it, waving frantically, stood Fiona—Fiona, in high-heeled shoes and a town hat with a veil!

Guy braked carefully, so as to avoid a skid, then wrenched open the car door.

"What's happened? Where is Ian? Is he hurt?"

"Hurt? No, of course he isn't hurt!" snapped Fiona, with chattering teeth. "I expect he's in Crianlarich by now. Oh, Guy! Look at my car! The idiot skidded and went into the ditch, and look at it! It's almost in the waterfall!"

"Well, I don't suppose he did it on purpose," Guy said. "But anyway, if he was driving when it happened, how can he be in Crianlarich, now?"

"Because he got a lift in a lorry," said Fiona. "He w-went for h-help."

"Oh, we met that lorry!" exclaimed Mariella. If "we'd only known that Ian was on it, we might have stopped it."

"Well, I don't really see what good we could have done if we *had* stopped it," said Guy. "What puzzles me, Fiona, is why you didn't go with him? You're doing no good here, you know."

"What? Me go and leave my precious car here?" exclaimed Fiona. "My twenty-first birthday present! You must be mad! Ian's gone to get help, and he'll be back to pull her out."

"I think it's you who are mad," said Guy. "In the first place, to come in that little sports car, and without chains, and second-ly for staying here. In all probability Ian will never get back to-night, and if it hadn't been for our coming past, you'd have been marooned here all night by yourself, and that would have been the end of Fiona Frazer. Get into my car, and be quick about it! We haven't a moment to lose, if wer'e going to get through ourselves. I'll scratch a note for Ian and leave it on the seat of the car, just in case he does get back, and we can ring him up at Tyndrum or Dalmally. Be quick! Get in Fiona!"

He stood there, holding open the rear door, but Fiona didn't move.

"I can't leave my car like this! I won't leave my car!" she wailed. "Besides, there's my evening frock!"

"Your evening frock! How can you stand there and talk about a stupid frock at a time like this!" exclaimed the exas-perated young man.

"It's not a s-stupid f-frock! It's a m-model, and it cost the earth!"

"Well, bring it along with you, then," said Guy. "Why not?"

"Because I c-can't. Because it's in the boot, stupid, and the b-boot's jammed," chattered Fiona. "It's jammed against that rock."

"It certainly is," agreed Guy, walking round his own car, and tugging at the luggage boot of the Frazers'. "No use— you'll just have to leave it where it is, Fiona."

"I w-won't!" answered Fiona, stamping her foot in the snow. "The water's rising. It'll get into the case, and my frock will be ruined."

"You can't do anything about it, anyway—even if you stay here," argued Guy.

"Oh, yes, I can. I can guard it. If Ian and the men come back, I can make sure they rescue my frock first. If I'm not there, they just won't bother about it. I know men! They'll just leave it to be r-ruined, and I can't go to a Ch-charity Ball without my frock!"

"You won't go to the ball in a frock, or without one, if you don't do as you're told, and quickly," Guy told her in exasperation. "Can't you see, you stupid child, that you'll be buried in the snow by morning? You'll freeze to death!"

"I'm n-not a s-stupid ch-child! How dare you! I'm a m-married woman!" yelled Fiona in a fury.

"Oh, Fiona—do come quickly," said Mariella, hopping out of the car, and dashing into the fray, while Jane pressed her nose against the car window in an effort to see what was happening.

"Mariella! Get back at once!" ordered Guy. Then he hastily added a "please", as though realizing that what he had said sounded rather peremptory. "Leave this to me!" Then he turned again to the shivering girl: "Now are you coming, Fiona? For the last time I ask you."

For answer, Fiona made a dive for her own car, which was sinking rapidly deeper into the ditch at every moment, and wrenched open the nearside door. But Guy was too quick for her. He grabbed her by the arm and hauled her back.

"No, you don't! You're coming with us, now, this minute. . . . Open the door, Jane!" He picked up Fiona, and bundled her unceremoniously into the back of the car. Then he got in himself, and started up the engine.

"You might give her a spot of coffee, Jane, if there's any left," he said as they moved off. "Not that the little idiot deserves it, but I suppose we can't let her freeze to death. Gosh! What some girls will do for the sake of clothes! Imagine sticking there just because your stupid frock——"

"It's *not* a stupid frock," came Fiona's furious voice from the back of the car. "How many times am I to tell you? It's a m-model. I'll never forgive you, Guy Charlton!"

"Oh, well—I expect I shall survive," answered Guy. "If you ask me, I think I'm a regular boy scout, saving people from icy deaths, when they aren't even grateful for being saved. It would have served you right if I'd left you to your dismal fate. If it hadn't been for your parents——"

"Oh, do shut up!" ordered Fiona, beginning to cry. "I wish I'd never come to the hateful dance! Everybody's always down on me! I wish I'd never been born! I wish I was dead!"

"In another minute I shall stop the car and come round there and spank you!" threatened Guy. "Then you'll have something to cry about! So take warning!"

Evidently Fiona took warning, for the only sound from the back of the car was a hiccough or two, and a pathetic sob.

"There's nothing so queer as weather in Scotland," declared Guy as they neared Dalmally. "It's nearly raining now, and everything looks quite green. When you think of all that snow farther back, you'd hardly believe it was the same world."

"You see, if you'd left me where I was I should have been perfectly all right," said Fiona's aggrieved voice from behind his left ear.

"Not at all. I expect if you could see that place at this moment, your car would have quite disappeared," answered Guy. "What it's doing here isn't any criterion as to what it's doing away back there."

"It's awful to think of my dance frock under all that snow," said Fiona pathetically. "How can I go to a dance without a dance frock? How can I, Guy Charlton? Answer me that!"

Before Guy could reply, Jane said quickly: "I know what we can do! You can wear *mine*, Fiona. We're about the same size. I'm not sure whether I have a partner, anyway, if, as Nigel says, Vivien Chator is coming. Josef may want to dance with her."

"Oh, no," interposed Mariella positively. "I'm pretty sure Vivien will be Nigel's partner. He as good as said so."

"Well, anyhow," insisted Jane, "you can still have my frock, Fiona. I don't care much about the dance itself. I get quite enough dancing as it is. I only really came because I should meet all my friends—you, Mariella, and the Listers, and Guy, and all of them."

"Oh, but I don't know——" began Fiona.

"It's quite a nice frock," said Jane.

"W-ell, perhaps—where did you get it?" Fiona asked cautiously.

"Oh, it's a Christian Dior model," Jane said casually. "It's black slipper-satin, with huge roses embroidered on an enormously full skirt. There's a lot of jet jewellery—ear-rings and so on—to go with it. Really, it's quite nice, Fiona, and it would look lovely with your fair hair."

Fiona began to brighten up.

"Perhaps it would. Well, if you really don't want to go to the dance——"

"Oh, I didn't say that. I said I wasn't as keen as you are, perhaps," began Jane.

"Well, you know what I mean. Everyone knows that ballet dancers are the world's worst ballroom dancers," said Fiona quickly. "So, if you don't mind, Jane, I might try your frock. It mightn't look too bad."

"Oh, I expect by to-morrow morning we'll be able to get a breakdown gang along that road and haul your car out of the ditch," put in Guy. "I think we're in for a proper thaw. Then you'll be able to wear your own frock, Fiona. It seems a shame for poor Jane not to be able to come to the dance."

"My frock will be quite ruined," declared Fiona positively.

"Even if the water hasn't got into the suitcase, it will be hope-
lessly crushed—quite unwearable."

"Oh, I don't know—we might borrow an iron," Guy said
helpfully.

"If you think I'm going to start being a laundry-maid, then
you're mistaken," said Fiona. "Anyway, if Jane doesn't want
to wear her own frock, then it will settle everything if *I* wear it."

Guy said no more, but Mariella, looking at his profile lit up
by the faint gleam thrown off by the dashboard light, knew that
it wasn't because he had nothing to say, but because he felt it
was quite useless trying to argue with Fiona when she had the
chance of wearing a real Dior creation.

"This is Dalmally," Guy said as they drove up a wooded
stretch of road and into a small village. "I'd better drop into the
hotel and ring up Ian, as I didn't do it at Tyndrum. Shan't be
five minutes!"

It wasn't long before he was back.

"They were just on the point of setting out on foot to rescue
Fiona," he said. "Ian was no end relieved when he knew she
was here with us. By the way, he says they'll have a shot at
hauling the car out of the ditch in the morning, and if they
manage, he'll come straight on here. If they don't, he'll come
by train. This is where we take the Inverary road. Our hotel is
just a few miles farther on, by the side of the loch."

"Lock Awe?" said Mariella.

"Yes. The tiny village of Inveross is on the south side of the
loch, nearly opposite the Loch Awe Hotel—that's the hotel that
looks like a fairy-tale castle—all turrets and things. There's a
little stream beside our hotel called the Allt nan Coire Rhos,
which means 'The Stream of the Corrie of the Rose', and that's
why the village is called Inveross—'mouth of the Ros'—and the
hotel the Allt nan Ros. Allt is the Gallic for stream—the rush-
ing, tumbling kind."

"You seem to know an awful lot about it," Mariella said
enviously.

"Well, I've been here before—quite a few times," he answered.

As Guy had said, it wasn't long before they came to a tiny

village. Although by now it was quite dark and a curtain of sleet was falling, Mariella declared she could *feel* the mountains all around.

"Mostly opposite," corrected Guy solemnly. "Yes, I can feel them, too. Well, this is Allt nan Ros Hotel. It used to be the family seat of the Campbells, but when money got too tight they decided to make it into a hotel. It's a first-class one, too. Come in, all of you! They'll deal with the luggage, and I can see about a lock-up for the car later on. Dinner first!"

"By the way, what time is it?" asked Mariella with a yawn. "I haven't the faintest idea. It might be six o'clock, or it might be ten. Nothing like a long motor ride to make you lose track of time!"

"It's half-past seven," said Guy, consulting his wrist-watch. "Well, how's this for a beautiful hotel? All these paintings are originals, and they're all of this district. Many of them have been done by well-known artists who have stayed here. Come into the lounge. I expect most of the others will be here already."

The lounge seemed to be full of people. Besides their party, there were quite a lot of other visitors who, it turned out later, had come specially for the dance the next evening.

"Oh, hullo!" exclaimed a girl who was sitting near the roaring log fire. "It's Guy! Hullo, Guy! And Mariella and Jane! Come and sit by the fire. You must be frozen! Oh, and Fiona, too! I thought you were coming up with Ian, Fiona?"

"Hullo, Elizabeth," said Fiona. "Yes, I did come up with Ian, but the idiot got stuck in the snow. I expect he'll come on by train, unless they manage to haul the car out of the ditch."

"Hullo, Josef!" exclaimed Jane, as she caught sight of her partner slumped gracefully in an easy chair at the other side of the fire. "You've beaten me, after all! When did you get here?"

"Several dreary hours ago, *chérie*," said the young man, getting up and bowing from the waist in his usually rather spectacular fashion. "I arrive at four o'clock. All is empty and silent. Outside——" he shivered. "Ah, you should see outside! It is of the most depressing! Mountains, and then mountains again—many with snow upon their dismal tops! And after this, a lake with waves upon it—cold as charity! Not a shop any-where, nor any brightness!"

"No, of course not!" put in Mariella. "You didn't expect a regular lakeside resort, did you, Josef? Like you get in Switzer-land. Or a sort of Blackpool—with the lake all lit up with electric lights?"

"I do not know what I expect," said Josef with a shrug. "But it is certain that never have my expectations been so badly shattered! It is in truth the place with the one eye, as they say!"

"Oh, poor Josef!" said Jane. "I'm so sorry we weren't here to welcome you. Then perhaps it wouldn't have seemed so bad."

"What's all this?" demanded Guy. "Are you running down one of the loveliest spots in all Great Britain? Don't believe him, Jane! Wait till the morning, and then judge for yourself. Meanwhile, how about some dinner to brighten us up? There's the gong."

H

🏵 15 🏵

Loch Awe

"Oh, it's lovely! Lovely! Guy was quite right!" said Jane next morning, running to the window of the room she and Mariella were sharing. "Come and see, Mariella! There's a simply enormous mountain with two heads right opposite, across the lake, and a lot of others as well. And there's a most beautiful little island with a castle on it, and there's no snow anywhere, except on the tops of the mountains. Everything's as green as green! Oh, I can see the hotel Guy told us about—the one on the other side of the loch. He's right—it's just like a fairy-tale castle—all turrets and towers!"

By this time Mariella was by her side, and was standing lost in admiration of the lovely scene spread out before her eyes.

"That will be Ben Cruachan, the mountain Guy told us about last night," said Jane. "The one with the double top. Oh, how lovely to climb it! It looks quite easy if you started from the other side of the loch. You could just walk straight up it. Mariella, are you listening?"

But Mariella's eyes had left the mountains and were on the drive leading up from the road to the hotel. She flung the window open in excitement.

"Jane! Jane! Look who it is! Look who's come! They're getting out of the car now! It's Caroline and Angelo! You never told me they were coming."

"I didn't know they were," Jane said. "Lady Blantosh must have asked them at the last minute. I wonder if——" She stopped suddenly and then laughed aloud. Mariella was no longer there. She had dashed out of the room and was now down in the hall welcoming the newcomers.

"Oh, hullo, you two! How lovely to see you again! Did you

come by car all the way, or only from the station? It's a wonder you didn't get snowed up like we did! Are you going to dance, Caroline—professionally, I mean, or are you here quite privately? How are Sebastian and Veronica getting on? Did you see them in London? How did Sebastian's concert go? Why didn't you let us know you were coming?"

Poor Caroline sat down in the nearest chair.

"*Mariella!* Do stop firing questions at me like machine-gun bullets, and I'll try to answer a few! No, we didn't come all the way by car. We travelled from London overnight and arrived at Dalmally station half an hour ago. By the way, someone else got out there—a girl. A young man met her with a car and they went down towards the Dalmally Hotel, but she's coming on here because I saw the label on her suitcase. I wonder who they were?"

"Well, the young man would be Nigel," Mariella said soberly. "I expect he drove up to Dalmally yesterday and stayed the night at the hotel there, so that he could meet the train. They would probably go back there for breakfast so that Nigel could collect his things."

"You mean that horrible boy, Nigel Monkhouse?" exclaimed Caroline. "The one who used always to be bossing poor little Jane about? Well, I wish her luck, whoever she is! I wonder if she's coming to the dance to-night."

"I can answer that one," answered Mariella. "She *is* coming to the dance. Her name's Chator—Vivien Chator, and she's a member of the Sadler's Wells Ballet. Perhaps she's dancing to-night—professionally, I mean."

Caroline shook her head.

"No, she won't be able to do that—not without permission, and an awful lot of fuss. Angelo and I are going to dance, because, at the moment, we aren't under contract. Our new engagement doesn't begin till next week."

"Oh, I see. And, of course, that applies to Jane, too," said Mariella. "I wondered why she hadn't any clothes with her—I mean dancing clothes. Of course, dancers can't just go dancing anywhere—not when they're professionals. I ought to have known that, being the daughter of a *ballerina*! But it's a fact—

you lose touch. I've lived a country life so long that I feel much more a huntin', shootin', fishin' kind of a girl than a famous dancer's daughter."

"If I might venture to break into the conversation," said the young man who accompanied Caroline, "I would say that the life of the country agrees with you, Mariella."

"Oh, thank you, Angelo!" explained Mariella. "I can always rely on you for a compliment! But tell me all your news. I haven't yet heard how the Spanish tour went off."

"It went off very well indeed," said Angelo. "Caroline is now a Spanish dancer in her own right, and I——" He shrugged his shoulders expressively. "I am——"

"You are only the famous Rosita's partner!" said Mariella with dancing eyes. "Angelo, you old humbug! You know perfectly well that you'll always be the one and only Angelo Ibañez."

"Yes, you're right," said Caroline. "However good I become, Angelo will always be just a little better. I think he does it to spur me on!"

Suddenly Mariella jumped off the small table where she had perched herself.

"I don't know why we're sitting out here in the hall," she said. "The others will be in the lounge waiting for the breakfast gong to sound. Come in and meet them! I think you know everyone, as a matter of fact."

"Oh, Guy!" said Jane after breakfast was over and they had gone back into the lounge. "Are you going climbing? What perfectly enormous boots!"

"Yes, I shall need them, I expect," Guy told her, putting down the map he was studying, and looking with amusement at the awestruck expression on Jane's small face. "I thought of going round the lake by car to within a mile of the Loch Awe Hotel, then up to the right, round the flank of Beinn a' Bhùiridh. Look, you can see it here on the map." He traced the route with his finger.

"It calls that mountain Beinn a' Bhùiridh on the map," put in Jane, spelling out the letters. "Why did you call it 'Bane Avouri'?"

Guy laughed.

"That's how it's pronounced although it's written Beinn a' Bhùiridh. It's one and the same. Not many of these mountains are pronounced the way they're spelt! Well, then I shall make use of this convenient railway track——" He traced it with his finger.

"You—you don't mean to say that a *train* goes up there!"

"Oh, no. It's an old railway line to the discarded mines," Guy explained. "But it provides easy going for a couple of miles into the corrie."

"Which mountain will you climb then?" asked Jane eagerly, her eyes on the many peaks of the great range.

"I thought of climbing up to Point 3100, and then on to Stob Garbh, and then, if there's time, doing the ones right over to Cruachan himself, and coming down by the Falls of Cruachan. The only difficulty is that I shall have a long walk back along the road to the car. Still, if the weather holds out, it would be worth it."

"Oh, it sounds lovely!" said Jane with a sigh of envy. "How I wish I could come, too!"

"I'm afraid it's impossible to-day," said Guy with a smile. "You see, although it looks all right just now, the weather may easily change. In fact, the forecast wasn't too good, and it would be no place for a delicate girl up there"—his eyes lifted to the bulk of Cruachan, etched black against the pale winter sky—"in a storm—even if you had the right clothes and footwear. Some day—later on in the year—I might take you climbing—if you really want to climb."

"You think I'm nesh, as the north-country people say!" exclaimed Jane. "Just because I'm a ballet dancer! A delicate girl, indeed! . . ." She looked down at her ankles, slim as any ordinary person's wrists, and Guy's amused glance followed her eyes. "Oh, I know they don't *look* tough, but they *are*. When you think of all the *pirouettes* I do, the *entrechats*, the *battements*—all making my feet and legs as strong as steel. I bet they're a lot stronger than yours, anyway!"

"Have it your own way!" laughed Guy. "But I'm not taking you with me to-day. You've no footwear——"

"Why *will* you keep on harping about footwear!" exclaimed Jane in exasperation. "I'll guarantee I could walk better in my shoes—high heels and all—than I could in those twin battle-ships. But never mind—go all by yourself, you horrible boy, and when you get lost we'll come out and find you!"

"That's a bargain," said Guy, pushing the map into his ruck-sack, and hoisting the same on to his broad shoulders. "And I promise to take you up something before long, Jane—honest injin, as we used to say when we were kids. But you must have a really good strong pair of boots."

He strode out of the lounge, six foot of graceful young man-hood, and Jane couldn't help giving a little sigh. Josef was graceful too, but she did wish he wouldn't sit in the lounge with such a discontented scowl on his handsome face. If only he would come out with her for a walk beside the lake—it was so lovely! But when she suggested it, Josef merely huddled further into his greatcoat that he would insist upon wearing, even in the beautifully warm lounge of the hotel, and declared that he wasn't going out into the wilderness to please Jane or anyone else. He'd catch pneumonia!

"But it isn't any colder here than in London," Jane argued. "In fact, I don't think it's as cold. And at least it's a *healthy* cold —not fog and petrol fumes and soot."

"For me, I prefer the soot," said Josef with a shrug. "All these dismal mountains! They make of me a—how do you say it? —pessimist—one who is sad of the mind. I like them not! No, my dear Jane; I stay here, where at least one can drink coffee and warm one's hands at the logs." He held out his beautiful white hands towards the glowing fire.

"Oh, well—I suppose I shall just have to go by myself," said Jane. "Mariella insists upon waiting here for Nigel, and all the others have gone round the lake to Oban. I was counting on you, but if you *won't* come——"

"Excuse, please!" muttered Josef firmly. "I, too, will wait with Mariella for—Nigel."

"All right—then I'll go by myself," Jane said, a funny little feeling in her heart telling her it wasn't Nigel that Josef was waiting for, but Nigel's companion—Vivien Chator.

She went back to the lounge, and stood looking at the panorama of mountains and loch spread out before her eyes. Light cloud covered the main top of Ben Cruachan, but the other peaks stood out clearly. Then she noticed a small table standing near the window. It wasn't an ordinary table, but made in the form of a large map with glass covering the top. On the map Jane picked out the different peaks: "Stob Dearg, Meall Cuanail, Ben Cruachan, Drochaid Glas, Stob Diamh, Sròn an Isean, Stob Garbh, Beinn a' Chochuill, Beinn Eunaich, and Beinn a' Bhùiridh in the front," she said, stammering a little as she tried to get her tongue round the strange Gaelic names.[1] "How lovely to climb some of them! I do think Guy might have taken me. It's a perfect day—not a cloud in the sky—at least only that small, grey one behind Beinn a' Chochuill—oh, now Beinn Eunaich has disappeared in the mist. How funny! I expect he'll appear again in a minute."

Suddenly an idea came into her head. If Guy wouldn't take her mountain climbing, why shouldn't she go by herself? What fun to meet him on the top of Ben Cruachan! And, after all, it was quite a short distance—only a mile or two. The map said so. If one went in a boat across the loch, and then climbed straight up, one would be there in no time—especially on a day like this. Very little mist, and no snow to speak of—only a fleck or two on the sides of the mountain, and a bit on the top. From here it looked just like little bits of paper left behind after a paper-chase. So argued Jane to herself. Certainly no danger there. How

[1] Stob Dearg (3,611 feet)="the red peak", pronounced Stob Jerrack.
 Meall Cuanail (3,004 feet)="seaward-looking hill", pronounced Meal Coonull.
 Ben Cruachan (3,689 feet)="the mountain of peaks", pronounced Ben Krooackan.
 Drochaid Glas (3,312 feet)="the grey bridge", pronounced Drochadg Glass.
 Stob Diamh (3,272 feet)="the peak of the stags", pronounced Stob Jeeve.
 Sròn an Isean (3,163 feet)="the nose of the young bird", pronounced Stron an Eeshun.
 Stob Garbh (3,215 feet)="the rough peak", pronounced Garrer.
 Beinn a' Chochuill (3,215 feet)="the peak of the hood", pronounced Bane a Hockull.
 Beinn Eunaich (3,242 feet)="Fowling Peak", pronounced Ben Ooneech.
 Beinn a' Bhùiridh (2,936 feet)="Hill of roaring" (stags), pronounced Bane a Vouri.
 (In all cases the "ch" is pronounced in the Scottish way, as in "Loch".)

utterly ridiculous of Guy to set off armed with an ice-axe, of all things! She would tease him about that when he returned.

She ran up to her room, and put on her shoes—the only pair she had brought with her. She remembered vaguely the sort of shoes she had worn when she lived in Northumberland, and for a second she wished she had a pair like that to put on now— shoes with flat heels, big enough to take an extra pair of socks— but it was only for a second. "I couldn't walk in them now, even if I had them," she said to herself. "They would feel like boots —far too big and clumsy! No, I shall climb much better in these. After all, the heels aren't *really* high, and they're quite water-tight." She was to remember those words in the very near future, and laugh ruefully at her ignorance. London streets, even on a wet day, cannot compare with a stretch of boggy ground on the flank of a Scottish mountain. When she came down to the entrance-hall, ready dressed for her excursion, she found it deserted, except for a maid polishing the floor.

"I beg your pardon," said Jane, going over to her, "I wonder if you could tell me how one gets across the loch? Or does one have to go all round it in a car?"

The maid looked up and smiled.

"Och, no, miss, there is no need for you to be doing that. You can go across in the boat. Andrew is taking her across in a wee while. Andrew is the gillie."

"That sounds lovely," said Jane. "But where do I find Andrew?"

"He'll be down by the loch side," answered the girl in her unaccustomed Scottish voice. "If you'll tak' yon wee path"— she pointed out of the window to the far side of the terrace— "ye'll see it. Ye canna miss it."

"Andrew is the gillie," repeated Jane to herself as she followed the girl's instructions. "I wonder what a gillie is? It sounds like a shoe to me, but I have an idea it's some sort of a servant. Perhaps he's the boatman."

In a few minutes she came to the end of a sandy path, and a small beach appeared, complete with boat-house and miniature jetty. A young man was busy untying a boat from a ring in a nearby post—a large young man wearing a very old and shabby kilt, and a jacket with large leather patches on elbows and pockets. "This will be Andrew, the gillie," said Jane to herself. Aloud she asked: "Are you taking the boat across the lake? Can I come with you?"

The big young man straightened himself and looked down at her for a moment. Then he smiled.

"Yes—of course," he said in his soft, Scottish accent. "I am going now. Can I help you?" He held out a large brown hand, and Jane found herself seated in the prow of a small motorboat. "You wish to go across to the Loch Awe Hotel?"

"Oh—er, yes. I think so," Jane answered. "At least, somewhere near there." Then she added: "Isn't the mountain lovely?"

The young man followed her gaze.

"Cruachan Beann," he said. "Yes, he is a noble mountain."

"Have you ever climbed him?" asked Jane.

"Oh, yes," said her companion. "Many times I climb him, but I am not climbing him in the winter."

"Why not?" asked Jane. "There's no snow now—at least, not much."

"There is more than you imagine," said the young man. "Those little patches are quite large stretches when you are up there."

"Where do you start climbing him from?" asked Jane.

"Oh, most people go up the track by the Falls of Cruachan," answered the young man, "but for myself I prefer the cart-track that starts from nearly opposite the hotel. It becomes very faint farther up, but you can just follow it. It goes round the flank of Beinn a' Bhùiridh and into the corrie, and is a more interesting route."

"Oh, what a lovely island!" exclaimed Jane, forgetting the mountain in her excitement. "That one over there to the right. There's a castle on it!"

"That is Kilchurn[1] Castle," said her companion. "It is very old and is in ruins, but inside the castle walls a small house has been built—just like a doll's house! It, too, is in ruins, but it is worth a visit. For many years an old woman—one of the

[1] Pronounced Killhoorn.

Bredalbane Campbells—lived in the house all alone, with only her dogs for company. One dark and stormy night she is returning across the water from Dalmally, and she is drowned. Since then no one is living there."

"What a pity!" said Jane. "It would be such a romantic place to live in. But oh, the poor old woman! What a sad end to her life! Oh, here we are, across the loch already. Is this the Loch Awe Hotel? What a lovely place! But it looks as if no one lived there."

"It is closed in the winter," said the young man. "Just as we, also, at Allt nan Ros are closed, but we have opened for the ball of Lady Blantosh because she is a great friend of the family."

"Oh, I see," said Jane, accepting his offer of a hand over the narrow landing-stage. "Yes, I expect not many people would want to stay here in the middle of the winter. Well, thank you very much, my good man. How much do I owe you?"

The young man shook his head.

"You do not owe me anything," he said firmly. "It was a pleasure. I was coming over in any case."

Firmly Jane slipped half a crown into his hand. After all, one couldn't accept free lifts—if you could say that of a boat—from strange gillies, could one, especially if one had *asked* for the lift?

16

Lost on the Mountain

AFTER leaving the loch side Jane tried to remember what Guy had said about his movements. He had intended to begin the climb somewhere to the east of the hotel. Yes, that was it—something about a railway line. Well, why shouldn't *she* take the gillie's route, and strike straight up the mountain? Here was the cart-track, right opposite the hotel. All she had to do was follow her nose, and she'd reach Ben Cruachan in the end. How surprised Guy would be when she met him on the top! She might even get there first by taking the short, direct route.

The path was well marked at first, and Jane set off up it at full speed. Before very long she was well up the steep, lightly wooded slope of the mountain. Before her enchanted eyes Loch Awe came into view. To the west, the Pass of Brander; in front, and to the south, the main arm of the loch. Dotted over its blue, glittering surface were islands, some of them wooded, others with ancient buildings upon them. Away to the south-east rose the mountain Guy had pointed out at Crianlarich—Ben Lui. His crest rose black against the pale, winter sky.

The path had become much less distinct, and was now little more than a sheep-track. Sometimes it almost disappeared altogether. After a while it wound away westwards and was no longer climbing so quickly, so Jane forsook it and set off up the steep hillside on her own. Soon she reached a ridge, and over the top she could look down over splintered rock into a corrie below where a mountain torrent thundered with the noise of an express train, flinging itself over the rocks and boulders in its path. The top of the mountain behind it was covered in mist. In fact Jane saw with astonishment that most of the tops were now shrouded, though where she stood was still in sunshine. As she stood there, however, a finger of mist crept over her face, blotting out the sun. She shivered. It was cold standing here, so she set off again, striving to keep herself warm by sheer speed.

On and on she climbed, and still the top of the mountain seemed to get no nearer.

"I wish I'd brought something to eat," she said, thinking longingly of lunch at the hotel, "but I never imagined it would take as long as this. It looked such a short distance on the map. And oh, I wish I'd borrowed a pair of Mariella's shoes! Guy was right—these aren't heavy enough. I can feel all the stones through them, and they're getting wet, too. . . . Oh, well—I've climbed an awful long way—I *must* be coming to the top of Ben Cruachan soon. I've been climbing for"—she consulted her wrist-watch—"goodness! No—it's impossible! It can't really be two o'clock already! My watch must be fast. Perhaps I'd better go down. . . . Oh, look! There's a cairn at last! This must really be the top. Imagine reaching the top of Ben Cruachan!"

As she sank down beside the cairn with a sigh of utter weariness, she felt the thrill that every mountaineer or climber feels when he has reached his object. No matter that the mist had closed down all round her, and was now drifting like cold fingers of chiffon over her face, so that she couldn't see anything at all except a few feet of frosty grass and glistening rocks directly in front of her. No matter—she had reached the top—the very top—of one of Scotland's loftiest mountains. She stood up and gave a shout of victory.

Poor Jane! Her triumph was short-lived. At that moment the soft woolly blanket of mist in front of her parted and disclosed before her horrified eyes the whole main Cruachan range. Peak after peak appeared for one brief moment, and then vanished like ghostly giants from another world, and between them and Jane lay a deep and dangerous gulf that even she, in her inexperience, knew she could never cross from this point.

"Then I'm *not* on Ben Cruachan at all!" she said, almost in tears. "I'm not anywhere *near* Ben Cruachan! I must just go down the way I came up." But this, she found, was easier said than done. Which *was* the way she had come up? She wasn't at all sure now. The mist was so thick that there was no view of any sort, no object to tell her where she was. There wasn't even a glimpse of sun to tell her which was east and which was west!

"I suppose I ought to have brought a compass," she said aloud. "But after all, a compass wouldn't have been much use because I have no idea how to use it!"

To make matters worse, flying sleet had begun to fall, and she had no mackintosh. Large holes had appeared in the thin soles of her town shoes, and the water was coming in fast. Every now and then she had to take one or other of them off and empty out loose stones.

"I must just go on straight down," she said firmly. "As long as I keep my back turned to that awful place and go straight down, I'm bound to come to that little path I left—oh, it seems such hours, and *hours* ago."

The queer thing was that she didn't seem to be going down at all. In fact, sometimes the ground actually seemed to be going *up*! Presently a large dark object loomed in front of her out of the mist, and Jane gave a gasp of dismay. There was no mistaking it. It was the cairn she had rested against quite half an hour ago!

"Oh, I must be going round in circles!" she cried. "I've read about people doing that, but I never thought it was really true!" A thrill of fear ran through her. Then she pulled herself together. "I must turn my back on this stupid cairn and walk *straight*," she told herself. "No going round!"

Then it dawned upon her that as the cairn itself was round, how was she to know she was walking in the right direction? She might walk right over that awful precipice she had seen for a brief second when the mist had parted!

Just as this moment the worst happened. She found herself on the edge of a precipitous outcrop of rocks plastered with icicles. Sheer at her feet they leapt down to an enormous corrie far below where, on the far side, glimmering eerily out of the mist, roared a torrent, joined by several others farther down.

"Well, I certainly can't get down there," cried poor Jane aloud. "Even if I wanted to! Anyway, I'm sure it's the wrong direction. I ought to walk due south, where the lake is—but how can one tell which *is* due south when there isn't any sun?

I'm pretty sure this isn't south—it feels more like north! All this snow, for one thing! I'm sure I didn't pass this before. . . . If only it wasn't all so *white*! Everything is white—the ground, the sky—what one can see of it through the mist—*everything*! It makes me feel almost giddy! You can't tell where one begins and the other ends. Goodness! How funny!"

A gleaming white line appeared in front of her, a few yards away. What could it be? She dashed forward over the snow, then pulled up in horror. Not more than five feet from where she stood, the ground disappeared altogether. Below was no-thing—nothing! The glittering white line was the fine, powdery snow on the lip of a precipice. From far below came the distant sound of a waterfall, roaring dully.

"Oh!" said Jane, drawing back with a shudder. "I'm scared! In fact, I'm more than scared. I'm terrified! I wish Guy was here! I know now that I'm lost in the snow on this horrible mountain, and every way I go it's the wrong way, and if I don't die of cold I'll die of hunger! How I wish I'd never come!"

But it was no use wishing. She had got herself into this mess, and she must get herself out of it. She must just keep on going downhill. In spite of her fairy-like appearance, Jane was quite tough. A dancer must have plenty of stamina and determination. She certainly never thought of giving up. On and on she struggled. The sleet turned to snow, and as the ground grew whiter, the more difficult it became. She slipped and slithered over patches of rock which, not so very long ago, had been dry and climbable. She fell in and out of streams which had risen suddenly and were now roaring cataracts. She fell over hidden boulders against which the snow had drifted.

On coming out from behind an outcrop of rock, the wind and blown snow caught her full in the face, and drove her to her knees, gasping. It was as if someone had thrown a handful of steel shot full in her face. She struggled on in a downward direction, and presently the wind decreased, the slope eased and the ground became soft. Here the snow was deeper, and with every step she sank down almost to the knees. She grew ter-ribly tired. One of her shoes came off, and she was forced to leave it stuck in the bog. The other squelched at every step. The great tumult of a waterfall sounded in her ears, and presently she found herself on the edge of a wide, raging torrent.

"If only I could follow it down, I should come to the lake eventually," said Jane, her north-country upbringing coming to her aid, even in her half-conscious state. "If I could only find a path!"

Completely exhausted, and so cold that her feet and hands had no longer any feeling in them, she clung to a boulder, while the water flung itself from rock to rock in a fury of tormented cascades. Suddenly her foot slipped, and her ankle turned under her weight. A shaft of pain like a red-hot needle shot through her. . . .

"Guy!" screamed Jane. "Oh, Guy! Guy! Where are you?"

Then, through the waves of pain that flowed over her it seemed to her that someone answered. But, of course, that was quite impossible. . . . There was no one here. . . . She was all alone on this terrible mountain. . . . Someone called her name . . . no, it could only be the clamour of the waterfall, sobbing, sighing in the pools. It could only be . . . It grew dark. . . .

🏵 17 🏵

Rescue

Guy didn't spend much time on the main top of Ben Cruachan. For one thing it was after two o'clock, and if he intended to be back at the hotel in good time to dress for the dance—always remembering the long walk that lay before him when he reached the loch side—he had no time to lose. For another, the weather had worsened, and it seemed to his experienced eyes that a storm was blowing up. Although he was an expert climber, and knew all these mountains like the back of his hand, he still had no mind to be caught up here in the dark and in a blizzard. He wasn't one to take unnecessary risks. He'd had a wonderful day, climbing from peak to peak of the splendid Cruachan range, and now he was tired and ready for a hot bath and a good meal. It was a pity he hadn't time to bag the other top—Stob Dearg—too, especially since he had given up going over the actual top of Drochaid Glas to gain a few minutes. However, that awkward bit he had just come up, where the ridge narrowed and steepened, and the rocks were iced, with a snow cornice above, had proved quite sporting, even if it had taken him rather longer to negotiate than he had expected.

As he shouldered his rucksack once more, the mist rolled away from his feet, and he had a brief glimpse of Loch Awe and beyond that the sea. To the south, the top of Beinn a' Bhùiridh appeared for a brief second or two. Over to the east, a shaft of wintry sunlight gleamed on the Allt Coire Glas, and then on Allt Coire Chreachainn, and the slopes of Beinn a' Chochuill beyond. But as he watched, entranced, as he always was, by the magical effect of sun and mist on the mountains, a cloud boiled up at his feet, and he was once again in a white, clammy world, one young, strong figure against the whole force of nature. He

Guy on the main top of Ben Cruachan

gave a sigh of happiness, and his tiredness vanished. It was good to have conquered this great double-topped mountain in such wintry conditions, and, having conquered it, he felt it to be more than ever his friend.

Slipping and sliding on the great slabs of rock (many with a covering of snow upon them) which form the main top of Cruachan, he began the descent. In a quarter of an hour he was on the col. Then he began the long scramble down the mountainside into the corrie far below, kicking steps in the snow as he went. After some time he stopped. In front of him stretched a smooth, steep slope of crisper snow, which disappeared into the mist after about two hundred feet. To the uninitiated it looked as if it went on for ever, but Guy knew it led down to the floor of the corrie, about five hundred feet below. This step-cutting business was too slow for him, so he decided to glissade it. With the ice-axe on the right side of his body, his left hand firmly gripping the head, and his right hand the shaft, Guy launched himself down the slope, using the point of the shaft to check his speed. What fun glissading was! Nearly as good as ski-ing. He knew there was an outcrop of rock somewhere below him which must be avoided. Very soon this appeared, and, picking himself up, he skirted it, and then continued across the floor of the corrie.

It was growing dark down here, and though the mist had thinned somewhat, it still did not allow him to see across to the other side of the corrie, where he could hear the Allt Cruachan roaring on its downward path. Presently the noise died away as he trudged steadily downwards, leaving the stream far away to his left. After about twenty minutes he heard it again as the allt curved towards him, just before it took its dramatic plunge into the gorge below. There was something else, too, a thin, sad wail—like the cry of a new-born lamb, or a child in distress. He listened intently. Above the noisy clamour of the waterfall it was hard to catch any other sound. Perhaps it was his imagination. . . . But no, there it was again! There was no mistaking it Someone was calling for help—and calling his name!

"G-uy! G-uy!" Then the cry died away, and there was nothing but the roar of wind and water.

Guy cupped his hands and yelled back.

"Hullo! Hullo! Is there anyone there? Where—are—you? Hullo! Hullo!"

"G-uy!" came the weak answer. "I'm here—by—the—stream——"

"Jumping Jehoshaphat!" exclaimed the young man. "It's a girl! I'll bet a pound to a hayseed it's Jane!" Then he cupped his hands again, and yelled at the top of his voice: "Hold on! I'm coming! Keep—on—shouting! Where — are — you? *Shout!*"

Guided by the faint cries, he crossed the torrent, taking flying leaps across the foaming water, slipping and falling over rocks that he could see only faintly in the gloom, plunging into deep pools, often nearly up to the thighs in an effort to get across with the greatest possible speed.

He found her at last, lying at the foot of a boulder, her un-gloved hands blue with cold, one slender foot twisted beneath her, the other with the remains of a silk stocking still clinging to the ankle.

"*Jane!*" cried Guy in horror, and dashed forward.

"It's my ankle!" moaned the girl. "My ankle, Guy! I think it's broken!"

Guy had often idly wondered what he would do if one of his climbing companions was injured, or if he were to find someone in need of help lying on the mountain, but never in his wildest imaginings had he thought of anything quite as awful as this. Thoughts raced through his mind as he knelt by the half-conscious girl and gently straightened her injured leg, feeling it with skilful fingers to see if it was broken or only sprained. . . .

"Get the person to shelter," said his thoughts, "any sort of shelter . . . a cave, an overhanging shoulder of rock . . . somewhere out of the wind . . . go for help . . . keep him warm and cheerful, if you can . . . reassure him."

Yes, that was the trouble—it was always a man he had pictured in his imaginings. You could talk to a man. You could say: "Look, Jack—or Dick, or whatever the name was—we're in quite a spot! Can you manage to hang on while I hare back to the nearest house? I'll strap up your ankle before I go, and you'll be more comfortable. Lucky you're in such a get-at-able spot! What about a pipe, old man? I'll be back in two shakes of a duck's tail. I've got a packet of raisins in my rucksack, and some cheese. Coming over!" . . .

But what did you do when the injured person was a bit of a girl who had never been alone on a mountain in her life, even in the day time, let alone at night? A girl who was obviously in intense pain, and scared to death. If you left her alone, she'd probably freeze to death, or become delirious, and wander goodness only knew where—into the waterfall, most likely—or over into the Cruachan gorge. No, he couldn't leave her alone. Quite impossible! . . .

While the snow drove in stinging clouds down the corrie, Guy drew Jane gently farther into the slight shelter afforded by the boulder, and then opened his rucksack. . . . Maps, compass, ropes, rope-soled shoes . . . several pairs of socks, woolly scarves, a pair of gloves . . . a tin with a few raisins and some boiled sweets in it . . . a couple of sandwiches. . . . Ah, yes! A couple of old sweaters. . . .

"Come, Jane—we must get you into these." He tried to pull one of the sweaters over her head, but she moaned so pitifully that he had to stop.

"Guy! My foot!"

"Right-ho—I'll see to it first," said Guy, stuffing his surplus clothing back into the rucksack so as to keep it dry—for it was still snowing—and pulling a couple of hankies out of his pocket. "Something for a splint. . . ." He rummaged in all his pockets and finally drew out a folding foot rule. This he padded with one of the hankies, and with the other bound it to Jane's foot, so that it was held rigid.

"Now then—the sweater." This time he managed to pull off the girl's soaked costume, and substitute his own garment. Over this he pulled his wind-jacket, warm from his own body, putting on the other spare sweater himself.

"Now for some gloves and socks." He pulled off his gloves —first a waterproof pair, then a woollen pair—and, after rubbing Jane's blue hands, he put them on her. This left the spare woolly pair for himself. Then he pulled all the spare socks he had over her cold feet.

"Now you must have something to eat," he told her when he had finished. "Sorry I've nothing drinkable. Come along, Jane! Just a mouthful or two. Yes, you really must—you don't want to peg out, do you? Besides, you won't make it any easier for me to get you down from here if you go fainting, you know! It's going to be hard enough as it is!" Obediently Jane ate the sandwiches he put into her mouth, bit by bit, and after that a few raisins.

"I don't think I shall *ever* get down from this dreadful place!" she said at length. "I think you'd just better leave me here, Guy——"

"Be quiet!" ordered Guy. "That's not to be thought of. I can't and won't leave you here in the snow to freeze to death, which is what it would amount to. When you've had a little rest, I'm going to carry you on my back over this rough stuff."

"*Carry* me?" exclaimed Jane. "How could you? Why, I'm quite grown up!"

"We'll see," answered Guy. "As for being 'quite grown up', well, you don't look it, that's all I can say! You look about twelve years old, sitting there, so little and helpless. For two pins I'd put you in my rucksack, like I once did little Patience Eliot! Seriously, if I can carry you over this rough stuff, when we get to the grass you'll be able to walk—or anyway, hobble along somehow. Put your arms round my neck! Heave-ho! 'Hold tight!' as the London bus conductors say! Down we go! . . ."

And down they went, step by step, the girl's arms clasped tightly round the boy's neck, her cold, wet cheek against his own warm, wet one. . . . Over the loose stones by the side of the waterfall, Guy's big boots crunching and grinding on the rocks. When they came to the lip of the corrie, where the stream takes its first dramatic plunge into the Cruachan Gorge far below, he set her on her feet. Leaning on his arm, she descended slowly and painfully. It was no longer so cold. They were now sheltered from the wind by the mountain at their back, and the snow had turned first to sleet, then to rain. New strength seemed to flow into Guy's tired limbs, now that the life of this frail girl depended on him. He insisted upon thinking of her as a frail girl, and always would. "Little Jane Foster" was how he thought of her, ever since he had rescued her from the bullying clutches of Nigel, her cousin, long years ago on another snowy New Year's Eve.

"Are you warmer now?" he asked her, as they stopped for a breather after an especially steep stretch of turf.

"Oh, yes—a lot," she answered. Then suddenly she looked down and caught sight of the clothes she was wearing. "Oh, Guy, it's your coat I've got on. I must take it off at once! I can't wear your coat. . . ."

"Now don't get in a flap!" said Guy. "I've got on a spare sweater out of my rucksack."

"Yes, but it's your *waterproof* coat——"

"Don't you worry your little head about me," said Guy. "I'm as hot as—well, never mind what. Feel me!" His fingers closed round her wrist in a warm bracelet. "Come along, now, and don't talk a lot of rot! We don't want to sit on this old mountain all night, do we? It's New Year's Eve, you know!"

"Oh, so it is," said Jane, getting up painfully. "I'd forgotten. I'd forgotten all about the others, too. They'll wonder where I am."

"*I* hadn't forgotten them," declared Guy. "I've been seeing in my mind the search-parties that'll be in full swing when they realize you haven't come back from your mountaineering expedition!"

"Oh, but there won't be any search-parties," said Jane, "because no one knew I'd gone climbing."

"No one knew—you told no one?" Words failed Guy. Then, looking down at his companion's pitifully white, strained face in the light of the moon, he realized that this wasn't the moment to be lecturing her on her follies. He contented himself with the promise that he would have a straight talk with her at no very distant date.

"Do you see what's happened?" he said, when they reached the railway cutting and were out on the road. "It's a lovely, starlight night down here!"

And indeed he was right. The loch lay before them, a ruffled expanse of molten silver. The silver-birch trees swayed in the light wind, and the clouds raced past an almost full moon.

"It's often like that," said Guy. "A wisp of cloud on Ben Cruachan, and if you're are weather-wise you know that you're in for squalls up there——" He nodded over his shoulder towards the wooded slopes of Beinn a' Bhùiridh, behind which lay those other, wilder slopes, corries, and precipices leading to that giant of Scottish mountains, Cruachan Bean.

"Oh, it's an awful, terrible place!" said Jane with a shudder.

"It's not awful at all," corrected Guy. "As long as you treat it with the respect it deserves." Then he noticed that her steps were flagging, and he stopped in the road. "I'll carry you for a little way," he said. "It will give you a rest. If we were living in a book, it is at this precise moment that a car would come round the bend—the Listers' car, with Richard and Elizabeth waving wildly. 'We've just come back from Oban!' they'd shout. 'Fancy meeting you here! Get in!' But, as we aren't living in a book, I suppose we shall have to leg it!"

It was seven o'clock that night when the two weary figures staggered up to the door of Cluny Cottage, near Loch Awe Station. The owner of the cottage, a dark-eyed, soft-voiced Scotswoman, held up her hands in horror when she beheld them.

"Och! The wee bairn!" she exclaimed, when she had heard Guy's story. "And what would a wee bairn like that be doin' all by hersel' up on yon great mountain!"

"That's what *I* want to know," Guy said, depositing Jane gently in a huge armchair the woman had pulled forward. "But just now she's about all in—far too exhausted to tell us anything. A hot drink, bath, and bed is what she needs."

"And she shall have them, too," said the good-hearted Scot. "I'll away and get her a cup of tea, and she shall have a bath as soon as she has drunk it."

"Well, Jane—I'll leave you here for a bit," said Guy, looking down at his companion. "I think I ought to crash across to the station and ring up the Allt nan Ros. Even if they haven't got as far as a search-party, they may be worried. I'll ring up a doctor,

too, while I'm about it. We must have that ankle seen to as soon
as possible. After I've done that, I'll pick up my car, and go
back to the hotel for a bath and a change of clothes. I'll come
back here for you later on."

He set off wearily for the station. Now that the crisis was
over, and he'd got Jane safely down, he realized how desper-
ately tired he was. Every muscle in his body ached, and he was
ravenously hungry. Suddenly he caught sight of himself in one
of the blacked-out windows of the little station waiting-room.
The hail and sleet had made dirty runnels down his cheeks,
there were great smears of mud on his forehead, and he badly
needed a shave. He laughed aloud. Anything less like a guest
at a Charity Ball you couldn't imagine! He looked more like an
escaped convict, or a tramp!

Meanwhile, back at the hotel, Fiona was in a proper tantrum,
as Trixie, her old nannie, would have put it. Dinner was at
seven, and it was now six forty-five, and there was no sign of
Jane. Not that this would have worried Fiona at any ordinary
time, but just now it was all important, because to Jane belonged the wonderful ball dress that Fiona was to wear that
evening—the Christian Dior model. Fiona had already invaded
Jane's bedroom, and demanded the frock, but Mariella had
declared she had no idea where it was.

"But it *must* be here," Fiona insisted, flinging open the ward-
robe door. "No—it isn't. Well, then, it must be in her case. . . .
Where *can* it be? You're sure she brought it, Mariella?"

"Well, I *think* so," Mariella said, not too helpfully. To tell the
truth, she was much more worried about Jane herself than
about the frock. "Where can she be?"

"Oh, I expect she went out walking somewhere, and forgot
all about the time," said Fiona. "You know what a day-
dreamer Jane is. Really, she might land up *anywhere*!"

"That's what I'm afraid of," said Mariella. "I'm afraid she's
got somewhere, and now she finds she can't be back again—for
instance, on one of those islands in the middle of the loch, or
half-way up a mountain, or somewhere. . . . And Guy Charlton
hasn't come back, either; but, of course, we all knew he'd gone

climbing. Still, it's quite dark now, and he knew dinner was at seven, and he's my partner. It isn't like Guy——"

"Oh, do stop *fussing*!" broke in Fiona. "You might help me to look for my frock——"

"You mean *Jane's* frock," corrected Mariella. "Really, Fiona, I don't see what you want it for now. Your own's perfectly all right. Not a drop of water got into the case—Ian said so. Your own frock is lovely. It's not even crushed."

"Oh, yes, it is," retorted Fiona. "It's a frightful mess. I can't possibly wear it. Where else could Jane's frock be, Mariella?"

"Really, I don't know, Fiona," answered Mariella, slipping her own frock—the green taffetas—over her head. "I'm beginning to think she didn't bring it, after all."

"But she *did*!" yelled Fiona, stamping her foot. "How annoying you are, Mariella! Jane told me distinctly she had it with her. and offered to lend it to me. You heard her yourself when we were in the car last night."

"Well, what do you expect me to do?" exclaimed Mariella in exasperation. "Say 'abracadabra' or something, and conjure it out of a hat? . . . Oh, there's the telephone. It *would* ring just when I'm half dressed. Answer it for me, will you, Fiona, please."

Fiona went over to the telephone that stood on the little bedside table, and picked up the receiver. The receptionist's soft, Highland voice reached her:

"Is that Miss Foster? I have a call for you. . . . One moment, please. . . ." Then a deeper voice—a young man's voice—broke in: "Hullo, Mariella! This is Guy speaking. I rang up so that you wouldn't think Jane and I had eloped, or anything! I'm afraid she's had an accident. Now, don't be alarmed—it's only a slight accident. She sprained her ankle. At least, I *think* it's only sprained, but it's very swollen, and it's hard to tell just yet. . . . Yes, I'm here at the Loch Awe Station."

"It's not Mariella—it's me, Fiona, speaking," said Fiona. "We were all wondering where Jane was. We didn't know she'd gone with you. . . . Oh, she didn't? Well, anyway, never mind. What does it matter? The question is—what has she done with her frock?"

"Her frock?" Guy sounded bewildered. "What on earth has her frock——"

"I'm wearing it to-night, stupid," said Fiona. "Don't you remember? Nobody seems to remember *anything*! She offered to lend it to me. Well, it isn't there. We've looked everywhere, and it's nearly seven o'clock now. I ought to be dressed——"

"Look," broke in Guy. "Is Mariella there? Sorry, Fiona, but I want to speak to Mariella. . . . Oh, is that you, Mariella? Thank goodness for somebody sensible! I must explain about Jane. She went out climbing . . . no, not with me. By herself. Well, she got lost . . . yes, on Beinn a' Bhùiridh. . . No, I can't think what made her do it. Anyway, the mist came down, and she wandered from the path and came down the wrong side into Coire Cruachan. I found her there. She was about all in, poor kid! She'd lost one shoe and sprained her ankle. I was just telling Fiona. . . . Are you still there, Mariella?"

"Oh, yes," said Mariella, a wave of horror sweeping over her. "D-did you say she'd hurt her foot? Oh, Guy—how *awful*!"

"Cheer up!" said the voice at the other end. "It might be a lot worse. It's not broken, I think—only sprained. She'll be about again in a day or two. I shan't wonder if she doesn't manage to hobble in to the dance to-night, after she's had a rest."

"But Guy—she's a *dancer*," said the horrified Mariella. "She's billed to appear as Guest Artist with the Theatre Ballet in Edinburgh the day after to-morrow."

"Well, she may be O.K. by then."

Mariella sighed, and thought how impossible it was even to *try* to explain to a young man who didn't know the first thing about ballet—about those exacting *entrechats* and *pirouettes*—how difficult it was to do them with two whole feet, let alone with one of them damaged!

"Where is Jane now?" she asked him.

"She's in a cottage over here," said Guy. "They've put her to bed. She'll be O.K. It's bad luck about the dance to-night, though. I'll be over at the Allt nan Ros myself shortly—I'm badly in need of a bath and a change. I'm pretty wet. I could do with some dinner, too! Afterwards, perhaps, I could come back here with the car and pick up Jane. After an hour or two's sleep she ought to feel better. But, of course, it depends on you—I'm not forgetting that I'm your partner to-night. . . . Yes, but of course it matters. . . . Oh, yes, it was quite a spot of luck that I happened to find her. . . . What's that? Oh, it's Fiona again? Well, what is it *now*, Fiona? . . . No, of course I can't wake her up to ask her anything so unimportant! . . . *I* think it's unimportant anyway. You'll just have to wear your own dress, or a jumper, or something. . . . Well, I don't see why not. People will understand if you explain. . . . Yes, I expect you're right— I *am*! You've told me so often enough, anyway! So long!"

"I think he's the most aggravating person I've ever met!" exclaimed Fiona. "Wear a jumper, indeed! As if I would!"

"Oh, poor, poor Jane!" thought Mariella. "The awful thing that haunts all dancers has happened to her—she's sprained her ankle. It's worse than if it were broken because a clean break can be mended, and the ankle is often as strong or even stronger than before. But an ankle that's been sprained is never quite the same again. Everyone knows that. Oh, poor, poor Jane!"

18

The Highland Ball

IMAGINE a long room, oak panelled, with a gallery at one end. Out of the high, pointed windows you could see the moon sailing in and out of the racing clouds, and the fir trees on the hillside opposite the window bending in the light wind. It was cold out there, but inside all was warmth and light. The floor had been waxed until it shone like a lake, and reflected the colourful scene. Flowers had been banked against the low rostrum underneath the gallery—crimson and cream azaleas, and pink primulas, scarlet geraniums, and yellow and white chrysanthemums. The antlers of the stags' heads on the walls still wore wreaths of holly and evergreens. It was New Year's Eve—Hogmanay, in Scotland—and a time of jollification for everybody.

The dancers themselves were colourful, too. In England the ladies provide the colour, the gentlemen the background. Here, the men were as gay as the women. In fact, it was hard to say whether the male dancers, most of whom were in full Highland dress, or the female in their ball dresses draped with the tartan scarves of their respective clans, were the more decorative!

"It makes me wish I were married to a Scot!" said Mariella enviously. "You *are* lucky, Fiona, to be a Frazer! I think your tartan looks lovely with that white frock. And what a gorgeous brooch!"

"It's a cairngorm," said Fiona without enthusiasm. "It cost a lot of money, but really, after Ian had bought it for me at MacIntyre's, in Princes Street, I saw heaps of others I liked better. I asked him to take it back and change it, but he said the others were too expensive. Ian is frightfully mean, sometimes!"

"It looks very nice, anyway," insisted Mariella. "I wonder

when Guy will be back? He had a bath, and changed into his evening things, had some dinner that they'd kept hot for him, and went straight back again for Jane. He said he felt a 'new man'! Everyone is frightfully sorry for poor Jane. Josef was quite distraught. But of course he *would* be! He was counting on Jane to pull him a few more rungs up the ladder of success!"

"He doesn't look too heart-broken!" Fiona remarked nastily. "He's making a great fuss of Vivien Chator, though what for I really don't know. She's not a beauty, is she? Her mouth is far too big, and her hair looks awful, scraped back like that."

But Mariella was no longer listening to Fiona. Her mind was summing up the dramatic situation. Jane, with a sprained ankle, obviously could not dance at Edinburgh on Thursday. Who was to take her place? Why, Vivien Chator, of course. She was here on the spot. She had been understudying Jane. What more likely? And of course Josef knew it—that was why he was making such a fuss of her. Poor Nigel's nose was quite put out of joint! Oh, well—he might have time, now, to dance with her, Mariella. His voice asking her for the eightsome reel made her heart sing. Although he wasn't wearing a kilt, he was more handsome than any of them, thought Mariella proudly. His fair head towered over the other men's—all except one young man, whose name appeared to be Robin, and Mariella had reluctantly to admit that Robin was even taller.

She found herself in a set with the tall young man and a crowd of other Scots, and to the skirl of the pipes the wild dance began. She noticed that Vivien Chator and Josef Linsk shrugged their shoulders expressively and retired to the balcony. Josef knew his powers as a dancer—no one better!—but he was too wise to compete with a crowd of lightfooted Highlanders on their own ground! He murmured something in his own language that, being translated, meant: "Discretion is the better part of valour!"

"They're fascinating, though, aren't they?" Vivien said, leaning over the balcony rail and staring at the dancers below, as if studying the antics of a herd of wild animals. "The men dance even better than the women!"

"What do you think about Jane Foster, *ma chère*?" said Josef, lighting a cigarette. "A sprained ankle is a serious thing for a dancer, is it not?"

"Serious? I should just say so!" Vivien said. "She will probably never dance again. Or, if she does, it will always worry her."

"Yes," said Josef thoughtfully. "It is a most serious thing to have happened. A weak ankle for a dancer is like a weak ankle for a race-horse—only worse, for the horse can have his ankle bandaged. Moreover, he still has three legs remaining! There is the performance on the night of Thursday. How will it go, think you?"

Vivien shrugged her shoulders, a habit she had caught from Josef.

"I will do my best, of course. You understand what I mean— what we were discussing before. It is the chance in a million. The chance every dancer waits for."

"Leave it to me. I will arrange it," said Josef confidently. "I myself will make the telephone call to London. I will be of the most diplomatic—and oh, yes, of the most helpful. You shall see! We will together dance the *pas de deux* from *Lac*, and the Blue Bird, and you shall dance the lead in *Pineapple Poll*. I am sorry for Jane, *naturellement*, but——" He shrugged his shoulders. "Ah, well—these things happen. . . . So! The reel, he has stopped himself! Shall we go down now? Or perhaps you had better stay here until the next dance has established himself. If he sees you, the young man whose name is Nigel will upon you make the pounce, as they say!"

"Oh, Josef—you are funny!" laughed Vivien. "But you're quite right. I *shall* be pounced upon by that frightfully serious and bossy young man if he once catches sight of me!"

"The 'country pumpkin', does one not call him?" said Josef.

"*Bumpkin*, Josef, *bumpkin*!" corrected Vivien. "One of these days I shall teach you to speak English."

"That will be a pleasure," said Josef with a bow. "In fact, dear Vivien, it will indeed be a privilege to be taught anything by you."

At a quarter to ten that night Guy's car was speeding round

the head of Loch Awe for the fourth time in twenty-four hours. Jane, her creamy cheeks even paler than usual, sat wrapped in rugs in the front seat beside the driver. Except for a line of pain round her sensitive mouth, she seemed to have recovered from her ordeal.

"I still can't make up my mind whether I oughtn't to have left you in bed in that cottage, instead of dragging you round here," said Guy anxiously, glancing at her pale cheeks in the moonlight.

"Oh, no, Guy! I feel quite all right now," she assured him. "What a blessing there wasn't a doctor to be got hold of anywhere! If he'd ordered me to stay in bed, I'd have been frightfully disappointed. It would be a most awful waste to spend Hogmanay in Scotland—in bed!"

"Well, we must get you up to Edinburgh first thing to-morrow morning," said Guy. "I shan't be happy until a doctor has seen that ankle."

"Yes, and I must telephone to London and Edinburgh the very minute I get to the hotel," said Jane. "Or perhaps Josef would do it for me. You see, I may not be able to dance on Thursday. How long does a sprained ankle take to mend, Guy?"

"Oh, a few days' rest, and it ought to be O.K.," Guy said lightly. No use frightening the poor kid more than was necessary. "But you must certainly telephone, or let Linsk do it for you."

"As a matter of fact, my foot feels wonderful," declared Jane. "You've bandaged it so well. Guy, anyone would think you were a real doctor!"

"Well, I *am* in the doctoring line, you know," said Guy with a smile. "They always say that a vet is half a doctor."

"Yes, he is, isn't he!" laughed Jane. "I think a veterinary surgeon is an awfully nice thing to be. Curing sick animals. . . . Oh! What are you stopping for? We haven't run out of petrol, have we?"

"No, we haven't run out of petrol," said Guy, drawing in to the side of the road.

"Then——"

"I want a word with you, young lady," said Guy. "That's

why I'm stopping here, where it's dark. If I could see your little childish face, looking so pathetic, I could never say all the stern, fatherly things I intend to say to you."

"Guy—you make me rather frightened," said Jane in a small, solemn voice.

"I should hope I do!" said Guy. "Now, tell me, please, what were you doing on that lonely mountain all by yourself?"

"I——" began Jane. "It was mostly you, Guy."

"Mostly me? What *do* you mean?"

"Well, you see—you would go off climbing," explained Jane. "And I wanted to go climbing, too, only you wouldn't take me. You don't know how much I wanted to go climbing."

"Poor kid!" Guy said, half to himself. Then he went on resolutely: "But you do see now, I hope, that you couldn't have gone with me, Jane—not in that weather, and wearing those clothes. By the way, that woman has dried them quite successfully, hasn't she? No one would guess they'd been through such an ordeal! One day I might take you climbing with me, if you really wish to go, but not until the spring or the summer, and only provided you get yourself some suitable footwear. Just now, you must promise me never to do such a stupid thing as to go climbing mountains all by yourself when you haven't an idea how to do it. Promise, Jane?"

"Supposing I won't promise?"

"I shall spank you!" Guy threatened.

"Oh—then I suppose I shall have to promise," Jane said meekly. "But only provided that *you* promise, too."

"What must I promise?"

"That you'll take me up that very mountain—Ben Cruachan —right to the very top!"

"That's a bargain!" laughed Guy. "Shake on it!" His strong, brown hand found her little white one under the rug, and they shook hands solemnly. "I promise to take you up Ben Cruachan when——"

"When what?"

"Oh, nothing," Guy said lightly. "It was just an idea I had." He was silent for a few minutes, then drew an envelope out of his pocket, opened it out into a flat sheet, and began to sketch

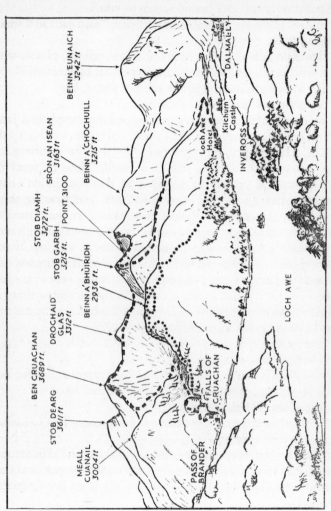

BEN CRUACHAN 3689 ft.

STOB DEARG 3611 ft.

MEALL CUANAIL 3004 ft.

DROCHAID GLAS 3312 ft.

BEINN A'BHÙIRIDH 2936 ft.

STOB DIAMH 3272 ft.

STOB GARBH 3215 ft.

POINT 3100

SRÒN AN ISEAN 3163 ft.

BEINN A'CHOCHUILL 3215 ft.

BEINN EUNAICH 3242 ft.

Loch Awe Hotel

Kilchurn Castle

DALMALLY

INVEROSS

LOCH AWE

FALLS OF CRUACHAN

PASS OF BRANDER

Guy's sketch for Jane showing where they had been

rapidly. . . . "Look, Jane. This is where you went this afternoon, and where I found you."

By the light of the dashboard Jane watched the range of
mountains come to life under Guy's clever fingers. . . . "Beinn
a' Bhùiridh in front here. . . . Behind, Ben Cruachan, himself
. . . and here are all his satellite peaks. . . . Drochaid Glas . . .
Stob Garbh . . . and so on, ending with Beinn Eunaich. You
see my route? I'll mark it by an oblong-dotted line, and yours
with a round-dotted one. Here are the Falls of Cruachan,
where I found you. Now you can see what happened to you,
and where you wandered in the mist."

"Oh, thank you, Guy," said Jane. "I'll keep your map, may
I—as a souvenir?"

"Yes—and as a solemn warning as to what happens to
naughty girls who go off climbing all by themselves!" laughed
Guy. "And that reminds me—if ever you do go off climbing
mountains, Jane—with other people, I mean—you must always
leave word with your friends at home saying exactly where
you've gone—or intended to go. Then if anything happens to
you and you don't return, the search-party will know where to
look."

"Yes, I see now that's what I ought to have done, but at the
time I just never thought. It looked so easy!"

"Things that look 'ever so easy' and perhaps really *are* ever so
easy in fine weather have a nasty way of becoming ever so
difficult if the weather changes," said Guy. "Well, now I think
we'd better be getting along. It must be nearly ten o'clock.
Only two hours to the New Year!"

The skirl of the bagpipes reached the ears of the two late-
comers as they crossed the entrance-hall of the hotel just after
ten o'clock. Jane managed to hop along on her sound foot, one
arm on Guy's shoulder. Judging by the lusty shouts coming
from the ball-room, the dancers were enjoying an especially
lively reel.

"What about going up to the balcony?" said Guy. "Just to
have a look at things. It might be quite a good idea for you to
sit up there, Jane, out of the way of the madding crowd. We
could all retire to it, now and then, to keep you company.

Personally I'd find it a great relief, when I feel I'm getting out of my depths down in the ball-room."

"Don't you like dancing?" asked Jane.

"Oh, I like it well enough," answered Guy, "except this modern stuff—tangos, fox-trots, and so forth. I never can see the fun of them. But, as a matter of fact, I've always been too busy to go to dances. Riding, swimming, and suchlike—and, of course, my job."

"And climbing?" added Jane.

"Yes—and climbing," agreed Guy.

"Well, I think the balcony is a good idea, too," Jane said. "Especially as I'm not exactly dressed for a ball." She looked down ruefully at her once immaculate town suit. "I'm afraid this is rather the worse for wear! But I don't know how I'll manage the stairs."

"I do. Very simple," Guy said, picking her up and depositing her on the top step.

"Oh, thank you, Guy! . . . Oh, doesn't the ball-room look gay! And isn't the Highland dress lovely?"

"Yes, it's quite attractive," admitted Guy, looking down over the balcony rail at the vivid, ever-changing pattern of swinging kilts and flying scarves. "Especially when they're dancing their own reels and strathspeys. The Campbell of In-veross is a splendid figure, isn't he? He's that tall chap over there dancing with the girl in green."

"The Campbell——" began Jane. Then she stopped suddenly, and clutched the rail in front of her. "You don't mean that young man in the kilt, with the dirk in his stocking and the lace cravat?"

"Yes—Robin Campbell," said Guy. "He's the Laird of In-veross—the head of the family here, and he's usually referred to as 'Himself of Inveross'. He owns the hotel, you know."

"Oh, *no!*" exclaimed Jane in agony.

"What's the matter? Do you know him?"

"I tipped him half-a-crown," said poor Jane. "I called him 'my good man'. You see, I saw him getting out the boat, and I thought he was the gillie. *Guy*, don't laugh! There's nothing the least funny about it. It's *awful!*"

"Not at all. It's a huge joke!" roared Guy. "The best I've heard for a long time. Robin will be the first to appreciate it. Fancy tipping Himself of Inveross! Oh, Jane—you're incorrigible! Wait till I see Robin!"

"If you laugh with him about it, I'll never speak to you again," threatened Jane.

"In that case, I suppose I shall have to restrain myself," Guy said solemnly. "It will be difficult, though. By the way, Robin is following in my footsteps. He's studying veterinary surgery at Glasgow. I must introduce him to Mariella. They ought to be kindred spirits. He must have nearly finished there now, and be ready to take a job. Well, that's the end of the reel, and we've been spotted. Here is Linsk, hot foot, to ask how you are!"

Josef was being his most charming self, asking after "Jane's most sad foot", running to get more cushions for her back.

"As if Guy hadn't got me plenty!" she laughed, as he returned with yet another.

"That is Charlton, is it not—the one you call 'Guy'? He is that most tough young man. In his—how do you say it? 'Crude' I think is the word—in his crude fashion, he is quite useful to you, is he not?"

Into Jane's mind flashed a picture of Guy as he had carried and helped her all those miles down the mountain track back to safety and warmth, with never a word of blame or a hint of the weariness she knew he must have been feeling. And though she wouldn't admit it, she knew in her heart that Josef, with all his outrageous good looks and all his charm couldn't hold a candle to Guy.

"Useful?" she echoed. "I hardly think that 'useful' describes what Guy did for me to-day. Why, he saved my life! If it hadn't been for Guy, I should still have been up there on that awful mountain, probably frozen to death in the snow."

"Snow?" echoed Josef in his turn. "But, *chérie*, there *is* no snow! Not even one little snowflake. It is a starlight night. See!" He waved dramatically towards one of the pointed windows. "There is a moon, also."

"I know it's a fine night down here," said Jane. "But up

there——" In her imagination she saw again the icy slopes of
Ben Cruachan, the snowdrifts piling up in the corries, forming
into shells and cornices over the edges of the gullies. She heard
again the roar of the cataracts thundering down the faces of the
precipices, and she shuddered. But it was useless trying to explain all this to Josef, sitting there in his dress clothes, the last
word in sophisticated elegance.

The band struck up a tango, and the young man rose.

"I must go," he said. "I am dancing this tango with Vivien.
It is a 'request' number. Excuse, please!"

He bowed and left her, and strangely enough Jane didn't
mind. It was quite pleasant sitting up here all by herself. She
could watch the guests and note their antics. A tango was always
rather an amusing dance to watch. Not many English people
could do it, and even when they managed the steps, they always
seemed to look faintly ridiculous—the men, especially.

Leaning over the balcony rail, Jane saw that Josef and Vivien
were giving what amounted to an exhibition dance. At first one
or two couples had braved the floor, but now everyone was
standing round watching the slow, beautiful movements of the
professional dancers.

"They dance most awfully well together," thought Jane.
"Really, as a partner, she suits him better than I do." And
strangely enough, this thought didn't hurt as it would have
done once.

Presently the one or two brave couples plucked up courage
again and joined the professionals, and soon the floor was filled
with languourously swaying couples, all dipping and hesitating
to the compelling rhythm of the famous tango 'Jealousy'.

"I ought to be jealous of Josef, dancing so wonderfully with
Vivien," said Jane to herself, "but the queer thing is—I'm not.
. . . I wonder where Guy is? He certainly won't be dancing this
—it's one of his *bêtes noires*!"

While she scanned the couples standing round the walls, or
sitting in the alcoves, Guy's voice at her elbow said: "Hullo,
Jane! All by yourself? I've brought you some sandwiches and
coffee. I expect you're hungry. The meal you had in that cottage
was a long time ago, and you missed dinner. By the way, they've

all spotted you, and you're in for shoals of visitors. One young lady in particular! She's out for your blood, by the sound of her! Something about a frock you offered to lend her."

"My goodness!" exclaimed Jane. "Fiona! I'd forgotten all about that frock. How awful of me! I gave it to the chambermaid to press. I wonder what she's done with it? Oh, poor Fiona!"

"I shouldn't worry too much about Fiona," said Guy. "That frock she's wearing is obviously quite all right. It's my opinion she only wanted to wear yours because it was a model by Frank Sinatra, or somebody."

"Oh, Guy! Frank Sinatra is a crooner, not a dress designer!" giggled Jane.

"Is he? All the same to me," Guy said solemnly. "Well, here is the angry young lady herself. I'll return, shall I, when the battle's over—to bury the dead!"

"You coward!" teased Jane. "I shall be torn limb from limb!"

"*Jane!*" came Fiona's querulous voice before she had reached the top of the little spiral staircase. "Jane, I do think it was too bad of you to go and get lost on a mountain the very night of the ball, and me not knowing where your dress was or anything."

"I think the one you're wearing is lovely," said Jane. "The white lace looks beautiful with that tartan scarf, and it's not crushed or anything."

"That's not the point, Jane," argued Fiona. "You offered to lend me yours, so naturally I didn't even iron my own frock."

"I thought you didn't have to iron lace dresses," put in Jane. "I thought you just shook them out, and that's why people took them on cruises and things."

"Oh, they *say* that," retorted Fiona. "I mean, the people in the shops do when you buy them. But it's not true, really. Anyway, I didn't even take it out of my case. You've ruined the ball for me, Jane, if that's any consolation to you—you and Ian, between you. If he hadn't skidded into the ditch, it would never have happened. It's too bad!"

"I'm so sorry," said Jane. "But really I didn't do it on purpose—get lost, I mean. I ought to have told you that the maid had my frock, but you see I thought I'd be back in time. By the way, there's poor Ian looking for you—over there by the pillar."

But Fiona wasn't so easily got rid of.

"Well, he can just go on looking for me!" she declared with a shrug. "He can't tango for toffee, anyway! Really, he's the worst dancer ever! It's painful to do anything more complicated than a fox-trot with Ian, and, even then, he just walks round and round as if he was exercising a horse or something. Never anything the least bit original."

Jane had to laugh. Fiona's picture of Ian exercising a horse, Fiona being the horse, was too much for her.

"Well, I'm glad *something* amuses you!" Fiona said huffily. "Oh, now that tango has finished, so perhaps I can get something to eat. I haven't had a thing since dinner—not even a lemonade—but I don't expect Ian would care if I starved to death!" She went off down the stairs, and Jane breathed a sigh of relief.

"Thank goodness, that's got rid of *her* for a bit!" she said thankfully.

It wasn't long before she had another visitor. A large, untidy girl with a good-humoured face bounded up the little staircase.

"Oh, Jane!" she exclaimed breathlessly. "How are you? What a simply frightful thing to happen! I mean, getting lost on whatever its queer name is. I just came up to tell you—she's arrived!"

"Oh, hullo, Sylvia!" said Jane. "Who's arrived?"

"Lady Blantosh. She's been staying in Edinburgh, and she's come over just for the night, because this dance is in aid of her destitute babies, you know. . . . Oh, sorry, Guy! I didn't know you were just behind me with some lemonade for Jane! Can I mop it up?"

"No, it's all right, Sylvia," laughed Guy. "Most of it has gone on the floor. Look *out*! Here's Richard with some ice cream, and Elizabeth with a plate of meringues. You're getting spoilt, Jane!"

"Forward march! At the double! Spring to it, my hearties!" said Richard, balancing a plate of ice cream on two fingers and a thumb. "Look snappy, you folks! We must see the royal entry

What is the good lady wearing this time? Oh, *no*! Look, you people. Do you see what I see?"

They all craned over the balcony just in time to see Lady Blantosh shaking hands with Himself of Inveross. They all knew Lady Blantosh's genius for wearing the wrong clothes whenever she could, but they had hardly expected this.

"A kilt!" exclaimed Elizabeth in amazement. "But she isn't Scottish! Anyway, this is a ball—not the Highland Games! My goodness, and look what she's wearing with it! A lace blouse, high-heeled, satin slippers, and—believe it or not—nylons!"

"I need some strong drink after that!" exclaimed Richard, collapsing into a chair. "Anyone got any cider-cup?"

"You can have some of my lemonade," said Jane generously. "Quick! Something's happening!" Her ears caught the exciting sound of the castanets. "It's Angelo and Caroline! I ought to call her Rosita, oughtn't I, now that she's so famous. Oh, aren't they lovely!" Spellbound, Jane watched the Spanish dancers as they circled each other, holding one another's gaze all the time, their slim, strong fingers clicking out the rhythm with their castanets, their feet beating softly on the polished floor. Softly at first, then louder—louder—until the hall was filled with the wild, swinging, stamping Flamenco Gypsy dance. Rosita's many petticoats swung round her like the petals of a great silken poppy, her flying dark hair hid her like a cloud. Angelo's body, strong and supple as tempered steel, bent and swayed, his dark, aquiline features expressed all the pride and arrogance of the Spanish gipsies. Then the feet of the two dancers beat softer and yet softer, until the sound was like the tapping of the rain on the window-pane—until it died away altogether, and the dance was finished with a last proud gesture of the head and upflung hands.

A positive roar of applause broke out. There were cries and stamps, and yells of: "Encore, Rosita! Another one, Angelo! Encore! Encore!"

So, after a few minutes, the two of them appeared again. Rosita was now wearing a beautiful dress of Catalonia. A black net covered her hair. Her dress had an enormous skirt of blue and green shot-silk, with flowers embroidered on it. The tight-

Spellbound, Jane watched the Spanish dancers as they circled each other

fitting bodice was of black satin, and underneath the dress bil-
lowed many starched petticoats. She wore a little apron of black
lace, matching her black lace mittens. A white scarf, embroidered with scarlet, was folded demurely round her shoulders, and fastened with a large brooch. Her white stockings
were criss-crossed with black ribbons.

Angelo wore a suit of dark blue cloth, with tightly fitting
trousers reaching to below the knee, and a fitting coat with cut-
away fronts. It was ornamented with white braid. Under this he
wore a white satin shirt, and a red sash with long fringed ends
wound, cummerbund-fashion, round his waist. His stockings
were white, and on his head was a long black net cap, something like a fisherman's jersey cap. His hands were held at the
height of the shoulders, fingers pointed. Rosita held her apron
delicately, whilst her eyes were demurely cast down.

At one end of the balcony Jane watched entranced, whilst at
the other Josef and Vivien stood together, talking softly.

"I think he is too conceited, that young man!" exclaimed
Josef, his eyes on Angelo's lithe figure. "He is good-looking,
and he knows it!"

"Oh, I don't agree," said Vivien. "I think he is a great artist.
I have heard of Angelo, of course. Who hasn't? Well, now I've
seen him, and I think he surpasses his reputation. As for the
girl—she is much more beautiful than I expected. She is warm
and glowing, and full of fire and *joie de vivre*—supremely exciting
to watch."

"I agree about Rosita," said Josef. "In my mind I see her in
Tricorne, the Three-Cornered Hat, and I think to myself: 'How
beautiful is Rosita in that ballet!' Perhaps one day we shall see
her in it, and it will be a case of 'Rosita Rejoins the Wells', eh?
For you know Rosita *was* at the Wells until quite recently."

"Yes, I know," answered Vivien. "She is rather like me. I
was at the Wells at first. Now I am back there once more. That
sometimes happens. But somehow I do not think it will happen
to Rosita. I think she and Angelo will reach the stars on their
own."

Jane, hearing snatches of the conversation, thought to herself: "She's generous. I believe Vivien Chator is quite a nice

girl. I think I'd like her very much, if only she weren't my rival." Yes, the truth must be faced—Vivien Chator *was* her rival. Josef had put a long-distance 'phone call through to London, and another to Edinburgh, and it had been arranged that if Jane, herself, couldn't dance as Guest Artist, Vivien Chator was to take her place. It might well be the beginning of Vivien's rise to fame, and the end of Jane's career. Jane sighed. How awful to think that a dancer's career hung on so small a thing as a sprained ankle! She had never thought about it before, but it was true.

❧ 19 ❧

Edinburgh

JANE spent the most miserable week of her life in the Trossachs Hotel, Forfar Street, Edinburgh, where she had been taken on New Year's Day. Guy had driven them all up in his car—Josef, and Vivien, and Jane herself, her poor injured foot propped on a cushion. Mariella was going back home with Nigel, who was now curiously attentive to her, since Vivien seemed to have forgotten his very existence in her excitement at her sudden and unexpected rise to fame as Jane's substitute.

The Edinburgh doctor had pronounced Jane's injury to be merely a sprain, and had been very cheerful about it until he had heard that she was the famous Jane Foster of the Sadler's Wells Ballet. Then he had suddenly become very grave indeed, and had ordered an X-ray. He had also made an appointment for Jane to see a world-famous bone specialist. The latter had also been cheerful, it is true, but Jane wondered if it was an artificial cheerfulness. Would she ever dance again? Would she? As she sat gazing down on the huddle of roofs that marked out the Royal Mile, and beyond that the King's Park, with Arthur's Seat towering in the background, she asked herself this question. Would she ever dance again? And if she didn't, what was left for her?

Last night she had hobbled to a taxi, and, seated in a box at the King's Theatre, she had watched Vivien Chator dancing Columbine in the ballet *Carnaval*, the Blue Bird *pas de deux* from *Swan Lake*—the dances that she, Jane Foster, had been billed to dance. She had watched Vivien receiving bouquets, taking innumerable "curtains", and heard the praise showered upon her: "Isn't she beautiful? . . . Yes, my dear, quite a romantic story. She came up in the first place to understudy that other dancer—

what was her name? Jane something. Well, if you ask me, this girl is quite as good, if not better. . . . Oh, no—I've never seen Jane What's-her-name, but I'm sure she *couldn't be any better*. For one thing, this girl's Russian. At least so I've been told, and it's a fact, you can always tell these Russian dancers, can't you? They've got a 'fire' the English ones simply don't possess. Of course, Margot Fonteyn's different, but she's an exception. Oh, yes, and of course Moira Shearer, and Beryl Gray. . . . Josef Linsk is good-looking, isn't he? I expect he's Russian, too. You can tell he's in love with her, can't you? So romantic, I think!"

Jane glanced sideways at the three large women in the next box, talking so loudly, and wondered if what they said had any truth in it. Was Vivien Chator so very good? Was she better than Jane? Was Josef in love with Vivien?

As for the women, never for a moment did they dream that the slender girl with the sad, pale face, sitting so quietly in the adjoining box, was the very "Jane What's-her-name" they had been talking about.

After the show, Jane had managed to hobble round to the stage entrance, and up to the stage dressing-room where Vivien Chator, still in her Swan Queen dress, her almond-shaped eyes looking even longer and darker than ever with their heavy make-up, was signing autograph books.

"I'm so sorry I haven't got a photograph," she was saying to a couple of entranced schoolgirls, "but if you'll leave me your address, I'll send you one. I'll sign your books here, shall I? Oh, and here is Jane Foster—you'd like her autograph, too, wouldn't you? Yes, below mine—there's just room. Sorry! I seem to have taken up most of the page!"

Jane signed the book underneath the flourishing signature of Vivien Chator, and talked to the girls for a moment. But very soon they forgot about her. Their eyes strayed back to Vivien in her snowy *tutu*, crisp and virginal as a Christmas rose, to her glittering crown with the jewelled swan in front, to her make-up table covered with the floral offerings of an admiring audience.

Oh, the flattering, worshipping, fickle audience! How quick it is to acclaim, and how quick to forget!

With a sad little ache in her heart that hurt much more than the ache in her foot, Jane left the theatre, and stepped into the waiting taxi. For the first time for many months, no one noticed her go. No one rushed forward with an autograph book for her to sign, no one asked her breathlessly what she was dancing in to-morrow, or what she thought of Edinburgh. No one came forward with a camera to take her photograph by flashlight.

Back at the hotel, she undressed wearily, and was about to get into bed when the telephone at her bedside rang.

"Oh, Guy!" she said when she heard his warm voice at the other end of the wire. "How lovely to hear you! I was feeling frightfully blue! . . . No, of course, it's not too late to ring me up. As a matter of fact, I've been to the theatre, just to see how things were going. It was pretty grim, seeing someone else taking my place! Oh, I know I shouldn't have gone, but somehow I just *had* to. . . . Oh, yes, my ankle's O.K. At least, I *think* it is. I've got to go back to Mr. Arkroyd to-morrow and he'll pass judgment! . . . No, I'm not doing anything at all this week-end. Mummy did think of coming up, but you see, Mr. Arkroyd and Dr. Jacobs say I can't possibly dance for a bit yet, so I may as well come home to Monks Hollow, so Mummy isn't coming after all. . . . What? You mean you're coming up here, to Edinburgh, yourself, to-morrow, Saturday, and you'll take me out in the car? . . . And you'll take me home on Sunday, too? Oh, Guy—how wonderful!"

It was amazing, thought Jane, how just hearing a person on the telephone can cheer you up. Guy had such a warm, friendly voice, and he'd obviously been thinking about her, and planning how to make things easier and happier for her. Whereas Josef— she realized with a pang that Josef had hardly spoken to her since their arrival in Edinburgh. Of course she knew he was frightfully busy, but still he might have spared time just to ring her up and ask how she was.

On Saturday Guy duly arrived.

"Just in time for lunch," Jane said, eagerly going forward to meet him. "You must have started off at crack of dawn to get here so soon! Oh, it's lovely to have someone to talk to. Several of the company are staying here, but they go out after breakfast, and one doesn't see them again until next morning. I suppose I was the same myself when I was dancing!"

"You look as if you're walking a lot better," said Guy as she led the way to the dining-room.

"Oh, yes. Dr. Jacobs says I must use my ankle now to stop it getting stiff, but of course I can't actually walk very far yet."

"I've brought you a letter from Mariella," Guy said as they waited for their soup. "What on earth did I do with it? . . . Oh, here it is!" He held out a large, blue envelope with Jane's name scrawled across it in Mariella's dashing handwriting.

"Do you mind if I read it?" asked Jane.

"No, of course not," answered Guy. "Go ahead!"

"Dearest Jane," said the letter. "I do hope that by now you're feeling better, and that the doctor has given a good report on your ankle.

"Nigel and I got home on the Wednesday night. We passed the place where Fiona's car got stuck in the ditch, and would you believe it?—there wasn't as much as an inch of snow anywhere! Oh, Jane—it was the most wonderful drive home! Nigel was most awfully kind, and looked after me like anything—just as if I was an ordinary girl. I mean, not just Mariella, whom he's known since childhood. He even remembered to ask me if I wanted any tea, though he never bothers with any himself, and he was so pleased when I said it didn't matter, and we'd just crash on. He said I was a sport! I can still hardly believe it! Isn't it funny how things that begin badly often end well, and vice versa? I was so miserable the day we came, and now I feel I could jump over the moon! Just because Nigel was so sweet. Of course, I don't mean that Guy wasn't sweet, too. He *was*— bringing us like that in his car. In fact, Guy is the nicest boy I know—next after Nigel. But of course he *isn't* Nigel, and that's that. There's only one Nigel."

"If I may ask and not seem awfully inquisitive," put in Guy, "why the funny look?"

"*You'd* have a funny look if you read this letter," exploded Jane. "From beginning to end, it's all about Nigel Monkhouse and how wonderful he is! Will Mariella ever find Nigel out for what he is, I wonder?"

"Oh, I expect so," said Guy. "Give her time! She's only a kid, after all. As a matter of fact, Nigel Monkhouse is quite a decent chap when he's with other fellows. It's just that he's known Mariella so long he forgets she's grown up, and bosses her about as if she was his kid sister. One of these days——" He stopped.

"Well, one of these days, what?"

"I was going to say that one of these days, Nigel is going to wake up and realize that Mariella is a very pretty girl, and as sweet as she's good-looking, and then——"

"Then? Guy, why *will* you keep stopping without finishing what you were going to say!" exclaimed Jane in exasperation. "It's most aggravating!"

"Sorry!" apologized Guy. "Well, when that happens, either Mariella will love him more than ever, or else she'll have found him out for what he is, as you said just now, and she'll tell him to 'go and find another', as the song says!"

"Well, I hope the latter," said Jane fervently. "Mariella is far too good for Nigel."

"I rather hope so, too," agreed Guy. "But I don't expect it will matter much what *we* think!"

After they had finished lunch, they went out to Guy's car and drove slowly up Princes Street.

"One of the most famous streets in the world!" exclaimed Jane. "I still can't believe I'm really seeing it! All the beautiful shops on the one side, and the lovely gardens on the other! One can buy a tartan skirt, and then dash across the road and smell the carnations; then dash back for a sweater to go with it! I think it's a lovely way to go shopping! I like the Burns monument, too, and the Floral Clock, and, of course, the mountains in the distance, and the castle on the hill."

"In short, you've joined the Edinburgh worshippers!" laughed Guy.

"Yes, I'm afraid I have," confessed Jane. "I think it's a very beautiful city."

"So do I, but I like the other end of it best," said Guy. "The Old Town, where I'm taking you now."

"I know!" said Jane. "You're taking me to the King's Park. You must have second sight, Guy! I've been looking at it out of my window all this week, and aching to go there—it looks so lovely! It was most aggravating!"

"I was hoping," said Guy, "that no one had thought of taking you there, and that I should have the pleasure of showing you my favourite bit of Edinburgh first."

"By the way—before we go any further, Guy," broke in Jane, "if you want to do any business—I mean the business you came up to Edinburgh to do—you needn't worry about me. I'll wait outside in the car, and I shan't mind how long you are. I'll be quite happy. You don't know what a relief it is to be out of that hotel!"

Guy smiled.

"What makes you think I came up here on business?" he asked.

"But of *course* you did," said Jane.

"Of course I *didn't*! Saturday is my off-day, and I came up expressly to see how you were, and—well, because I wanted to see you, Jane."

Jane said nothing for a moment. Then the colour rose to her pale cheeks, and a warm glow stole round her heart. After the neglect of the past week, it was lovely to be wanted. Moreover, to be wanted when she was down on her luck!

"How kind of you," she said. "It was very sweet of you, Guy, to come all that long way just to see me."

"Not at all," said Guy. "I was pleasing myself. I wanted to come. . . . Look, Jane—this is the Royal Mile. I thought, perhaps, you hadn't seen it, either. At least, not at close quarters. It's a picturesque part of Edinburgh, isn't it?"

Jane looked up at the "lands"—the tall old tenement houses, with their crazy rooftops, rising higgledy-piggledy against the grey wintry sky, and nodded.

"It's a wonderful old street," went on Guy. "The heart of Edinburgh! The place where all the historic things happened. Mary Queen of Scots must have ridden up and down here on horseback many and many a time, and Sir Walter Scott, too, in later times. I can just see Robert Burns stopping outside that

L

funny little shop there, and scribbling a poem to his latest 'bonnie lassie'! Why, John Knox must have preached on this very spot. Look! There's the house where he lived!"

"Oh, and there's the Palace of Holyroodhouse!" exclaimed Jane, as they left the narrow thoroughfare and came out into a wide road. "Now I've really seen it! The palace where the Queen stays. I've often heard about it. Oh, and there's Arthur's Seat! What a pity my ankle isn't strong yet. I could have persuaded you to take me up there."

"Yes, it is a pity," agreed Guy. "But never mind. I have another idea. I thought that, as you couldn't walk, you might enjoy a ride, so I rang up the McCreedy Livery Stables and booked two mounts for this afternoon."

For a moment Jane said nothing. Her heart was filled with dismay. Ever since she was a child, and had been made to ride whether she wanted to or not, she had hated riding. She had always been terrified of horses. But how was one to explain this to a young man who had gone to such trouble to provide her with what he obviously thought would be a great treat? How was one to tell him about the childish vow she had made—that never, never would she mount a horse once she was grown up and able to do as she pleased?

"I—I haven't any riding clothes," she faltered.

"I thought of that," answered Guy. "I've brought some for you. I borrowed them from Elizabeth Lister. She's about the same size as you, I think. I've brought some togs for myself as well."

"Oh——" faltered Jane. Then she smiled at him. It was no use—she must just go through with it, and hope for the best. Fortunately Guy was too busy manœuvring the car through an archway in a long, low building to notice that his companion wasn't very enthusiastic.

"The usual sort of place," said Jane to herself with a sigh. "Smelling of clean straw, and leather, and *horse*! Hateful, hateful smell! The same bandy-legged stable-boys staggering about under enormous loads of hay, and sacks of oats, or carrying buckets of water. The usual awful horses, all showing the whites of their eyes, and putting back their ears, and yawning and showing their frightful teeth! Don't I know it all!" Aloud she said politely:

"The McCreedy Livery Stables? No, I don't think I've heard of it. It's quite a big place, isn't it?"

"Yes. I always come along here to ride when I'm up in Edinburgh," said Guy. "I booked the nags for two-thirty, and it's now just a quarter past. I expect you can change in a quarter of an hour, eh? You ought to have had plenty of practice in changing quickly!"

"Yes," said Jane, "I certainly have!" To herself she added: "I feel I want to take a long, long time over changing. So long that there won't be any time left to ride!" But she made herself hurry, because, after all, Guy was paying for this, and it must be horribly expensive. Moreover, she didn't want to spoil his ride.

He was waiting for her when she limped out of the changing-room, and with him was the inevitable stable-boy holding two horses—a large, black gelding, and a small, chestnut mare.

"You *have* been quick," Guy said approvingly. "Well now, I hope you approve of Lady Jane, your mount. I chose her partly because of her name, and partly because she struck me as exactly the horse for you. Up you go!" He lifted her carefully into the saddle, and Jane waited fearfully for the antics to begin. But no—Lady Jane stood like a rock while Guy took the black horse from the stable-boy, and swung himself into the saddle. Side by side they clattered out of the stable-yard, under the archway, and out under the rolling hills of the King's Park.

"What's the matter?" Guy said, glancing with surprise at his companion's white strained face. "Is the foot hurting?"

"Oh, no—n-not at all," faltered Jane. "I w-was just wondering—you see, it's a long time since I rode on horseback, and I thought——"

"You mean, you thought you might not be able to manage her?" said Guy. "Is that it? Well, don't worry about that. She's the quietest little mare imaginable, despite the fact that she's no slug. She won't play you any tricks. I tried her out myself first, just to make sure."

"She mightn't play *you* any tricks, but she might *me*," said

Jane, with the knowledge born of past experience. "Once she knows I'm frightened of her——"

"Oh, look—I'm sorry if you're really scared," said Guy. "I had no idea it was as bad as that, or I wouldn't have suggested it. We'll go back if you like——"

"No," said Jane. "She hasn't done anything yet, and it's very nice out here, with the frosty sun going down like a ball of fire, and the seagulls mewing. I'd forgotten we were so near the sea! Perhaps you're right"—she leaned forward and gently stroked the mare's satiny neck—"perhaps I just had a bad time when I was a kid. You see, Nigel——"

"I understand," said Guy quietly. "I've often thought about it, and been sorry you were spoilt for riding. It's such a lovely pastime, and, being a Northumbrian, you ought to love it! You see? The mare is beautifully behaved. Like to try her in a canter?"

They cantered together over the springy turf, and Lady Jane was as smooth as silk. They passed two little boys flying a kite, and another kicking a ball. The mare took no notice at all, even when the ball bounced right under her feet. Once a paper bag, caught in the hedge along one side of the road, blew off, and came dancing towards them. Jane steeled herself for the worst, but the worst didn't happen. The mare might never have seen it for all the notice she took.

"I don't believe she's true!" Jane exclaimed, relaxing in the saddle.

"She's a perfect mount for a slightly nervous young lady," said Guy. "And incidentally, I'm thinking of buying her."

"Buying her?" echoed Jane. "But you've got two hunters already. Surely you don't want any more horses? Besides, she's far too quiet for you."

"Oh, I wasn't thinking of riding her myself," said Guy. "She's far too small for me, anyway. No, I had someone else in mind for her. Or I might, perhaps, sell her again. There's never any trouble in finding a buyer for a mare such as this one."

"No, I expect there isn't," agreed Jane.

The hours flew by, and, to her astonishment, Jane loved every minute of it. Not for a very long time had she enjoyed anything so much.

"I'll tell you something," she confessed. "When I was a kid —about twelve, or thereabouts—I made a vow never to ride when I was grown up. I meant it, too!"

"Well, I hope Lady Jane has made you change your mind," laughed Guy, "and that you've had a restful afternoon. It must be a nice change after rehearsals, and performances, and what not, just to sit on a horse's back and relax!"

"That's just what I thought one must never do on horseback —relax!" said Jane. "I know if ever I relaxed when I went out riding with Nigel and Mariella I always found myself lying up-side down in the ditch, or sticking in the hedge! But you're right, Guy—it has been restful this afternoon, and I *have* re-laxed, and thank you so very much!"

It was when she was changing back into her ordinary clothes that she realized with a shock of surprise that for a whole after-noon she had never once thought of the Wells.

"It's almost as if I'd already left the Wells," she said to Guy, as they drove back towards the city again. "Perhaps it's an omen! Perhaps I *have* left the Wells!"

Guy was very silent as he manœuvred the car skilfully in and out of the maze of traffic as they approached Princes Street. As the gardens came into view, he said suddenly:

"If ever you *do* really leave the Wells, Jane, I'd like you to know there's an alternative. Something else you could do."

"What could I do?" asked Jane in surprise.

"You could always marry me," said Guy. "You know, Jane, I believe I fell in love with you that night years ago when we met at the Frazers' party. Of course, I didn't realize it at the time—one doesn't—but coming down from Cruachan I sud-denly knew that I couldn't live without you. At least, I suppose I shall have to, if, perhaps, there is somebody else, but I had to tell you—to find out how you felt. That's the real reason I came up to Edinburgh."

"There isn't anybody else," said Jane. "I used to think I was in love with Josef, but now I know I wasn't. I only loved his dancing, and was flattered by the pretty things he said. I know now that he's not nice, really, and doesn't mean the things he says. He says them to every girl he meets! But you see, Guy, there's my dancing. It takes the place of my sweetheart. I'm in love with the stage, and with the ballet."

"Yes, I was afraid so," said Guy. "Still, if ever you find you can't, or don't want to, dance any more, I shall still be waiting, Jane."

"It's very sweet of you, Guy," said Jane. "I shall always be proud of winning your love, because you're such a darling. Oh, Guy—in another minute I shall cry! If only there weren't so many people about!"

"That was why I asked you to marry me right in the middle of Princes Street," said Guy. "It sort of eases the tension to have taxis hooting at you, and policemen signalling, and pedestrians dashing about everywhere. Now if we were on the top of Ben Cruachan——"

"Yes?" said Jane.

"You remember you asked me once to take you up that mountain?" went on Guy.

"Yes, and you said you would if—then you stopped, and you never finished what you were saying," said Jane.

"I meant that if we fell in love, I would take you up Ben Cruachan," explained Guy, "and when we were right on the top, where the cairn is, I would kiss you and I would say: 'Will you be my wife, Jane Foster?' And you would say: 'I will, Guy Charlton,' and our promise would be solemn and binding, made, as it was, in the very heart of the hills."

"You have funny ideas, Guy," said Jane, with a catch in her breath. "I think I like them. If only it wasn't—well, you see how it is."

"I understand," said Guy simply.

❦ 20 ❦

More News About Veronica

Jane's ankle got well rapidly. Her case had now been put into the hands of her own doctor and a Newcastle bone specialist. She was to go to the latter for a report in a week's time after her return.

"It seems silly, when I can walk as well as ever," she said gaily at breakfast on the fateful morning. "Why, I can even dance!" She turned a couple of *pirouettes* just to assure herself that this was so, and, seeing that there were no bad after-effects, she tried an *entrechat*. This, too, seemed to be quite all right.

"I believe I'm going to be O.K.," she said. "I believe I'm not going to have to leave the Wells, after all."

The doctor's report was encouraging, too. It had been a very slight sprain, seemingly—a mere nothing if it had happened to an ordinary person. But, of course, with a dancer—any injury to a foot was serious. Still, he thought all would be well. There was certainly no reason to think she would never dance again. She could go back to work now—to-morrow—if she wished, so long as she took things gently at first. It *was* possible, after a very strenuous performance, she might feel fatigue, but she was very lucky—very lucky indeed.

"Very lucky indeed!" echoed Jane as she left the doctor's house. "I hardly think 'lucky' describes it. I think an angel must have been guarding me!"

She almost danced for joy as she crossed the road and joined her mother in the car.

"Mummy! Guess what? My ankle is perfectly all right again, and I'm going back to the Wells to-morrow. We'd better go round by the station, and I'll book a seat on the pullman."

After a week's practice Jane was dancing as well as ever. The sprained ankle was like a bad dream. During the day she forgot about it. Only sometimes at night, when she was all alone, she thought about her adventure on Ben Cruachan, and the way Guy had rescued her. Once she dreamt she was standing on the top of the mountain, watching the mists rise about her feet, and then disperse, disclosing the shining waters of Loch Awe far below. There was someone with her on the mountain, and though she couldn't see his face, she knew it was Guy. Then suddenly she slipped and fell—down, down, into a dark crevice, where last winter's snow still lingered, and the sun never shone.

"Guy!" she cried in a panic. "Oh, Guy—where are you?" But Guy didn't come. "*Guy!*" she shrieked at the top of her voice, and with the shriek she woke to find Aunt Irma standing by her bedside in alarm.

"Whatever is the matter, Jane?"

"I've just had the most awful nightmare," said Jane. "I thought I was lost on Ben Cruachan, and Guy didn't come——"

"You're very fond of Guy, aren't you, Jane?" said her aunt.

"Oh, I love him dearly," confessed Jane, "with one side of me. But of course it's no use—no use at all—my loving him. I'm a dancer."

Aunt Irma nodded wisely.

"Yes, that is so, Jane. Unless one marries into the profession, like Veronica has done, or someone like your uncle, who is content to move round with his wife——" She shrugged her expressive shoulders. "*Que faire?* What can one do? When ballet comes in at one's door, love must perforce fly out at one's window, as the saying goes! At least it's not quite like that, but it's near enough."

"You're right, Aunt Irma," said Jane with a little sigh. "I've chosen my life, and I must live it. And of course I'm quite happy. I'm outrageously happy."

But was she? Well she certainly thought so the next day when the amazing thing happened.

"Aunt Irma!" she cried as soon as the lift put her out on the fourth floor of 140a Fortnum Mansions, her aunt's flat. "Aunt

Irma! Uncle Oscar! The most wonderful thing has happened! You'll never guess—not if you live to be a hundred!"

"Well, in that case, how about telling us what it is? Neither your uncle nor I have the least wish in the world to live to a hundred—not even to guess your news, Jane!" said her aunt.

"This morning, at dress rehearsal, something very strange happened," said Jane. "As you know, we're doing a new production of *Lac* for the Gala performance. I was dancing the *pas de trois* with Josef and Mavis, and understudying Veronica. Well, I was watching Act Two from a box, and suddenly I noticed something queer about Veronica. It wasn't that she danced less well—in fact, she was dancing wonderfully. Never, never, have I seen anyone dance like that. It was as if she was inspired! Then, she sort of hesitated—I can't describe it, and I don't believe anyone else noticed. Oh, yes—Sebastian did. He held up the orchestra for just a second. I don't believe even the orchestra noticed, but, of course, being a dancer, I expect I've got the habit of counting in split seconds——"

"Oh, Jane, Jane—*do* go on!" exclaimed Aunt Irma. "Your uncle and I are nearly frantic! Veronica didn't collapse, or anything?"

"Oh, no Aunt Irma. She went on dancing wonderfully . ."

"Well, then—what are you talking about, Jane, and why all the fuss? I expect you're just imagining it."

"Oh, no I'm not!"

"All right, then go on!"

"I *am* going on, Aunt Irma—if only you'll let me," exclaimed Jane. "But you will keep on interrupting. It was just when Odette greets Siegfried—you know, the *mime* scene—that Veronica—well, I'll call it hesitated, though it wasn't really that. At the end of Act Two we were all on stage ready for the next act, when suddenly Veronica said in that dreamy voice of hers: 'I don't think I'll dance any more to-day.' Well, you can guess what a sensation that made! The dress rehearsal, the full orchestra there, Madame—everything! Sebastian took one flying leap right out of the orchestral pit, and rushed over to Veronica. . . . 'Oh, it's all right,' said Veronica, still in that dreamy voice. 'I'm not ill, or anything——'

" 'But I saw something was the matter,' persisted Sebastian. 'I saw it!'

" 'I'm not ill,' said Veronica firmly. 'I don't know what was the matter with me. I felt—a little strange, that's all. I'm perfectly well now, but, if you don't mind, I think I won't dance any more to-day.' Then she turned to me and said: 'Jane, dear—you'll take my place. You always seem to be taking my place, don't you!' "

"And what *was* the matter?" burst out Aunt Irma and Uncle Oscar both in the same breath.

"She's—she's—Veronica's having a baby!" exclaimed Jane. "Now wasn't I right? I said you'd never guess."

"Well, it certainly *is* an awkward moment to announce the fact that you're having a baby—at the dress rehearsal, just before the Gala performance!" exclaimed Aunt Irma. "Your uncle and I never did it! But, of course, it *has* been known for young married couples to have babies . . . but what will happen now about the Gala performance? The other performances will be all right—you'll be able to take over, Jane. I must say you have all the luck! But the Gala performance—they'll have to have someone special for it."

"That's the exciting part about the whole affair!" exclaimed Jane. "It's not 'someone special'. It's *me!* Yes, it really is, Aunt Irma. Don't look so—so—flabbergasted in the only word for it. It's really me, Jane Foster."

"You, Jane?" echoed her aunt. "You haven't had a great deal of experience——"

"Oh, I know it *oughtn't* to be me," admitted Jane, "but you see, it's very awkward. They were depending on Veronica. Things like babies never entered their minds. Then an awful lot of people are either ill or away. There's Wendy Wesley on tour in Australia, and Yvonne Chévier dancing as Guest Artist at the Scala, Milan, and Rosalie's in hospital with appendicitis, so I'm to get my chance. Don't look so disapproving, Uncle Oscar. It makes me shudder to think of the review you'll give me!"

"I shall say that young Jane Foster danced at the Gala performance, that her youth and inexperience marred an otherwise promising performance, and it will be true," said the famous critic. "I think it is a mistake, Jane, to force you, but of course, if what you say is true, then it is unavoidable. These things happen. *Quel dommage!*"

"Well, you're all very gloomy, I must say!" exclaimed Jane.

21

Nigel Asks a Favour

MARIELLA heard the great news in the village post office, as usual; and, as usual, it was Ann Musgrave who exploded the bombshell. When Mariella tethered her horse, Jasmin Flower, to the railings on that morning in March—the Friday of her half-term holiday—she was met by a wild-eyed, wilder-haired Ann.

"*Mariella!* Look what it says here about Veronica!" she exclaimed, waving the latest number of the *Ballet Weekly*. "Oh, but of course you're sure to know."

"I don't know anything about Veronica," said Mariella. "I haven't had a letter from her for ages, so let's hear the news."

"She's—she's having a *baby*!" exclaimed Ann.

"A baby? But how wonderful!"

"Yes, that's what I thought at first, but it says here that she isn't dancing at the Gala performance, after all."

"Well, of course not," said Mariella. "Whoever in their senses would want to dance at anything—even a gala performance—if they could have a baby instead? I wonder whether it will be a girl or a boy?"

"Oh, a boy, of course," declared Ann. "A boy just like Sebastian—not frightfully good-looking, but ever so *attractive*. A boy with sooty black hair, dark blue eyes, and that funny crooked smile."

"And if it's a girl," said Mariella, "in a few years' time the poor little thing will be doing *battements tendus* at the *barre*, and trying her best to follow in her famous mother's footsteps—like me!"

"Of *course* if she's a girl, she'll be a *ballerina*," declared Ann. "What could be more romantic?"

"Lots of things!" said Mariella cryptically. "Matter of fact, following in your mother's footsteps isn't the least bit romantic. It's awful! Nothing is so frustrating as trying to live up to someone else's reputation. I know! I've suffered from it! But let's not dwell on the gloomy past. Does it say who's taking Veronica's place at the Gala?"

"Yes, it does, and that's the other thrill," proclaimed Ann. "Guess what? It's Jane!"

"Jane?" said Mariella. "Oh, no—I expect that's a mistake. These journalists will say anything! Jane couldn't dance in a gala performance. Why, she's only nineteen. She isn't experienced enough. I expect they're wrong."

"No, they're not," said Ann. "It says quite plainly: 'To Jane Foster, the newest member of the Sadler's Wells Ballet to reach the stars, has been given the honour of dancing Odette-Odile at the forthcoming Gala performance. This may well be because of the absence through illness, or other reasons, of so many of the older and more seasoned of the company's dancers, etc., etc. You see—it's true! There's a whole article here about Jane. All about her getting lost on Ben What's-its-name, and spraining her ankle, and there's a paragraph about Veronica, too. They've raked up all that about her riding to her audition in a mist!"

Riding home, Mariella thought how queer it was that everything went on just as usual day after day—one might almost say year after year—in the country, while in London, world-shattering things were happening all the time. When last she'd seen Jane, she'd been convalescing after a sprained ankle. Now here she was taking the great Veronica Weston's place as *prima ballerina* at a Gala performance at Covent Garden. Royalty would be there. Perhaps Jane would be presented to Princess Margaret—perhaps even to the Queen! "All the same," thought Mariella, cantering smoothly along the grass verge of the country road, "I'd rather be up here in Northumberland where it's quiet, and, yes, *sane*—where there are *real* things to do, like riding, and planting out the wallflowers, and learning how to cure sick animals. Less glamorous, perhaps, but more satisfying!"

She had come to the place where the Bychester road climbed up and up over the rugged moorland, under the very shadow of Raven's Eyrie. Here, the Monks Hollow road—her own road—wound away between the shadowy larch woods, past the heathery hillside, where the rabbits played in their dozens on moonlight nights, when she saw Nigel coming towards her on horseback. He gave her a view-hullo in his usual hail-fellow-well-met fashion, and they stood talking, while a couple of sheep rubbed themselves against the dry-stone wall bounding one side of the road, and ba-aa'd dismally.

"I always think sheep are the most melancholy-sounding animals," said Mariella. "Even in the spring you feel they're pessimists and are telling their lambs all about the wicked world!"

"Yes, they *are* pretty dismal," agreed Nigel, "though I can't say I ever thought of it before you mentioned it. . . . Look, Mariella—I'm glad I ran into you this morning. I was going to ring you up, as a matter of fact, but now I'm saved the trouble. I suppose you aren't going to the Horse Sports over at Dewburn to-morrow?"

"Well, I had been thinking," began Mariella, but Nigel cut her short.

"No, I thought you wouldn't be—or anyway, that you wouldn't be riding in anything, seeing that you go back to college early next morning. Too hectic for you, eh? Well, what I want to know is will you lend me Jas for the afternoon? Castor's gone lame, and as you know, Pollux can't jump for toffee!"

"What about Bessie?" asked Mariella, her eyes on the gleaming mare he was riding.

"Bessie?" exclaimed Nigel, clapping the mare's neck jocularly. "Why, you know, Mariella, that I simply wouldn't stand an earthly on poor Bessie. Stand still, old girl! She's nothing but a hack! So you see, it's really essential that I should borrow a horse from *somebody*, and I thought to myself: 'Mariella's the one! Always ready to help a chap out of a spot of trouble is Mariella. You can count upon her. That's what makes her such a decent sort of girl! Besides, Jasmine Flower is one of the best goers you could meet in a month of Sundays. She's like her mistress—a real winner!' That's what I thought. Now how about it, Mariella?"

"Well, if you put it like that, Nigel," said Mariella, falling for his flattery, as usual, "I expect you can borrow her. As you say, it would, perhaps, be rather tiring for me to ride to-morrow afternoon, and then get up early on Sunday morning to catch my train."

"Yes, of course it would," Nigel assured her. "But of course there's nothing to stop you coming to watch *me* ride, is there? That wouldn't tire you at all, and it would buck me up no end. I'd *like* to know you'd come specially to see me ride." He grinned at her engagingly. More than ordinarily handsome, Nigel looked his best on horseback. His bright, curly hair shone in the wintry sunlight, his blue eyes challenged her, and poor Mariella's heart melted within her.

"When do you want her?" she asked him. "To-night? Or will to-morrow morning do?"

"Oh, I'd better have her to-night," answered Nigel. "Give me a little time to get used to her. Perhaps you could ride her over for me—I don't expect you're very busy, seeing you're on holiday. You could go back by the bus. There's one at six. I'd come over for her myself but I don't finish at Harry Foster's till five, you know, and by the time I've had a meal it'll be darkish."

"All right, Nigel—I'll bring her over for you," promised Mariella, thinking at the same time that Nigel's mother would almost *have* to ask her to stay to tea, seeing that the one and only bus didn't go till six, and that therefore she might just see Nigel before she caught it.

"And don't forget you're to be there to cheer me on to victory," added Nigel. "I shall be looking out for you! 'Bye, Mariella. Many thanks!"

He dug his spurred heels into Bessie's flanks and rode away at a smart pace towards the village, and Mariella walked her own horse slowly along the grass verge towards home, thinking how wonderful Nigel was. How he would win every race at the sports to-morrow, and that it would partly be due to her, Mariella. Of course, most of the credit would be due to Nigel, himself, because there was certainly nobody who could touch him when it came to the Mile Over Fences, or the Handy Hunter, but still it would be *her*, Mariella Foster, who would share the honours with him. People would say: "Oh, of course, Nigel Monkhouse was riding, so naturally no one else had an earthly. Yes, my dear—he was riding Miss Foster's Jasmine Flower. It looks rather as if—yes, everyone says——"

It was well worth missing the Horse Sports, Mariella decided, turning in at her own gate, to hear her name coupled with Nigel's—even by a lot of old gossips! Yes, it was well worth it, even though it was actually to take part in the sports that she had come home in the first place.

22

Gala Performance

Do you remember that autumn morning, months ago now, when you saw Covent Garden Theatre during rehearsal? Remember the lighted stage, standing out starkly against the darkened body of the great theatre, the dancers, themselves, in an amazing motley of costumes—ballet tunics, old crushed *tutus*, tights, and hip-length jumpers, slacks and cricket shirts, skating skirts, and even a bathing costume or two! In fact, every conceivable sort of dress that he, or she, found it most comfortable to dance in.

Now picture Covent Garden just before the curtain rises on the evening of the Gala performance. Below you is the huge bowl of the stalls, filling up with the flower-like dresses of beautiful women, jewels glittering on neck and hair, sweet-scented floral sprays pinned with jewelled pins to low *décolletages*. Picture the boxes, filling up with more lovely women, and their more soberly dressed escorts. They lean on the plush ledges, their bare arms gleaming in the subdued lights, their priceless fur capes slipping from their white shoulders to disclose fabulous creations by famous dress designers. In the closely-packed horseshoe tiers above, so high that you see the audience only as a moving mass of colours, there comes the faint thud of seats going down, the rustle of a thousand programmes, the hum of a thousand whispering voices. Out in the crush bar, the crystal chandeliers wink and sparkle, and everywhere there is an air of expectancy. Royalty has not yet arrived! The Royal Box is empty. And then, at last, the National Anthem sounds in our excited ears. She is here! Her Majesty, the Queen! . . .

We gaze at her from afar off, and there is a catch in our breath. How lucky we are to have so lovely and gracious a lady to be our sovereign! And now the Royal Box is full of flowers and bowing figures, jewelled tiaras, and gorgeous uniforms. The Gala performance has begun!

How many dancers have dreamt of being the *prima ballerina* at a Gala night at Covent Garden? This dream had now come true for one small girl—nineteen-year-old Jane Foster. Upon her slender dancing figure were fixed the many thousand eyes of that great audience. Yes, even Royalty marvelled at those supple, satin-clad feet, as they *pirouetted* with such effortless grace and perfection, executed *entrachats* with such precision. Her lightness and grace charmed the audience, and made them her slaves. Many of them had not seen her before, this newly arisen star. They acclaimed her! They took her to their hearts! At the end of Act Two they would not let her go. There seemed to be only one person in the theatre who had not completely lost his head. In one of the stage boxes sat Oscar Devereux, the famous critic, gravely jotting down notes for his paragraph in the Sunday paper, wherein he would say something to this effect: "I was agreeably surprised by the dancing of Jane Foster in the Gala performance of *Le Lac des Cygnes* last Friday. This very young ballerina—she is only just nineteen—brought to the Odette role a moving quality of youth and tenderness. Only her inexperience marred an otherwise charming performance."

Yes, it was true! She *had* charmed even him, hard-bitten ballet critic that he was! She *had* surprised him, too. She was dancing immeasurably better than he had expected. It was obvious that she possessed that gift that some *ballerinas* have—namely, of rising to unexpected heights upon an important occasion. Of course, she was no Fonteyn, or Weston. He wouldn't be surprised if this proved to be her greatest performance. You see, he knew Jane intimately, and he knew that her character was soft and affectionate, that it lacked that steel thread that must run through a *ballerina's* nature if stardom is to be reached and sustained. Yes, Jane had reached the stars, but would she stay there? He doubted it.

At the end of Act Three he knew his judgment to be correct. Her Odette had been moving, but her Odile was lacking in strength. To be brutal, it was insipid. She did not fill the stage.

Jane Foster in the Gala performance of Le Lac des Cygnes ...
brought to the Odette rôle a moving quality of youth and tenderness

But the audience didn't notice. They had accepted her, and, having done so, were now sitting back in their comfortable chairs, determined to be charmed. A gala audience is scarcely a critical one! Of all these lavishly-dressed people there were few as knowledgable, where ballet is concerned, as the fans standing in the gallery queue on ordinary nights.

The performance drew to a close—a beautiful performance. There were twice the number of swan maidens, and the huge stage was filled with them. Even a seasoned critic like Oscar Devereux drew in his breath as they wheeled and circled across the stage, their feet making a soft rustling sound, like the beat of many wings drawing back into a great "V", like a skein of wild geese crossing the moonlit sky.

s for Jane, the whole performance had for her a strange, almost dreamlike quality about it. It was as if she watched herself dancing, saw herself receiving bouquets of roses. In a dream she heard herself being presented to Her Gracious Majesty during the Second Interval, then, at the end of the performance, mounted the stairs to her dressing-room by her own side, and beheld someone else's face in the make-up mirror beside her own. Was this really Jane Foster?

As the autograph-hunters, pressmen, and well-wishers melted away, and she was left alone at last, she asked herself again: Was this Jane Foster? Was this the girl who had come to grief on far-away Ben Cruachan, the sad girl to whom Guy had proposed marriage in the middle of Edinburgh's famous Princes Street? The girl who had limped miserably into that Edinburgh theatre to see someone else taking over her rôles? It hardly seemed possible! She looked down at her ankle, and flexed the foot. Yes, it was perfectly sound. She was lucky, she knew. Lucky, lucky Jane Foster! Happy Jane Foster! And yet— was she? There was a little ache in her heart that surely ought not to be there. In her imagination, she saw Guy's strong, dark face when he had said: "I shall still be waiting, Jane."

Only this afternoon, as she had passed through the empty theatre after rehearsal, she had heard a group of dancers talking. They hadn't known she was there, of course, or they wouldn't have said what they did: "Jane Foster—well, she's no substitute for Weston, is she? Quite adequate, but just not top grade, and never will be. Oh, I don't expect the audience will notice the difference, given all the trimmings, but the critics will—some of them, anyway. Trust old Oscar! He knows a thing or two! I shall look forward to his ballet talk in the *Sunday Survey*! . . . What's that you were saying, Clara? What happens when you get to the top and begin to slide down the other side? Quite frankly, I'm not worried, because I shan't ever get to the top, not with my neck—or rather, the lack of it. Silly to think that just because my neck is one inch too short I've got to stay Leading Swan in the *corps de ballet* while others dance Odette-Odile, but there you are! It almost makes one wish one had been born in China—or is it Burma?—where they stretch one's neck at an incredibly early age! . . . No, I'm not getting away from the point; I'm just coming to it. What happens when the slide begins, you were saying? Well, look at Judith. Yes—Judith Craven, the Queen Mother. I suppose you kids don't remember that she danced Odette-Odile at a Gala in nineteen-forty-something or other? I'll bet you didn't see her dancing then, anyway. She was quite good. *I* remember her, because I've been here since the Year One. If I'd got to the top, I'd have been well down the Penny-on-the-Mat by now, but as it is, I stay 'put' in the *corps de ballet*, where technique counts more than personality. Besides, the *corps de ballet* is less wearing on the nerves! One lasts longer! . . . And what happens after one's past even being the Queen Mother, you were saying, June? Oh, one usually retires gracefully, and opens a dancing school. Then, when one dies at the age of eighty-nine or thereabouts—dancers live a long, long, time, my dears, goodness only knows why!—there's a nice little paragraph in the *Ballet Weekly* all about the things one danced in—eons and eons ago. Nobody even remembers now! What more could one want?"

"You sound depressing, Margaret. I can't see that happening to Fonteyn!"

"I never said it would. Fonteyn is one of the Really Great Ones. So is Veronica Weston. They will never be forgotten. They're like Anna Pavlova. Besides, Veronica's lucky. She married into the profession, so to speak, so she'll be able to

retire gracefully and bask lazily in her famous husband's lime-
light, even when her own dancing days are over—rather like
Irma Foster. Once upon a time, Irma was all important, and
poor, dear Oscar was a nonentity. Now the tables are turned,
and Oscar is the important one, and poor, dear Irma merely
basks! . . ."

Ever since hearing the hard, bitter voice of the disgruntled
ballet dancer, Jane had felt uneasy. Now, in her dressing-room,
surrounded by the floral offerings of the Gala audience, she
faced facts. Ruthlessly she forced herself to know the truth. She,
Jane Foster, was without doubt a beautiful dancer, but she was
not unique. There were many more dancers just as good as she.
She had been lucky, that was all. This evening she had reached
heights she might never reach again. She was on the top of the
highest peak. But she was no Fonteyn. She was no Veronica
Weston. She would stay on her peak for a little time—a very
little time—and then her place would be filled by someone else
—Vivien Chator, perhaps—and she would gradually descend.
Gradually, but irrevocably. One night—perhaps at some future
Gala performance—*she* would be the Queen Mother, and people
would say of her: "My dear, that's Jane Foster. No, of course
you don't remember her. She was *prima ballerina* at the Gala
performance in nineteen-fifty-something or other. I know,
because I was there! She danced quite well, too, but of course
everyone knew she wouldn't last. Oh, yes—I assure you it's
true! Pathetic, isn't it? You remember Josef Linsk? Yes, the
Magician, Von Rotbart. Well, I remember when *he* danced
Siegfried. It must be more than twenty years ago. He was quite
good-looking in those days. He's a little bald, now, but of
course he can always wear a wig—that's the best of the stage!
He and Jane have married, you know. I hear they've taken a
teaching job somewhere or other. Matter of fact, I believe this
is their last performance. A real Swan Song! . . ."

"No! No!" cried Jane, flinging out her hands, while the
mirrored room threw back her agonized gesture a dozen times.
"It mustn't be like that! I must stop now—*now*, while I'm at the
top! Besides—I don't want to marry Josef! I don't want to
marry anybody in the profession. I want to marry Guy!"

23

The Telegram

WHEN Mariella arrived at Bychester Tower that evening, her high hopes of being asked to tea were shattered. Lady Monkhouse was not at home, and the maid said a message had been left saying would she, Mariella, leave Jasmine Flower in the stables, please—the far right-hand loose-box—and many thanks for bringing her over. There was no word about tea.

As the bus wasn't due to leave the village until six o'clock, Mariella dropped in at the Monkhouse Alms and had a cup of tea, also a plate of dropped-scones which were the inn's speciality. After which she made her way to the War Memorial, which was the village bus-stop, and sat down on the edge of the coping to wait for the bus as patiently as possible. At about five minutes to the hour she heard the clip-clop of a horse's hoofs on the hard road, and her heart leapt. What if it was Nigel, come especially to thank her for bringing Jasmine Flower over for him? But once again she was doomed to disappointment. The rider was a tall, dark young man, with close-cropped black hair and rather serious grey eyes.

"Guy!" said Mariella, glad to have someone to talk to, even if it wasn't the person she would have chosen. "What are you doing in Bychester?"

"I might say the same to you, Mariella," laughed Guy, "except that I happen to know!"

"You know about Jasmine Flower?" exclaimed Mariella in surprise. "But how could you? I mean, has Nigel——?"

"I met Monkhouse in Monks Hollow village this morning," explained Guy. "I'd been doing a job of work, and he happened to be visiting the same farm on some estate business. He told me he was riding in the Bychester Horse Sports to-morrow, and that he was borrowing your Jasmine Flower. Aren't you going to the Sports yourself, Mariella? I made sure you would be."

"Oh, yes—I'm going," said Mariella. "Matter of fact, I came home especially."

"Then you're riding another horse?" questioned Guy. "Well, of course, it's not my business, but I think you're making a mistake. You won't get a better horse for the job than Jasmine Flower. She's a sure winner—with you in the saddle, of course!"

"Thank you, Guy," Mariella said with a wistful smile. "I know she's a wonderful horse, and I hate not riding her, but you see, poor Nigel——"

"You mean that Nigel is borrowing her, and leaving you without a mount?" exclaimed Guy in so stern a voice that Mariella was almost frightened. "Is that so, Mariella?"

"Oh, no—you're quite wrong, Guy," she assured him. "Nigel thought I wasn't keen. He thought it would be too much for me——"

"Too much for you!" exploded Guy. "When has a race or two at the local gymkhana been too much for you, Mariella? Tell me that?"

"Well, anyway—I *want* to lend Nigel my Jasmine Flower," insisted Mariella. "I'd be frightfully unhappy if I was riding and he hadn't a decent mount himself."

"Ah, now we're coming to the real reason!" commented Guy. "To change the subject, are you, by any chance, waiting for the six bus?"

"Yes," answered Mariella. "It's late, isn't it? I make it ten past six now."

"It's late," said Guy, "because it isn't coming at all. Didn't Nigel tell you, Mariella, that the six bus has been taken off for the summer months. It's now the seven bus."

"Oh, *no*!" cried Mariella. "It can't be! Why, I've been waiting here since four o'clock! But I expect you're right, Guy. I wondered why nobody else was waiting."

"Look!" Guy put in, "why not let me run you home in my car? Oh, yes, it's over there, parked in front of the Monkhouse

Alms. I've been exercising Dr. Jowett's hunter for him as a favour, but I intended to go home by car, so you won't be taking me out of my way. I'll just return the mare, and then come back here for you. Shan't be long!"

Without waiting for a reply, he cantered away across the village green, and Mariella breathed a sigh of relief. She was to be saved an hour's wait, plus a very uncomfortable journey in a country bus which went round by innumerable villages, picking up passengers and parcels—from rolls of wire-netting to crates of chickens—till it was so full it could hardly stagger along! It would be much more comfortable in the Charltons' big car, and poor Mariella was tired.

"It's funny," she thought, "how much more tiring it is just standing about waiting than it is when one's really busy!"

It wasn't many minutes before Guy was back again.

"You're always coming to my rescue, Guy!" she laughed as he opened the car door for her. "You're a real knight-errant!"

"Hardly that," expostulated Guy. "As a matter of fact, I had to come over your way, in any case, to pay old Sally Carruthers a visit. Her cat—her ginger Sammy, you know—was caught in a gin-trap, and I had to take his leg off, so I'm going along there to see how it is. The poor old soul can't come to me. Her varicose veins are very bad."

"That *is* decent of you, Guy," said Mariella. "Tell her how terribly sorry I am about poor Sammy. Those beastly traps! I'd like to put the man who sets them in one of them himself and leave him in it all night! He works for the Monkhouses, and I've tried to get Nigel to stop him using the horrible things, and Nigel said he would think about it, but so far nothing's happened. Every night all those poor rabbits tortured—besides the cats that get caught by mistake, like Sammy. Oh, Guy—what can we do about it?"

"Well, I'm a vet," said Guy, "and at the moment the best I can do is doctor the poor creatures that get caught. It's time a law was passed banning the beastly things. But there you are—most people just don't know about them, or are careful not to think about them."

"Oh, look!" exclaimed Mariella, forgetting about the gin-

traps in her excitement. "This is Hordon Castle, isn't it—your
home, Guy? Why are we coming here?"

"I thought I'd like to show you something," answered Guy,
driving under a stone archway and into an outer courtyard. "It
won't take a minute, and I thought it might be of use to you."

"You're making me very curious," said Mariella. "Whatever
can it be?"

"Wait and see," answered Guy, opening the car door, and
leading the way across the cobbled courtyard.

"I've never been to Hordon," said Mariella, looking up at
the historic grey pile that was Hordon Castle, Guy's ancestral
home. "Oh, what a lovely, lovely place! Look at all the daffo-
dils!" Through a door in the twelve-foot-high curtain wall, she
had caught a glimpse of the dene which surrounded the old
house like a moat. The stretch of smooth, green turf all around
the castle walls was a mass of golden blooms. They rippled
round the old building like a sunlit sea. "There are rhododen-
drons, too, all in bud."

"Yes," said Guy, "although the dene comes out on the high
open moorland, all among the bracken and the heather, where,
many a time, the snow lingers as late as May, down here it's
very mild. Well, come along and see my surprise." He opened
the door of a nearby stable, which incidentally had pointed
windows and had obviously been an ancient chapel at one time,
and stepped back to let her go through.

"O-oh!" said Mariella, drawing in her breath. "It's a horse!
A beautiful chestnut mare. Is she yours, Guy?"

"Yes—she's mine. I bought her a few weeks ago. Her name
is Lady Jane, and she's the perfect mount for a lady. Jane—
your cousin Jane, I mean—rode her when we were in Edinburgh that week-end, and it occurred to me that perhaps you
might like to borrow her for the Sports to-morrow. That's why
I brought you to see her. Oh, I know you wouldn't be as much
at home on her as on your own Jasmine Flower, but you're a
good horsewoman, Mariella, and she's a first-class animal. I
give you my word!"

"You don't need to!" laughed Mariella. "I can tell that all
right. She looks heavenly! Do you really mean it, Guy? That I

can really borrow her? I'd simply adore to—even if I didn't win a thing! To tell you the truth, I *was* feeling rather blue at having to watch you all riding, and me just watching, but of course," she added hastily, "I didn't tell Nigel so."

"Of course not," said Guy without a smile. "That's settled, then. Well, now I don't need to take you home in my car. You can *ride* home on Lady Jane! You'll get used to each other that way."

"What a good idea! That will be fun! . . . Oh, but what about poor old Sally Carruthers?"

"I'll look in at her cottage on my way to the Sports to-morrow," promised Guy. "I'll saddle up for you, shall I?"

It was when he was leading the mare out of the stable and holding her for Mariella to mount that he said casually: "By the way, have you heard from Jane lately, Mariella? I've been wondering how her ankle went on."

"I've done more than hear from her—I've *seen* her—on television!" said Mariella. "She was on the other day in that new ballet of Toni Rossini's—*Les Nuages*, Clouds. Jane was the Cirrus cloud, and she was perfect. You'd certainly never have known that she'd sprained her ankle. It was her first appearance since her accident. And, by the way, they're doing a Gala performance of *Swan Lake* at Covent Garden to-night, you know, and they're going to televise Royalty arriving. If you like to come over a bit later we might see Jane being presented!"

A flicker of something that might be pain passed over Guy's face.

"No," he answered gravely. "I don't think so—thanks all the same. I think I prefer to remember Jane the way she was the last time I saw her."

Mariella sighed.

"I think Jane is wedded to her art," she said simply. "Ballet dancers are like that. I understand, Guy—about you and Jane, I mean. Fellow feeling, you know! Shake on it!"

She held out her hand, and Guy took it.

All roads led to Bychester the following afternoon. Lines of cars and horse-boxes, shooting-brakes and bicycles—in fact, every kind of thing on wheels—filed in orderly fashion through the field gate leading to the improvised car park where the Horse Sports were to take place. Crowds of pedestrians rendered up their shillings at the hunting-wicket alongside. The sports field lay in a fold of the hills, like a Roman amphitheatre, and all around, on the short, sweet-scented turf, people were sitting in little groups, complete with car rugs, thermos flasks, and even the baby in the pram! Other enthusiasts, perched upon shooting-sticks, lined the fences, and discussed in loud, knowledgeable voices the horses and their owners, their merits and demerits.

"Have you seen Gillian? Oh, yes—she's here—it's her half-term. Matter of fact, if it hadn't been, she'd have staged an attack of tonsillitis, or something. That child lives for riding! . . . Look, there's Dorothy Mosscrop on Caraway-Seed. Hullo, Dorothy! Goodness! No. 13—it's a blessing you're not superstitious! . . . *I'm* not, either! I remember at the Lingfield gymkhana, years ago, I rode Challenger—you remember old Challenger—the mare I used to have before Flycatcher?—and I came in first in goodness knows how many events. I was No. 13 that time, so it just shows! What are you in for to-day? The Musical Ride, the Mile, and the Handy Hunter? You ought to do well in the Ride—Caraway's nippy, isn't he? As for the others, well, you've got the Foster girl against you. You know —the red-headed girl from Monks Hollow. Mariella Foster. She's hot stuff! She's not riding her own mare, though, so she's a dark horse. Excuse the pun! . . . Why not? Oh, she's lent it to the Monkhouse boy. He's riding it this afternoon. . . . Yes, I know. They *say* . . . Yes, wouldn't it? *Most* suitable! The Fosters and the Monkhouses. Both such well respected county families. Of course she's not really his cousin. No, her name isn't really Foster at all—it's Devereux. You see, her mother's on the stage, or something, so Mariella uses *her* name. Goodness knows why! Ah, here *is* the young man. . . . Hullo, Nigel! That's a nice horse you're riding. It's Miss Foster's Jasmine Flower, isn't it? We'll back you for a cert!"

"Thanks, Mrs. Musgrave," Nigel said complacently. "I hope I shan't disappoint you. Yes, she's a grand mare," he patted his mount's glossy neck with a proprietory gesture. "Yes, she belongs to Miss Foster. By the way, have you seen her about anywhere?"

"Oh, yes," put in the larger of the two women, whose name was evidently Shafto. "She's over there—talking to young Mr. Charlton."

Nigel scanned the crowd.

"I don't see—by George, yes, I do! That's Mariella over by the tent—on the chestnut mare! I wasn't looking for her on horseback. Now where did she get that animal from, I wonder? Looks a first-class bit of horseflesh to me. Somebody must have lent it to her. I must see what I can do—my mother would just like a mare like that. 'Bye, Mrs. Musgrave! 'Bye, Mrs. Shafto!" He cantered across the sports field and hailed Mariella.

"Hullo, Mariella! . . . How do, Charlton! I thought you weren't riding this afternoon, Mariella, old girl?"

"No, I wasn't, but Guy offered to lend me Lady Jane, so I changed my mind. I couldn't resist her! Isn't she beautiful?"

"Nice animal," conceded Nigel. Then his face darkened, as he took in what Mariella had just said. "Charlton lent her to you, did he? I like his cheek!"

"S-sh!" said Mariella warningly. "He'll hear you! Why shouldn't he lend her to me?"

"Oh, nothing," said Nigel. "It's all right, I suppose. But don't forget—you're to watch me win the Mile."

"I'll watch—provided you watch *me* win the Handy Hunter," said Mariella with a sudden burst of spirit. "I feel I could win anything on this horse! Guy's going to be there to cheer me on, too. He promised."

"The dickens he did!" exclaimed Nigel. "Right-ho! I'll be there, Mariella." Then he added to himself: "Can't be outdone by Charlton, and I must say Mariella looks rather well on that mare. No one in the field to match her, now I come to think of it!"

Mariella had one of the happiest afternoons of her life. Mounted on a perfectly mannered horse, she acquitted herself well in all the events she entered for. She won the Musical Ride, and came second in the Open Leaping, and she won the Handy

Hunter, which she had set her heart on. Added to this, was the wonderful fact that Nigel was paying her a great deal of attention, so much so that many heads turned, and many tongues wagged. . . . "Young Nigel Monkhouse, and the good-looking Foster girl. As good as engaged! . . . What a handsome pair! . . . Wonder if they will be married in the summer? . . . " Mariella couldn't help hearing some of the remarks that were passed, and her heart sang joyfully. Yes, it really looked as if Nigel liked her, after all!

The only fly in the ointment was the fact that Nigel won nothing himself. Several times he looked like winning, but always the victory was snatched from him.

"Of course, he's up against Guy Charlton of Hordon Castle," said the know-alls. "Young Charlton doesn't often compete in these affairs—he's above them—but when he does, no one else has a look in. He's a magnificent horseman. Always has been— ever since he was a lad. They say he was brought up in Canada —on a ranch, so it's no wonder he rides like a cowboy! Look at him now!"

Mariella, clinging to the rails, as she watched the Mile Over Fences, caught her breath as Guy came sailing over the jumps. Effortlessly, faultlessly, he took them in his stride, coming in a quarter of a mile ahead of the other riders. Nigel, his fair face red with temper and disappointment, arrived second.

"I wish to goodness I'd ridden my own nag!" he exclaimed, breathing hard, when he joined Mariella. "Can't understand this mare of yours, Mariella. . . . Used to think she was a good goer. . . . Don't now! . . . Think she's no earthly use! . . . Slowest thing I ever rode!"

"You don't think that perhaps Guy——" began Mariella tentatively.

"I don't think anything!" snapped Nigel. "Facts are facts! Charlton has the better horse. Anyone can win on a nag like his. Give me his horse, and I'll win every time! Of course, everyone knows that the Charltons have money to burn, so it's no credit due to Charlton that he's got a mount above all we poor paupers! Why, it's nothing but a race-horse! Oughtn't to be allowed in a gymkhana."

"No, it isn't, Nigel," Mariella said firmly. "Guy hunts Champion regularly. In fact, I've never seen him hunting on anything else. You're wrong there!"

"Well, anyway—I return Jasmine Flower to you without a regret. Another time I shall ride my own nag, I can tell you."

Mariella didn't say: "*Do!*" or "No one asked you to borrow my one and only mount," as she might well have done. She had far too nice a nature for that. Instead she murmured: "I'm so sorry, Nigel. It must have been one of Jas's off days. Horses have them, you know."

"So it seems!" retorted Nigel.

Riding home to his ancient Border stronghold, Guy's thoughts were a long way from the gymkhana he had just left. Above the road towered that landmark for miles around— Raven's Eyrie, and it suddenly struck him how like a Scottish peak it was in miniature. Sgurr nan Gillian, perhaps, one of the Cuillin peaks in Skye. A picture rose up in his mind of cloud shadows and misted hills, with the smoke of many a waterfall too far away to be heard. Then he thought of Ben Cruachan, and Jane, with her pathetic white face, looking to him for safety and comfort. How he would love to teach her to climb! How he would love to stand with her on the top of a mountain—just the two of them together in a world of cloudy peaks! Then, resolutely, he forced his thoughts back to earth. It was useless dreaming about Jane. Jane had a sweetheart already—the ballet. She wasn't for him.

His home rose up before him. Across the dene it stood— ancient bulging stone walls, quaint twisted chimneys, stone steps winding up to the turrets that no longer existed, glinting slit-like windows. When he got to the courtyard, where the wallflowers bloomed in scented warmth, he saw that someone was waiting for him. It was a boy in uniform with a telegram in his hand.

Guy leaned down from the saddle, took the orange envelope, and slit it open. It wasn't from a farmer about a sick animal, as he expected. It was from Jane. As he read, the castle, the waiting boy, everything faded from before his eyes. He was back on the shores of Loch Awe, and the Falls of Cruachan were sounding in his ears.

"Meet me on the slopes of Beinn a' Bhùiridh," said the wire. "Have changed my mind, and want to climb Ben Cruachan. Have left the Wells. Jane."

Guy sat staring at the bit of paper that had changed his whole life. The telegram boy waited somewhat impatiently.

"Any answer, mister?"

"None," Guy answered. Then he called the boy back. "Yes, there is! Wait a minute, will you." He scribbled on the back of the form: "Don't say 'I've left the Wells'. Say 'I've come home'. Guy."

━━━━━━━━

If you have enjoyed this book, you may like to read the previous "Sadler's Wells" stories:

Swan Lake